BELATED OMEGA

RAELYNN ROSE

Raeylynn Rose @2023
Published by Twisted Heart Press, LLC

ALL RIGHTS RESERVED: No part of this book may be reproduced, stored in a retrieval system, or transmitted, in any form or by any means, without the prior permission in writing of the publisher, nor be otherwise circulated in any form of binding or cover other than that in which it is published and without a similar condition including this condition being imposed on the subsequent purchaser. Your non-refundable purchase allows you to one legal copy of this work for your own personal use. You do not have resell or distribution rights without the prior written permission of both the publisher and copyright owner of this book. This book cannot be copied in any format, sold, or otherwise transferred from your computer to another through upload, or for a fee.

Disclaimer: This book may contain explicit sexual content, graphic, adult language, and situations that some readers may find objectionable. This e-book is for sale to adults ONLY, as defined by the laws of the country in which you made your purchase. Raelynn Rose will not be responsible for any loss, harm, injury or death resulting from use of the information contained in any of its titles.

This is a work of fiction. All characters, places, businesses, and incidents are from the author's imagination. Any resemblance to actual places, people, or events is purely coincidental. Any trademarks mentioned herein are not authorized by the trademark owners and do not in any way mean the work is sponsored by or associated with the trademark owners. Any trademarks used are specifically in a descriptive capacity.

❦ Created with Vellum

CONTENT WARNINGS

Before you start Violet's story, I think I should offer a few warnings. While this book does contain a happily ever after, it is intended for mature audiences only. As an alternate universe story, there are mentions of knots, heats, breeding, and lots of detailed and spicy sex scenes that may contain more than two participants as well as MM and MFMMM scenes. If that's not for you, turn back now.

Trigger warnings:

GRAPHIC SEX, violence, cursing, and dominant alphas abound in this book. I tried to do my best to broach varying subjects with as much sensitivity, but please take care of yourself and stop reading if anything triggers a sense of anxiety or fear.

CHAPTER 1

Violet

The pain was nearly overwhelming, shutting out sounds and smells and thoughts.

Assholes. Every single person in this place was a complete asshole.

No. Only the people who'd dragged us here were the assholes. The rest were victims like me.

For twenty-six years, I'd gone through life believing I was a beta. I was happy. It was so much easier to be…normal. Not a commodity or prize or toy.

Until I'd perfumed while walking home from work.

I'd done my best to rush home, and use every single scent blocker I had in my bathroom any time I had to leave the house. During my first two heats, I was able to lock myself in my tiny closet and ease some of the discomfort with a battery-operated toy.

The discomfort I suffered through those first two were nothing compared to this medically induced bullshit every omega in the compound were forced to suffer.

This was my first round of the experimental drug. There were others here who'd been drugged, who'd been raped as their hormone hazed brains convinced their bodies to present and beg for a knot.

Horror filled me as each wave crashed through my system and slick began to dampen the plain white cotton of the panties they'd provided. Would they come for me tonight? Would I bother fighting them? Or would I go into that same sex crazed mental state and spread my legs for whichever alpha visited my room?

There had to be a way to get out of this place. Or at least protect myself, to keep some modicum of my fight or flight in the forefront of my mind no matter how hard the heat came on.

Breathing against the pain, I searched the room for something to use as a weapon. Or maybe I could push the crappy metal framed bed against the door as a barricade.

How long would that hold, though? I had fought my ass off every time I'd been dragged to the infirmary for checks and injections. All I'd earned were cuts, bruises, a sprained ankle, and a black eye. Three weeks and I'd yet to earn my freedom.

There was an overwhelming urge to pile my blankets into a corner of the room or even under the bed so I could curl into a ball and pray I got through this cycle untouched.

When I perfumed, I'd made an appointment to see a doctor who was known for being discreet. No matter how many times she was questioned by the government, she refused to release the names or any information about a single omega she treated. I was going to get on birth control in case my *own* control slipped and I ended up begging some stranger for a knot. The last thing I needed or wanted was a pup.

I'd also gotten on a list for suppressants so I could continue my life as a beta. Unfortunately, I hadn't gotten the time to pick those damn pills up before I was taken.

A scream tore through the compound. Rushing to the window, I nearly smashed my nose against it to see three floors below me as a woman was ushered from my building to what I'd heard the guards refer to as the *fun room*. It made me sick what these assholes considered fun.

The woman doubled over, her arms wrapped around her stomach, but the guards simply continued pulling her forward until her bare feet were dragging across the asphalt. She was dressed the same way every single omega here was dressed, including myself – a plain, hospital gown that tied only at the nape of my neck and extended maybe three or four inches below my ass and crotch.

Easy access. That was what I'd heard one of the guards say, that the gowns were for easy access.

Every single second here felt like hell. Every single moment felt as though I were a ticking time bomb. Like the moment my heat fully came, the real me would implode and be replaced by a mindless breeder.

Tears burned the backs of my eyes as I stepped away from the window, refusing to watch another victim being dragged to that place, knowing exactly what would happen to her once she was behind closed doors.

Another ripple of pain stole my breath, but I did my best to hide each time, did my best to hide the fact my blood was boiling and my body was burning up with fever. I had spotted the camera the second they'd tossed me in this tiny ass room. They were watching for the telltale signs that I was primed and ready for them to knot me as much as possible.

What I hadn't quite figured out was the end game. Why try for so many pups? I hadn't seen any omegas transported away or any strange vehicles coming and going, so I didn't think we were being sold or trafficked. Were they hoping we could give birth to more omegas? Or maybe they were hoping to bring more betas into the world to reduce the number of alphas.

We could simply be part of some kind of medical experiment. After all, if they could find a way to send omegas into heat at will, they could form an entire population of compliant and overly willing men and women who would do anything and everything to please their alpha.

I didn't care. I didn't care what their reasoning was. I just wanted to go home. I would return to my crappy apartment, pack as much as I could fit in a duffel bag, and disappear. There had to be somewhere someone like me could go without constantly having to worry about covering my scent, without worrying about being in public when my heat hit and my perfume exploded from me and slick dampened my panties.

Pipe dreams. That was all I had. Fantasies.

And hope. The hope that I could find a way out before it was too late and I was carrying some stranger's pup.

Andrei

THERE WAS no reason to check on the location of my team. I knew they were exactly where they should have been. What made me nervous were the other two ORE – Omega Rescue and Extraction – teams joining us on this mission. I hated working beside someone I hadn't tested on the front lines.

As long as my pack made it out of here alive, I would consider this a successful mission.

No. We had to get as many omegas as possible out of this compound first. We were given the go ahead on kill shots if necessary.

But stealth was our first choice. It was far easier to sneak in and out undetected than it was to usher omegas through a combat zone.

Touching a fingertip to the comm in my ear, I clicked it twice and waited for the answering clicks that everyone was in position. We were ready to rock.

I was the first through the gate, slipping through a hole we'd cut far from any watchful eyes. My team was right on my ass. The other two teams would enter from the east and the west, staying away from lights and any cameras that might have been pointed toward the open spaces.

This was going to be tricky. Already, I spotted a camera high on a building that had been missed during drone flyovers. How many more would we struggle to dodge?

Mac appeared to my right, Chase to my left, with Liam directly beside him. The two had been in love far longer than I had known any of my pack. No way would they split during this mission. Or any mission. The fuckers were inseparable.

Something felt…wrong. Off. The intel had felt concrete, but I was already spotting so much that hadn't made it into the report.

There was a building on the south side of the property, and the intense level of pheromones rolling from that area damned near brought me to my knees.

My pack was to focus on the housing unit where there were reportedly at least a dozen omegas being held against their will and experimented on. The tall, narrow, nondescript building stretched ahead of us. We would have to make it across the open expanse of lawn and pavement without detection to get to the victims inside.

What sickened me was how often my team and others of our company had to execute similar missions. The rare omegas were targeted by the scum of the earth, dominated, raped, tortured.

It was my job to put a bullet in the head of any motherfucker I caught in the act of perpetuating such terror. And, honestly, I did it with a smile on my fucking face.

Omegas were to be cherished. They were to be held on a damn pedestal. It didn't matter whether they were male or female. Without them, the population could damned well cease to exist.

Betas could get pregnant in rare occasions, but their bodies were unable to accommodate the knot of an alpha. It could be painful for them. And pain was not something I could ever stomach inflicting on another living soul.

Lie. I loved to inflict pain…nah, I loved to inflict *agony* on people like those who'd locked up the omegas in this compound.

Focusing on the pack bonds, I checked in with each of the man flanking me on all sides. Excitement, anxiety, anger. No fear. The only fear any of us felt during these missions was for each other, the fear of losing one of our packmates.

Taps sounded through my earpiece. Everyone was in place. But those fucking cameras still gave me pause. If a single one of us was spotted, this mission would turn into a firefight. Not that I couldn't handle a firearm. But I didn't want to risk innocent people getting caught in the crossfire.

All we could do was use our training and hope for the best. Raising a hand, I motioned for my team to move forward, then tapped the comm in my ear twice, indicating we were on the move.

Every member of all the teams were dressed in all black, our weapons in a matte finish to avoid a flash of light catching someone's eye. But if any one of us appeared on the cameras and were spotted by security…

I had to push that shit to the back of my mind and focus on the mission. The other teams were in charge of covering our asses and collecting anything they could to ensure the perpetrators were prosecuted.

Personally, I would rather see every one of them dead, but that wasn't my call to make. Unless I felt they were a threat. And, yep, I would find anyone I came across as a threat. In my mind, I was saving the taxpayers money by avoiding a lengthy trial.

As though we had choreographed it, my team moved forward as a single unit, our steps silent and in unison like a march.

Staying low, my eyes darted everywhere, watching the windows, doors, trying to peer into the shadows of every tree or shrub.

Get in. Get the omegas. Get out. Go home alive. That was the mantra that repeated in my head as we finally reached a door that led into the residential unit of the omegas. Various scents permeated the air around me, coming from my packmates and those inside.

Turning my head to check on my team, I leaned against the door and tried the knob. Locked. There were only a few ways to get into a locked building. Since we were trying for stealth, I nodded Mac forward and covered his back as he pulled tools from deep pockets in his cargo pants. He began to fiddle with the various locks, trying to pick them with as much finesse as possible.

A pop sounded from somewhere to the west. Then another.

And then the fucking alarm began to blare with loud *wonk, wonk, wonks* as floodlights nearly blinded me.

"Fuck," I muttered under my breath.

So much for slipping in and out undetected.

Pulling Mac away, I took a step back and kicked at the door near the knob as hard as possible. It took three kicks before the door gave and allowed us entry into the building.

"Check every room. Kill anyone who doesn't look as though they're here against their own will."

No arguments from my team. No reminders that we should try to subdue and arrest the wrongdoers. While each of us had completely different personalities, we were as connected as a pack could be without being full mates. Different personalities, but we all had the same mission – protect the omegas.

Each of us had expressed a desire to have an omega of our own, to have one in our home whom we could pamper and spoil. But nearly a decade had passed since Chase, the youngest of our group, had joined and we had yet to find someone who filled that weird hole every alpha carried in their heart.

Whether we wanted an omega or not, there wasn't a chance in hell we would force one into our lives. We wanted a true connection; a mate who could love us as much as we would love her…or him.

I would definitely prefer a woman, but nature had a way of choosing our soul mates. And who was I to argue with fate?

As we split up and began forcing doors open, screams erupted one by one. They were terrified and had every right to be.

The more doors opened, the more the scent of omegas in heat began to permeate the air. How the fuck were this many people in heat at once?

They'd been drugged. The was the only solution I could form in my mind. They'd been given something to force them into heat.

Because if they were all in heat, they would be not only easier to dominate and control, but easier to impregnate. They would be putty in the hands of any alpha who could bring them relief from the fever and pain that struck during each cycle.

Fucking sadists. I could only imagine the shame and depression these people suffered at the end of each cycle when they realized what they'd endured simply because they were born with a specific gene.

"Upstairs," Mac barked out. There was no longer any reason for us to remain quiet. The rapid sound of gunfire echoed throughout the compound.

The enemy knew we were here.

Mac darted up the stairs with me on his heels while Chase and Liam continued clearing the first floor. I knew they would follow once they'd freed every prisoner in this place.

The trickiest part now would be getting everyone out and into the waiting SUVs without any casualties. The thought of a single omega falling made my stomach turn and a sour taste to enter my mouth.

"Clear," I heard Liam call out from below.

We had planned to gather all the victims and sneak them out at once. Now...we had to figure out a new plan.

Mac entered a room and ducked. Something flew over his head as a stream of foul epithets flowed from the room, mixed with a strong scent of cotton candy and the sweet stickiness of a lollipop; the kind we would get when we were good for the doctor. It mixed with the various other smells, but this one...

A craving for candy became nearly painful as the sugary sweetness entered my lungs and embedded itself into every cell of my body.

"Hey, hey, hey," Mac said with his hands out. Something else flew over his head. A pillow? Did this poor omega really think she could do any damage with a fucking pillow? "We're here to help. We're ORE. We're taking you home," he said as quickly as he could.

The curses cut off; various items no longer came flying from the room.

Rushing forward, I stopped beside Mac and peered inside. And felt my fucking heart nearly stop in my chest. Her eyes widened the moment they touched mine as though she felt the same odd magnetic pull as me.

Something about this woman's warm brown eyes tugged at my heart. Her smell awakened my cock. The fear that turned that cotton candy scent to cloyingly sweet and slightly bitter sent a protective and possessive urge to beat my own pack brother to a pulp rushing through my system.

Mac wasn't the enemy. And, by the looks of him, he was as affected by this high-spirited omega as I was.

In my forty-two years of life, I wasn't sure I'd ever met such an aggressive omega. They tended to be gentle spirited and just this side of meek. If I hadn't caught her scent, I would have guessed the victim as a beta. Maybe even an alpha with the way she was willing to fight for her life.

Her hand was still poised to throw the roll of toilet paper clenched in her fist, but her eyes stayed on me. Her chest rose and fell, her heavy and full tits slightly visible through the thin medical gown she wore.

"We need to go," Liam called from down the hall. "All rooms have been cleared and victims are waiting for escort."

The woman's eyes darted to the doorway then back to me. That seemed to snap her out of the same stupor I was lost in.

"I'm leaving? It's over?" she asked, suspicion warring with hope in her tone.

"It's over," I confirmed, extending my hand to her.

For a few heartbeats, she stared at my hand as though she wasn't sure this was all real. She still had the roll of toilet paper in her hand, ready to launch it at the first sign of a threat. It took nearly every bit of control to refrain from laughing. How much damage did she think she would do with a roll of thin ass paper?

Finally, she dropped the roll and darted barefoot across the room, sliding her small hand into mine. She was at least six inches or so smaller than me, but not quite as petite as other omegas I'd rescued.

She looked physically strong, albeit a little too thin. She also looked terrified. And so fucking angry.

Pushing through the cloud of perfume permeating every inch of this place and checking in with the connection to my pack, I escorted her out of the room and down the hall. Gunfire was popping from every direction. How the fuck was I getting these people out alive?

CHAPTER 2

iolet

Holy shit. Was this real? Was the Omega Rescue and Extraction team really here?

Never in my life had I thought I would need the assistance of ORE. But I'd always believed myself a beta until recently. It wasn't common for betas to be hunted or enslaved. I had really believed I was in the clear, that my life would be normal.

Stupid hormones. Stupid rare gene. Stupid asshole alphas.

But an alpha currently had his hand wrapped around mine, tugging me behind him as we joined the small group of other omegas huddled in the hallway, the sounds of terrified whimpers and sobbing mixing with rapid and repeated gunfire somewhere outside.

Glass shattered in the same direction we would need to run if we were to actually exit this building. I wasn't sure if there was a back way out. This was the only way I'd ever seen when I'd been dragged to and from the infirmary during the various testing and injections.

"Mac," the alpha holding my hand said over all the sounds, "check for an alternate route."

Mac. I had one name. But there were four men currently guarding myself and the other omegas.

Looking around, I realized there were people missing. They were either in the infirmary, or they were in that building, the building we all dreaded. I hadn't yet been taken in there, but I'd heard the stories, had listened in as guards had passed my door.

We had all been kept separate, but that didn't mean we hadn't found ways to communicate through the vents when it got quiet late at night. All I could do at the moment was scan over the bodies pressed together, but there definitely appeared to be a few missing.

The man holding my hand released it and pressed a finger to his ear. "Copy. Thirteen in my custody."

His eyes met mine for the briefest moment then darted away. The fact every single omega in this room was in a various stage of heat, I couldn't imagine how difficult it was for these men to remain professional. Years of training. Or perhaps the utmost control over their own hormonal urges.

Either way, I felt safe. None of them made a move to touch any of us. None of them leered or ogled. No one sniffed the air around us.

The fear was beginning to build as the sound of gunfire was punctuated with explosions that shook the floor beneath me. But the fear was helping override the pain that rippled through my middle half.

"We're going to die," a woman whimpered from somewhere to my left.

Any other day, I might have wrapped my arms around her and did my best to comfort her. I would have said everything I could to reassure her that we were going to be free and in our own beds within hours.

But I couldn't find those words. I couldn't guarantee her that every single one of us weren't minutes from death.

Honestly, death would be far better than what the fuckers who'd brought us here had in mind. I had seen pregnant omegas being escorted when I peered through the small window in my room. I had even heard an infant's cry at some point, though I never saw the pup.

They were using our bodies for whatever sick plan they had in their sick minds. And it wasn't like they indulged us with those plans. They were always careful about what they discussed in front of their little toys.

Anger. So much anger. It was quickly pushing aside the fever burning through my system and the intense cramping deep inside my body. Even if I hadn't been taken, merely finding out another person had been treated as nothing more than a sex slave, as something to be used and abused, as an incubator to a group of fucked up alphas, would have caused a rage deep inside my heart.

The fact I happened to be one of the omegas...

The man who'd dragged me from my room glanced at me again, his eyes narrowing a second before he touched a finger to his ear.

"Copy," he said. "Mac found a possible alternate exit. Down the hall. Through a basement. Can all of you walk unaided?"

No one spoke but we all nodded. Had they waited much longer, I wasn't sure I would be able to do much more than curl into myself and beg for a knot. And then I would end my forced heat cycle ashamed and disgusted that I'd begged those assholes to rape me while in a heat induced haze.

Two men raced ahead while the one who appeared to be in charge took up the rear. His touch was light on the small of my back as he urged me forward, not quite pushing me, but adding a sense of urgency.

Another explosion rattled the windows and shook the floor, pulling a terrified screech from a woman ahead of me. But no one stopped, no one hesitated. We had to get out of here and we couldn't escape if we cowered in a corner and waited to be carried out.

"Liam. Chase. Secure the basement," the man barked.

The two snapped into action.

I was right about the man being in charge because his bark made my omega snap to attention and a whimper escaped my parted lips.

Three names. I now had three names of our rescuers. I hated

thinking of myself as a victim, as a freaking damsel. I had taken care of myself for so long that it nearly grated to have to depend on another person, especially an alpha, for my independence. Hell, for my life.

"Clear," a male voice called from down the stairs.

A man with dark blond hair and carrying quite an impressive looking rifle appeared at the top of the stairs and began waving us all down. I stayed in the back. I wasn't sure what I thought I could do to help, but, unlike those ahead of me, I hadn't spent my life as an omega. I hadn't spent my life depending on others for my wellbeing. And I sure as hell hadn't been coddled. My parents had damned near tossed me out their door the day I turned eighteen and I knew it had everything to do with their only daughter being a beta.

If they'd merely waited a few more years, they would have gotten their dream of having a rare gem under their control. Something to use as a bartering tool, a daughter they could use to climb the social ladder to the top.

Part of me wanted to call them the moment I was free to let them know I was safe. But did they even know I'd been missing?

Another part of me wanted to call them simply to rub in their face that I'd perfumed and would be registering as an omega. Or maybe I wouldn't. Maybe it was better to keep my name and designation a secret after this whole ordeal.

The thoughts that pinged through my brain at a time like this...

I knew what I was doing. I was distracting myself. I was doing my best to keep my shit together so I could make it out of here in one piece. It was how I had always gotten through stressful situations.

Looking back, every single thing I'd been through up to this point had been freaking child's play. Simple. Laughable.

I was the last one to enter the basement. Mildew and dust tickled my nose while the scents of the omegas and the earthy, spicy, and nearly stifling scents of the alphas from ORE confused my senses until I wasn't sure whether I should growl, whimper, cry, or start screaming.

The blond – Chase? – raised the butt of his rifle and smashed out a window that looked barely large enough for me to climb through. How the hell were the guys going to climb out? And, as selfish as it might have sounded, I didn't want to leave without them. Who the hell would protect us once we were outside of these walls? I had no doubts the guards and whoever was in charge of this outfit would do whatever it took to keep their little pets, their experiments, their toys.

As I watched in awe, the man who'd gone in the basement with him – he had to be Liam – swung his rifle over his shoulder and made a ladder of his hands, deftly hoisting Chase through the broken window. Once he was through, Chase removed his rifle, tugged off what looked like a ballistic vest, and draped it over the frame to prevent us omegas from getting sliced.

We were going to get hurt either way. None of us wore shoes and there were shards of glass littering the basement floor.

As though I manifested that very thing, a sliver embedded itself right at the base of my toes when I moved forward behind the dozen others to wait our turn to get outside.

The man named Mac was now at our rear with the fourth man whose name I still didn't know.

His intense eyes watched me closely, glancing down at my feet, then frowning at all the bare feet that, like mine, were walking across the sharp slivers and shards on the floor.

He moved forward as though to lift me or one of the others, but I waved him away. We could deal with cut feet once we were far away from this place.

Another explosion caused dust to float onto us from the ceiling overhead and I had a brief bout of terror. What if this building collapsed on top of us. I would rather a bullet in my head than be crushed to death.

So many macabre thoughts. So much fear. So much anger.

So much regret. So many things I had never experienced. I had never fallen in love. I had never traveled. I had never pursued a meaningful career.

And I didn't have a family of my own. After they turned their backs on me ten years ago, I had no family at all.

Three more women, and I could climb through the window and be that much closer to freedom.

Screams erupted from outside. Screams of terror. Feet hit the hard, cold ground as they ran.

Shit.

"Hurry! Get them out! Now!" Chase said, turning and raising his weapon to fire at an unseen enemy.

We'd been discovered. I had no idea how many guards were at this compound, how many people these four men were up against. And the hope I'd felt when my door had been kicked open and I realized it wasn't the enemy but heroes was quickly dying.

"Fuck! The omegas are scattering," Chase said as he turned this way and that, the fire from the muzzle of his rifle lighting up his face each time he pulled the trigger.

"Let me out," Liam said, pushing me back so he could hoist himself through the window. He took his place on the other side of the window, covering his buddy's back and, hopefully, ensuring more of us would escape.

It was my turn. I was the last one left with Mac and the nameless man.

Turning to stare up into his face, I was momentarily taken back by the intensity in his stare. I couldn't name the emotions that swirled through his striking blue eyes, but there was obvious anger and determination. He was taking this personally.

It was his job. The Omega Rescue and Extraction teams made it their sole mission to protect those who were so often exploited. If we didn't make it out of here alive, their mission was a failure.

"Your turn," he said, his voice strong but soft as he turned me toward the window, gripped me by the hips, and hoisted me through the window.

Chase turned and grabbed one of my arms, making sure I was fully through and on my feet. "Please don't run. We can't protect you if we don't know where you are."

There were only two other omegas outside the window with me now. The others had scattered. And all I could do was pray they had made it away safely and could return to their lives they'd enjoyed before these monsters found us.

I sure as hell had no intention of running. Where would I go? I wasn't even sure where this place was located and didn't know if I could make it home. If I had a home anymore. I had been gone for weeks. Would the landlord assume I had abandoned my place? Would my stuff have been put on the curb for strangers to dig through?

Maybe I would get lucky and they had made a missing person's report. Jerry and Maggie had always been kind to me in the past. They had to have noticed I wasn't coming and going as usual since they were my neighbors in the small duplex.

The last two men climbed through the broken window and then I was being pushed and ushered away from the building. They created a living wall around us as they kept their rifles raised, pointing and firing periodically.

Now that I was free, the fear and anger built until I could barely breathe. So many sounds, so many smells. Blood. Gunpowder. Sweet and spicy and earthy coming from the alphas, the omegas, and even some betas.

A whooshing in my ears nearly drowned out all other sound. It was the sound of my heart pounding, the blood pumping through my veins. The sawing of air pulling in and out of my lungs as darkness began to creep around the edges of my vision.

Hell no. I would not pass out and end up either dead, thrown over the shoulder of one of these strangers, or dragged back to my own personal hell.

Pushing through, I reached forward and clung to the man whose name I hadn't heard uttered once. He reached behind him and patted my arm, then raised his rifle once more. He was doing his best to reassure me while trying to get us all out safely.

Horror turned my stomach when I spotted a female lying on her back in a pool of blood, her eyes wide and staring unseeing at the dark sky. An omega had been killed trying to escape. I couldn't tell whether it was one of the women who'd been in the same building, but assumed it had been one of those who'd run the moment they were through the window.

There were more bodies littering the ground, some were guards, some wore lab coats, and then…more omegas. One omega lay lifeless, his protruding belly proof that he'd been impregnated during his stay. Now neither he nor his pup would see another day.

Tears burned the backs of my eyes and blurred my vision, but I blinked them away. I could have a full break down another day. In this moment, my focus was solely on putting one foot in front of the other, staying between the tall, muscular bodies shooting at anyone who posed a threat, until we were at a gate that had been cut to create a gap large enough to squeeze a body through.

This was it. We were almost free.

And only three of us were still crowded between the ORE members.

"Andrei," Mac called over the noise, then jerked his head toward the gate. "Get them to the SUV."

Andrei. The final missing name. The leader of this group was named Andrei. Four names. Four Alphas. Four heroes. Four men who had risked their own lives to save ours.

"Teams two and three are through the gate with their cargo," Chase said after touching his ear.

As Andrei squeezed through the gap in the fence, I barely caught the glimpse of something in his ear. That was what they had been using to communicate, small earpieces like I had seen used in movies when bodyguards protected celebrities or politicians.

These guys moved more like military than some hired muscle.

Andrei held out a hand, waving us forward. I waited for the first two women to scamper through, then did the same, taking a deep breath once I was through as though the fence would stop the barrage of bullets that still whipped past in all directions like bees.

He lunged to his feet, wrapped a hand around mine, and began pulling, barking orders for the other two women to follow closely as the three remaining men covered each other as they slipped through the cut fence.

Twigs and rocks bit into my already sensitive and cut feet, but I ignored it as much as I ignored the pain from my induced heat. I would address all of it once I was behind my apartment door and could process everything that had happened over the past few weeks.

There was a moment when a breeze hit my bare ass and my back that I remembered the men following closely behind us were getting a full view, but at the moment, that was the least of my concern.

A bullet hit a tree inches from my head. I ducked and screamed, but kept running forward as the ORE members returned fire, covering us as we darted forward.

A black SUV came into view. Almost there. We were so close to safety. We just had to make it into that damn vehicle.

Something warm slapped across my face followed by a thud. I turned my head and opened my mouth as a soundless scream tore from my lips. Another omega had been hit directly in the head. It had been her blood that had splashed across my face and neck and dampened my hair.

"Oh my god," I whimpered.

But Andrei's hand clamped around my wrist and tugged me forward.

Of the dozen or so who'd been rescued from that building, only two of us were still running. I might never know how many actually escaped after darting into the woods surrounding the compound.

Bullets hit the SUV, but we continued forward. I was pulled around to the other side, my body now shielded by metal. The sounds of engines roared to life nearby. The other teams I had heard mentioned? *Please let them be good guys.*

The back door was yanked open and I was shoved inside, my head pushed down by Andrei. The only other remaining omega climbed in behind me, and we instantly sought comfort in each other's arms, huddling on the floor and trembling as the team climbed in and took their places.

The moment the vehicle lurched forward, I allowed a single tear to escape over my lashes. It was over. I was free. My nightmare was over.

As a fresh wave of pain caused me to release the other woman and double over, my arms wrapped around my middle, I wondered if a second nightmare was beginning. I had no idea what kind of chemicals we were dosed with and what kind of damage was done to my system.

All I could do was wait. All I could do was count the minutes until I walked through my apartment door and began the process of piecing my life back together.

CHAPTER 3

Mac

I PUSHED my foot against the gas pedal as hard as possible, cursing myself for not checking the intel we'd been given more thoroughly.

"Fuck," I muttered under my breath, fighting the urge to punch the dash.

How many had we lost? I had tried to keep the omegas from running once we were free of the building, but my attention had been split between the victims and the assholes firing at us from every direction.

Until we were able to speak with the other two teams, we wouldn't find out what had caused the explosions. I assumed the others wouldn't have set off any incendiary rounds without knowing whether all the omegas were freed. But that didn't mean the actors behind this particular compound wouldn't have wanted to hide any evidence of their actions.

The fuckers had killed omegas. They had targeted the men and women who'd been running for their freedom. They were already rare in society. They were to be protected and cherished. Yet those cock suckers had ended the lives of at least eight that I saw.

The scents of my pack, of pepper, leather, whiskey, peppermint, and chocolate cake mixed with the heady, intoxicating scents of the two omegas hiding on the floorboard of the backseat.

Cotton candy and bubblegum. I wasn't sure which belonged to whom, but that cotton candy scent made my mouth water and my cock twitch. Not something I needed to focus on when we still weren't out of the woods. Both literally and figuratively.

Now that the enemy was aware they'd been infiltrated, that they had lost some of their prizes, they would be out for blood.

"Any news from teams two and three? Any casualties?" I could easily communicate with them myself, but needed to focus on getting us out of the woods without the headlights alerting anyone to our exact location.

"Teams, report. Casualties? Injuries?" I heard Andrei say both from beside me and through the comm in my ear.

"Team two," one started. "No team members killed. Three injuries. No survivors in custody."

Growls erupted in the SUV as all four of my pack heard the same news.

"Team three. One death. One injury. Only four survivors in custody."

"Do you know how many omegas were with you at the compound?" Andrei asked.

Neither woman answered.

Turning in his seat, he hovered over the side to look down at them. There was a beat of silence followed by a flare of cotton candy and leather until I had to suck in a deep breath of air to remind myself where I was and what we were doing.

Andrei's scent had always affected me in a way very few did, almost forcing my alpha to submit under his power. But it was nothing compared to the way it filled the cab now, nothing compared to the way it mixed with the sweet smell of spun sugar and...lollipops? Like the kind we would get as kids.

My heart rate kicked up and my dick hardened until I had to reach down to shift it away from the bite of my zipper.

"Andrei," Liam said from the far back of the SUV.

Andrei shook his head in my periphery and tensed, as though getting back into fighting mode. "Do you know the number of omegas held in the compound? An estimate?"

The first response was a soft whimper that made my alpha want to find someone to kill.

The second response was in a voice sweet and feminine, yet strong.

"I don't know. There were those you saw in the building. And I know some were in the infirmary. Others were in the…fun room."

"The fun room?" Andrei growled.

"That's where they…that's where they take us when we're in heat," the woman said.

"What are your names?" Andrei asked.

He turned back in his seat and pulled out a small notebook and pen stashed in the glove compartment.

"Violet Henson," the sweet voice replied.

"Amora," the other woman said, not giving a last name. Maybe she still wasn't sure whether she could trust us. I didn't blame her.

Not only had I heard stories of what transpired in those types of compounds, but I'd witnessed it firsthand during dozens of raids through the years. Any survivors would need a lot of help to get through the trauma they'd suffered. They would need gentle guidance, a safe place to nest, and their families.

"I need to report in. But you can use any of our phones to contact your people," Andrei said, turning in his seat again to glance at the women.

He had shut the pack bond down, preventing me from getting a read on his emotion. It was pointless. The heady scent of his black pepper and leather told me all I needed to know about how he felt at the moment. Or at least how he felt about one of the women in the backseat.

I felt the same way. She was mine. She was *ours*.

Yet, after everything she had gone through, we might never have the chance to shower her with the love, affection, and devotion someone like her deserved.

"Can I call my mom?" the other woman asked, her voice so soft it was barely above a whisper.

"Of course," Andrei said, handing her his phone.

I didn't miss the fact he kept his body angled toward the backseat as though he couldn't take his eyes off the woman with the sweet smell.

There had been so much going on, I wasn't sure I knew what any of the omegas looked like. There had been both men and women. And only six omegas were currently in the custody of three ORE teams. Six out of how many? Two dozen? More?

Rage turned my stomach sour and added a red tint to the dark woods ahead of me.

It wouldn't be much longer until the tires hit asphalt. Then, I could turn on the headlights and speed toward the station.

Soft feminine murmurs met my ears as Amora assured her family she was alive and safe, that she would be home soon. I didn't know if she was one of the omegas who'd had a missing person filed on them with the police department, but I couldn't imagine any of these people's absence going unnoticed.

"Team one reporting," Liam said from the third row.

I glanced in the rear view in time to catch Liam waving off Chase as he checked him for injuries. I hadn't bothered checking myself, though nothing hurt. I wasn't hit. My pack was all in one piece.

"Two in custody. Several casualties. Team one intact," Liam reported.

Since he was using his phone, I couldn't hear the other side of the conversation but knew we would be under instructions to bring the survivors to the hospital first if needed then to the station for questioning.

As far as I could tell, neither of the women had sustained life-threatening injuries. But I could smell the tangy, coppery hint of blood coming from someone.

A thin, pale arm appeared between the seats and handed Andrei his phone back.

"Do you need to call someone?" he asked, offering the phone to Violet.

"There's no one to call."

Her voice was strong, but it was obvious she was fighting back emotion. Her voice held the slightest tremble and I worried shock would eventually settle in for one or both omegas. That kind of shit got to me and I had been doing it for nearly two decades. These two wouldn't be used to violence, to seeing dead bodies, to seeing someone's brains blown out right in front of them.

Taillights glowed red ahead. One of the teams was ahead of us, their headlights now shining the way as they traversed over a small ditch, rocking the SUV and sending everyone bouncing around inside.

"Oh my god," Amora cried out.

"It's okay. It's just the road," Violet reassured her.

She had gone through the same horror yet she was putting her own needs and feelings aside for the terrified woman.

Her sugary scent had taken on a slightly burned smell as her own anxiety spiked, telling me all I needed to know about the woman. She was afraid but was staying calm to avoid scaring Amora any further.

"We're almost out of here," I reassured them both. "The road is right ahead."

Relief filled me as the tires made full contact with the road and squealed as I pushed the SUV as hard as it would go.

Raising my eyes to the rearview, I caught a hint of bright lights a second before the ear-splitting sound of metal hitting metal filled the car. And then we were rolling, glass shattering and cutting my arms, my face, and any exposed flesh of my body.

The women weren't buckled in the back. They'd huddled together low on the floor to avoid the gunfire.

How the hell would they survive being tossed around like ragdolls inside of a fucking tin can?

. . .

Violet

I DON'T KNOW what made me peek my head up. But I caught bright light flooding the cab at the same time I saw Mac's eyes widen in the rearview mirror.

There was nothing I could do when something slammed into the side of the SUV, setting it into motion until I felt as though I was in a washing machine, being spun and tossed over and over. I grappled for the headrest, hoping to stop from being thrown around to no avail.

Glass bit into my forearms, scraped across my face, embedded in my side. My head smacked against Amora's shoulder, then the top ceiling of the cab as it flipped again.

The sound would stay with me forever. If I made it through this.

So much pain came from so many places in my body I had a hard time focusing on one.

Finally, after what felt like an eternity, the vehicle stopped rolling, coming to a rocking stop on its head. The men hung upside down, their seatbelts holding them in place. Amora and I were in a tangled heap, blood seeping from so many places I wasn't sure which was mine and which was hers.

"Fuck!" Andrei roared before hitting the button on his seatbelt and dropping hard. He was scrambling out of the broken window, rifle in tow before I could make sense of what was happening.

We'd had a car accident. Why did he need his rifle?

Unless...

We weren't safe. We hadn't gotten away. The assholes who'd taken us refused to let a single one of us walk away alive.

"Amora, get up. We have to move," I said, shaking her shoulder hard. She pinned my legs down, keeping me from climbing from the totaled vehicle and seeking safety away from the new barrage of bullets. The pops filled the night air, barely covering the sound of my panicked breathing when Amora didn't budge.

"Shit," I said, biting back a sob when I rolled her over. Her eyes were open. She wasn't moving. Her chest didn't rise and fall with each breath.

Another omega dead. I was the sole survivor with this team. That made only five of us who'd made it out so far. Unless the others were killed during this ambush.

"Get her into the other SUV," Andrei barked from outside as Mac climbed out to join him, his rifle raised and pointed before he'd fully climbed to his feet.

"Come on," Liam – or was it Chase – said as he grabbed me by the arm and started to tug.

I cried out as the move pushed more glass into my legs that were still pinned by Amora's dead body.

The blond crawled in through the broken passenger window and rolled Amora away. He checked me quickly before nodding to Liam at my back, who resumed tugging.

It still hurt, but at least there wasn't extra weight to shove the broken glass damned near to the bone.

Biting my lip, I choked back another sob as fear and pain threatened to pull me under. I couldn't lose it now. I couldn't lose consciousness. I had to fight. I had to survive. Even if only for Amora and the others who hadn't made it.

Feet gathering more glass, I followed Liam and Chase to a waiting SUV. Its team was standing outside of their vehicle with rifles raised. As I was ushered into the backseat, my heart clenched. There were no omegas here. This was the team who had been unable to save anyone.

"Let's go!" Liam bellowed as Mac and Andrei slowly retreated, never pulling their fingers from the triggers of their weapons.

The moment all the bodies were squeezed inside, the car lurched forward before the doors were pulled closed. The smell of burning rubber mixed with all the others, with coppery blood, with gunpowder, leather, pepper, chocolate, whiskey, sugary orange, and more.

My breathing became shallow the further we drove and the stronger the scents grew. I was a lone omega in the beginning stages of my heat with eight alphas who were full of rage and hormones.

Growling made it through the ringing in my ears, but no one

looked in my direction. Andrei was pressed to my left side, Mac on my right. Liam and Chase were squeezed into the hatchback space of the SUV while the four members of this team took the driver and passenger seat and the second row.

"Is it over?" I asked, begging my breathing and heart to slow down before I hyperventilated.

"Not yet, sweetheart," Andrei said from beside me.

He pressed his thigh against mine then dropped an arm around my shoulders, pulling me close to his side.

That was all it took for my body to nearly give up the fight. I collapsed against his side, breathing him in, letting leather and pepper chase away everything else until my lids grew heavy.

I wanted to sleep. I didn't want to be awake anymore. I didn't want to feel every cut and bruise on my body. I didn't want to think about the fever or the cramping in my middle.

I didn't want to think about the blood that covered me from various omegas including sweet Amora.

CHAPTER 4

iam

"CHANGE OF ORDERS," Andrei reported. "We're to take the omega to a safe house. You four are to make a few rounds to ensure no one is following before returning to headquarters."

"Copy," the driver said.

I pushed the side of Chase's vest aside to check the bullet wound, but he once again pushed my hand away with a frown. "I'm fine," he muttered.

It wasn't a deep wound, but it still needed to be cleaned and bandaged.

The little omega was bleeding in so many places I couldn't tell how badly she was injured. There was also blood from the tiny woman who'd died in the crash. Another team would have to be sent to locate and retrieve all those who'd fallen during the fucked up mission.

"This is fucking bull shit," I spit out, unable to hold back my anger any longer.

"Agreed," a member of team two – Micah? – replied.

"Does the omega need medical attention?" another replied. I thought his name was Wilder, but we didn't often work together.

"The omega's name is Violet. And, yes, I need medical attention."

And then Wilder's big body was turning in his seat and running his hands across Violet's face, across her scalp, down her arms, until he got to her midsection. I don't know what the fuck came over me, but a possessive growl rattled up my chest at the sight of his hands on Violet.

He wasn't molesting her. He wasn't hurting her, at least not intentionally. He was checking to see whether she would need a hospital instead of the halfway house.

Wilder's eyes darted to mine, then to each of my pack. Oh shit. All four of us had growled.

"Did you want me to check her over or not?" he asked, no anger in his tone.

With a shake of my head, I turned my attention back to Chase, doing everything in my power to refrain from dragging him into my arms and kissing him breathless simply to ensure myself he was, indeed, still in one piece.

Team three had lost two of their members. I didn't know whether they were pack or just worked together. But that could have easily been one of us. And our pack would have shattered to pieces.

Wilder returned to his examination, checking her legs, lifting them to look at the bottom of her feet. He winced as he set each back down gingerly.

"She – Violet has a lot of glass embedded in her skin and she'll need stitches in several locations. We'll drop you off, circle until we're sure no one is following, then I'll return with supplies. Unless you want to take her to the hospital."

I opened my mouth to suggest it might be best for her to see a real doctor, but she beat me to it.

"No doctor," she said through what sounded like gritted teeth.

A wave of cotton candy swam around me, filling my lungs and making me crave warm summer nights and carnival rides.

She was thin and pale. Her hair appeared black in the dim light of the SUV, but it was also coated in blood and sparkled with glass when she moved her head. She had a hell of a night ahead of her. And a huge part of me wished I could take it all away for her. I would gladly take the pain into myself if it meant relieving her, especially after everything she'd gone through up to this point.

"I have some pain killers on me. Do you want some now?" Wilder asked her.

Violet barely lifted her head from Andrei's shoulder to look into his face as though looking for the answer. And that odd possessive urge to growl bubbled up in my chest again. Why should I care whether she wanted Andrei's reassurance? The love of my life was currently sitting beside me with a gun wound to his side.

Okay. A gun *scratch*. It wouldn't require more than a bandage. No stitches.

Yet, even with Chase's thigh pressed against mine, with his delicious peppermint and green tea scent swimming around me, I had a strong urge to grab Violet, drag her over the seat, and wedge her between Chase and myself so we could keep her safe.

I wasn't even sure what she looked like. I'd barely gotten a glimpse of her when we'd pulled her from the totaled SUV, and that glimpse didn't tell me much with her hair half covering her bloodied and bruised face.

"It'll take the edge off," Andrei said, his voice gentle.

Violet turned back to Wilder and nodded, then waited as he dug through his bag until he found an orange bottle of prescription pills.

"They might make you nauseous if you haven't eaten in a while. So first chance you get, at least get some bread in your stomach," Wilder said, handing her a single pill and popping the cap on a water bottle before handing that to her, as well.

She popped the pill in her mouth and emptied half the plastic bottle in one long pull. When she was done, she dropped her head back against Andrei's chest and sighed.

The pill would help for now. And once they got the glass out of her skin, that would help, too. But she had at least a few days of pain to endure until the nerve endings no longer fired as her skin knitted itself back together.

Unable to help myself, I reached my hand forward and laid it on the back of Violet's head. The softest rumbling filled the quiet of the cab. Was she purring? Had my touch made her purr? Or could it be the collective scents and energy of my pack?

Either way, that made me nervous. I had heard of packs finding their omega in an instant. Had heard of packs building bonds and connections with an omega they barely met. But after so many years of only the four of us, I had given up hope that there was one out there for us. I had never been one to believe there truly was someone out there for everyone, not until I'd met Chase during ORE training and felt as though my entire life depended on the sound of his voice.

Chase's hand landed on my back and smoothed up to rest over the back of my neck, his fingers lightly touching the bond mark he'd left there years ago. I wasn't sure whether he was comforting me, warning me, or letting me know he felt the same thing I did – this little omega was made just for us.

We were meant to spoil her. We were made to cherish her. We were put on this specific mission so we could find her and protect her from the evils of the world.

First, we had to get her as far away from her abductors and to somewhere safe so we could get her wounds cleaned up and the blood washed from her skin and hair.

I would personally volunteer to bathe her if given the chance.

Chase's elbow jammed into my ribs. No doubt I'd just scent a waft of chocolate into the air as my dick hardened.

Maybe this wasn't a good idea. I wanted her. Without even truly knowing what Violet looked like or anything more than her name, I wanted her on a primal level. But she'd just been through the worst thing an omega could suffer. She'd been taken and possibly raped by psychotic alphas. The last thing she needed was another drooling all over her.

We could get her to the safe house, clean and dress her wounds, keep her out of the hands of the enemy, then help her get back to whatever life she'd left behind.

Did she have a pack of her own? Her hair was down so I couldn't see whether any crescent scars marred her neck. Maybe she had a mate. Or she could possibly want to get home to her friends and family.

There's no one to call. That's what she'd said when Andrei had offered his phone. She had no one who would be worrying about her, no one to protect her once she was no longer in ORE custody.

Nope. Not just nope, but hell no. That wasn't an option. Regardless of what our superiors had to say, regardless of what my pack had to say, I would personally see to her safety and wellbeing for as long as she needed.

I would just have to find a way to keep my fucking hormones from going into overdrive every time I got a whiff of her sticky sweet scent.

Violet

My lids fluttered as I struggled to get them to lift. When I finally got my eyes open, it was just as difficult to focus on any one thing.

Male voices made it to my ears as they spoke in low tones. So many scents surrounding me; some making me want to nuzzle my face closer to the source, some making me want to roll back over and let sleep claim me again, and some were simply there, neither good nor bad.

I laid on something soft, a scratchy blanket draped over me.

Lifting a hand, I winced as tape tugged at my skin and pulled the thin hairs that covered my arm.

It was several long minutes before my brain caught up to the moment, to the memories of the night, of why I was in a strange house covered in bandages.

And why I was no longer wearing that disgusting hospital gown but a soft t-shirt that smelled heavily of warm leather that seemed to wrap around me like a hug.

Tilting my head down, I lifted the corner of the shirt and brought it to my face, letting that warmth spread throughout my limbs until I realized all the male voices had silenced.

With aching muscles, I turned my head on the pillow to find eight male faces watching me closely.

"Do you know where you are?"

Liam? That was Liam, right?

"How the hell would she know where she is?" another guy said. I didn't remember hearing his name but he'd been the one who'd poked and prodded at me in the back of the SUV.

"Dumb ass." Chase. That was Chase.

Andrei, Mac, Chase, and Liam. They were the members of the team who had saved us.

Who had saved *me*. I was the only one remaining.

Bile churned in my stomach and I sat up quickly, searching for something to puke in.

"Oh shit," Liam said, hurrying over with a small black trashcan and setting it on the floor in front of me.

His hand was gentle as he rubbed soothing circles on my back.

"It's okay. You're safe. Wilder cleaned up and stitched what needed immediate attention. You'll need to see someone as soon as possible, but you're okay for now."

"*They're* not," I choked out between dry heaves.

I don't know why I thought I would throw up. It had been hours since food had been brought to my room. I was lucky to be fed more than once a day like a dog left chained up outside and forgotten about until it was convenient.

Liam lowered to his knees in front of me and I suddenly craved rich, moist chocolate cake. It was him. His alpha scent calling to my omega.

"I'm sorry. Were they your friends?" he asked, his voice so sweet and gentle.

Shaking my head, I leaned forward and put my head in my hands. I swore every inch of me ached or burned. At least the cramping was nothing more than an echo compared to everything else begging for attention.

"We never met. But they were still...they didn't deserve to die like that. We didn't deserve to be..." My voice broke on the last word as emotion threatened to drag me into a panic attack.

Not yet. I wasn't ready to give my emotions free range yet. I wanted to be safely enclosed in my own home before I fell apart.

"Did you kill them all?" I asked, lifting my head and jutting my chin forward. I might have been cracking inside, but I didn't have to let my outside reflect the splintering happening inside my heart.

"We got as many as we could," Andrei said from across the room. "You were our mission."

Not me. *We*. *We* were their mission. And I could tell by the looks on their faces they were angry, they felt like failures because so many had died while trying to escape.

"What about the others who ran?" I asked. There had been those in the basement with us who'd taken off into the woods.

"We won't know until a recovery team goes in to–"

Andrei held up a hand, cutting off Chase's words. "We don't know yet."

Until I was told otherwise, I could only assume five of us out of I didn't know how many escaped with our lives. I knew I should have been happy. Happy that I had made it out. Happy that at least a few of us were taken from that place.

But there were so many who would never see their families again. So many who would never see another morning. A mixture of survivor's guilt and pure white hot rage singed through my system.

"Will you find them?"

"The survivors?" Mac asked.

With a shake of my head, I winced. Every muscle in my body ached and bandages pulled every time I tried to move. "The assholes. Will you find them and make them all pay?"

Andrei crossed the room until he stood directly in front of me. Liam moved away, allowing enough room for Andrei to kneel in front of me. He gently parted my blanket covered knees so he could slip between them, took my face in both of his big, warm hands, and stared directly in my eyes.

"We'll find every single one of them."

Black pepper. Warm, soft leather. I felt as though he'd wrapped me in his scent, cocooned me in the safety of his alpha presence, and I fought the urge to lean forward and melt into his arms, to let him cradle me against his chest as he had in the car, to beg him to keep me safe from the world.

Stupid omega hormones.

Was it, though? Was this visceral reaction to Andrei's nearness due solely to my hormones?

I looked at him, truly looked at him. In the bright light of the room, I could see silver studs lining both ears. Another stud in his nose. There were tattoos peeking from the collar of his shirt, more on his forearms that were bared by the sleeves he'd pushed up to his elbows. The inky designs even curled over each of his fingers like a living piece of art.

But that wasn't what drew me in. There was something about his ethereal blue eyes framed by thick black lashes that almost lent him a touch of femininity. *Almost.* They were the lashes women spent so much time trying to achieve.

The dark stubble on his cheeks that was a shade lighter than his raven black hair was pure rugged manliness.

I hadn't truly gotten a good look at any of the men who'd rushed into the compound to attempt to free us. There had been far too much going on and it had been dark until the floodlights had flipped on and given the assholes enough visibility to pick us off one by one.

"Will they look for me?" I asked, voicing the fear that burned deep inside.

Andrei dipped his head once. "Until we locate the leaders of this outfit, we'll work under the assumption that you are still a target as are any of the omegas who were able to escape. Each of you will remain in ORE custody until the target is eliminated."

"Killed," I said. "Until those assholes are dead."

"Or arrested," one of the guys said from behind me.

Turning my head, I leveled each of them with a look, finally getting the first real glimpse of my rescuers. Every one of them was attractive, every one of them was large and imposing, and every one of them looked as though they could snap a person in half without breaking a sweat.

"I would prefer they were dead," I admitted.

I had never been a violent person. At no point in my life had I ever been in a fist fight. I hated the thought of wars because, regardless of who we were fighting, people died. On both sides. Even those whom were considered our enemies had families who would have to say goodbye.

Now? Something had been awakened in me, some beast that craved blood and vengeance. And I couldn't say it was all for me. It was for every single omega who hadn't been able to avoid being raped, for the pregnant omega who laid dead on the asphalt of that stupid compound…

For Amora.

Mac huffed a surprised laugh, then lifted a hand to his mouth to hide it. But I'd heard it. Either I had caught him off guard or he was in agreement with me. They hadn't appeared to have a problem shooting the assholes who were slaughtering omegas left and right. Hopefully, they wouldn't have any problem pulling the trigger again when they hunted down each and every person who'd had a hand in the atrocity I'd barely escaped.

"She needs to rest," Wilder said, pushing through the crowd and resting a hand on Andrei's shoulder.

A rush of black pepper filled the room a heartbeat before a growl rattled up Andrei's chest. He cleared his throat, leveled a look on me, and waited for…what?

"I'm fine," I said.

I wasn't sure why I said that. I wasn't fine. I was in pain. My heat would still barrel into me while I was in a house full of alphas. I would end up in a whimpering, whining puddle of slick soon. The pain and fever would linger until I received a knot.

Not true. It would eventually fade out on its own, but that would be a torturous five or more days.

Wasn't the first time I'd suffered through it alone. And definitely wouldn't be the last. My captors had made sure none of us were on any form of birth control so it would be easier to breed us.

How the hell had I made it weeks without being touched? Luck? More like a blessing.

Wilder took Andrei's place when he stood, lifting my lids and shining a light into my eyes.

"Any nausea?" he asked, then winced. "Other than…" He jerked his head toward the trashcan. Nothing had come up, but that hadn't stopped the dry heaves.

"That wasn't nausea. Or…I mean it was, but it was nerves. No. No nausea."

"Dizziness?"

"A little."

His hands were gentle as he lifted bandages and peeked under them. "I gave you a few stitches, but I would still prefer you get checked at a hospital. These guys can watch over you. You should get a CT scan, too. Make sure there isn't a brain injury. Those can sneak up on you and kill you. Or make you a vegetable."

At his words, the room exploded with alpha pheromones and growls.

"Mac, bring the car up," Andrei barked.

At his words, Mac immediately crossed the room and stepped outside. Hell, I wanted to jump to action under the alpha's words. I had been right earlier – Andrei was definitely the leader of this group. They were all alphas, yet he seemed to have power over them all.

"I don't want to–"

Andrei's eyes turned to mine, and my mouth closed so fast I swore my teeth clicked together.

Damn. I hadn't spent much time around alphas since I'd perfumed – other than the fuckers at the compound – and had no idea how intensely my body would react.

Was this normal? I hadn't been submissive to a single one of those other assholes. I'd fought them every step of the way until they had to sedate me any time they took me to the infirmary.

But with Andrei...I had this bone deep need to please him. And, honestly, that pissed me off. A lot.

I was not that woman. I did *not* submit to anyone. I did *not* mold my life around a man. I did *not* exhaust my energy looking for a mate.

Yet...I couldn't find my fucking voice as he kept that stare on me, as the heady smell of black pepper embedded itself in my pores, as the warm smell of leather seeped into my skin and chased away the fear of stepping through that door and being in public again.

I had been snatched right off the sidewalk. There had been people around me yet not a single person had stepped in to help as I'd screamed and fought with everything I had.

They would protect me. Andrei wouldn't let anything happen to me. Mac, and Liam, and Chase would make sure no one would touch me.

"Are you going, too?" I asked, turning to look into Wilder's face.

He didn't smell like this pack. He didn't carry any of their scents. But I felt safe with him, too. He smelled of oranges and sweet cream, and it unfurled and wrapped around me when I asked. Beta. Wilder wasn't an alpha. Yet I didn't feel any less safe with him.

"I would be honored," he said, dipping his head once, and was answered with a series of growls.

"Okay," I said, throwing my hands in the air. "Why do you all keep growling at him? Is he ORE or not?"

"He's not pack," Chase answered.

"And?"

No one had an answer for my question. Something tickled at the back of my mind, some kind of warning bells. Not the kind that made me afraid of these men, but rather afraid of what my reaction to each of their individual – and combined – scents meant.

I was too new to this life. Life as a beta was far easier, less complicated. Sure, I had noticed the scents of others, had been drawn to an omega's scent, had reveled in the warmth of an alpha's scent, or calmed by a fellow beta's.

But this? It was like I was drinking them all in and getting drunk.

Headlights brushed through the cabin and then everyone was on their feet. I stood, then immediately dropped down. My feet were bandaged but felt as though I'd walked over hot coals. Bull shit. It felt like I'd stood on hot coals for hours. The bottoms of my feet were raw.

Before I could say a word, I was scooped up by Andrei, the blanket settled around me by Wilder, then carried through the house and to the waiting SUV.

"Where are the other guys?"

A vague memory of orders to drop us off at a safe house then for the others to drive around before returning to headquarters felt like I'd dreamed it.

"We checked in and I returned with a vehicle. Can't leave you all stranded," Wilder answered.

But there was only the one SUV. Meaning he would be stranded with us unless he took the only vehicle there.

The thought of Wilder being with us in the cabin made me happy. He was a calming presence. And it didn't hurt that he had medical experience. Maybe he could help me avoid the medically induced heat.

That was a conversation I would have to have with him in private. If Andrei and the rest of the pack allowed us to be alone.

CHAPTER 5

ndrei

LIAM, Chase, and Mac stood sentry outside the door while Wilder and I waited with Violet.

Why the hell was this dude hanging around? It wasn't that I didn't appreciate his help with her wounds. He'd helped clean her up, though I'd made him turn his back when I had removed that fucking hospital gown that reeked of alphas from the compound.

As hard as I'd tried to remain professional, I couldn't help sneaking a peek at her full, heavy tits. Only a peek, though. I wasn't a perv and would never disrespect her like that.

But he was still here. He'd brought us an SUV, but no one had followed him to the safe house to take him back. And Violet…

Yep. Jealousy coursed through my system every time she looked to him for an answer, every time her scent poured from her when he grew near. She was in heat. Or nearing heat. We hadn't had a chance to discuss it with her, but we had to find a way to help her through the pain and fever without touching her.

That was going to be a bitch. Omegas tended to lose their fucking minds when their hormones took over. Could I turn her down if she begged me for release? If she begged for my knot?

The answer was yes, I could. And every single one of my pack better keep their dicks in their pants and their hands off her. We would have to find other ways to help her, cool baths to bring down the fever, pain killers to help with the pain omegas suffered for days on end.

I would do literally anything for this tiny omega. But I wouldn't fuck her. Not until she was in her right mind and understood what she was asking for.

And I really didn't know if she would be into my...tastes. My bedroom style.

Time. I would have to give her time. And hope that she felt the same connection each of us was obviously feeling.

"How much longer?" Violet asked. She was growing impatient.

No. She was nervous. Her eyes repeatedly darted to the door any time she heard footsteps in the hall.

I lowered onto the side of the bed and took her hand in mine. "You're safe, Violet. My pack is right outside that door. Wilder and I are in here. No one will get past any of us. I promise."

The nurse and doctor who'd tended to her, checking the stitches and bandaging before finally taking her for a CT scan – with four large alphas following closely behind – were betas. Good. Because Violet smelled entirely too good. I wasn't sure I would be able to keep my shit in check if someone tried sniffing after her.

She turned her hand over and thread her fingers through mine. Cotton candy filled the room as she looked into my eyes a second before she winced.

"What hurts?"

She snorted a laugh. "Everything."

Raising a hand, I touched the back of it to her forehead. Yep. She was warm and getting warmer by the second.

"Can I, um...can I talk to Wilder a second?"

I bit back the growl at her request. She'd just perfumed while I held her hands and now she wanted to talk to someone who wasn't pack…alone?

Fuck.

"Sure. I'll be right outside the door if you need me."

I couldn't resist lowering my head and pressing my lips to her forehead before nuzzling my cheek against hers. Dick move, but I felt the need to scent mark her before leaving her alone with another man.

Wilder cocked a brow at me as I passed. Asshole knew what I had done.

"She doin' okay?" Mac asked when I stepped out of the room and pulled the door closed.

"Yeah. Wanted to talk to Wilder alone."

Three heads whipped in my direction. "What? Why?" Liam asked.

"Don't know. Didn't ask."

Chase turned toward the door and stared at it as though he could see through and into the room. A soft growl vibrated up from his chest and his peppermint and green tea scent turned bitter.

Liam put a hand on Chase's shoulder, turning him until they were facing each other. Some private conversation passed between with nothing more than a look, then the growl faded. But his scent remained bitter, like tea that sat in the fridge too long.

With a deep breath, Chase turned his back to the door and stared straight ahead. He looked like he was fighting every instinct to rush into the room to check on our omega.

Not ours. Not yet.

But, fuck…I wanted her. Every second I spent with her it grew harder to ignore the urge to sink myself into her heat, to push my knot into her, to sink my teeth into her shoulder to make her mine. To make her ours. To make her pack.

Too soon. It was far too soon. We barely knew her. She didn't know us. There were four separate personalities she would have to learn. And there was no guarantee she would want to spend any more time with us than was necessary when the threat was eradicated.

That would give us time to win her over. The shitty part was we couldn't go about it the right way. We couldn't court her, couldn't shower her with gifts, couldn't take her on dates so she could get to know us each individually instead of the entire pack as a whole.

Too soon. I was getting ahead of myself. She had been through hell and I was planning her future with a pack of four fucking alphas. She might very well have wanted nothing more to do with another man after her ordeal.

So, we would protect her. We would dote on her. We would make sure she had everything she needed. And wanted.

A nest. Fuck. There wasn't a nest at the safe house. The place was rarely used and normally only for short periods. She would need somewhere to feel comfortable and safe while her body put her through the wringer.

The door opened and Wilder peeked his head out. "She needs to talk to you," he said, his eyes on me.

Opening the door wider, he stepped into the hall with my pack while I slipped back in. Violet had her head rested against the pillow, her eyes closed. I stood there watching her a moment. Her hair still needed to be washed of the dried blood and she would need a real bath at some point, more than the sponge bath I'd given her to clean up the wounds.

But even with the bandages, the cuts and scratches, the bruising along the right side of her face…she was fucking stunning. Her brown eyes were light and warm and reminded me of caramel. Her nose was a little long for her face but lent her almost a cat like appearance. Her lips…

Fuck, her lips. Full and pink and kissable.

Her eyes opened and landed on me.

"You smell good," she murmured.

My feet carried me closer as her candy sweetness filled the room. As I grew closer, I noted her blown pupils, her flushed cheeks. It was only a matter of time now before she was fully in heat.

Maybe I should ask my commander to send her to a home with betas. They wouldn't be as tempted to fuck her. They wouldn't be as driven by her hormones. They wouldn't have a primal need to fill her the moment she begged.

But I couldn't. *Wouldn't.* The thought of anyone else protecting her made me antsy.

"Everything okay?" I asked, lowering to the side of the bed as I had earlier.

"I'm going into heat," she said, pink washing over her cheeks as though admitting it embarrassed her.

With a nod, I took her hand and ran my thumb across the back of it. Her skin was so soft, so warm. Too warm.

"I know."

"I'm not supposed to be."

I frowned at her for a second and then anger squeezed my heart. They had induced her heat. How many times had the omegas been put through that over and over while they'd been held? Had she been...

Fuck. I didn't want the answer to that. I didn't want to know if they'd taken her against her will. Because I might not be able to keep my ass parked on the hospital bed. I would hunt down any and every mother fucker who'd so much as contemplated touching her, anyone who'd had any part of the horrors she and the other omegas had been through and rip their heads from their shoulders.

"What can I do to help?" I asked. Stupid question. There was nothing I could do. At least something I wouldn't do.

"I talked to Wilder. He's going to ask the doctor if it's too late for a heat blocker. I'm not..." She inhaled deeply. "I can't deal with that and all this," she said with a wave toward her face and her body. "It's too much. I'm not even supposed to be here. I wasn't supposed to be there."

"None of you should have been there."

"No," she said, turning her hand in mine again like she'd done earlier. I wasn't sure if she was aware she was clinging to me, but I didn't want her to withdraw her touch. "I'm not supposed to be a fucking omega."

It took a few moments for her words to register. "What do you mean?"

"I didn't perfume until later. My parents kicked me out at eighteen because they thought I was a beta. They wanted another trophy. My brothers are all alphas. Mom's an omega. Dad's an alpha. Then there was me."

I huffed a disgusted sound. They didn't want a trophy. They wanted a gem. They wanted to have power, to be able to use her as a step in the ladder of society. *Look at us. We gave birth to a rare gem.*

Fucking assholes. I might never meet any of her family, but if I did, I had every intention of telling them exactly what I thought of them.

"If I hadn't perfumed…" Tears glistened in her eyes and she squeezed them shut and made a sound in the back of her throat; a frustrated growl that shouldn't have been cute, especially not when she was in such emotional and physical pain.

Lifting my other hand, I smoothed it over her hair and rested it on her cheek until she raised her lids and looked into my eyes.

"We'll keep you safe. We will find those mother fuckers. And we will make them pay," I promised her. I didn't care how long it took. I would hunt them to the ends of the fucking planet, spend every minute of the rest of my life if necessary.

But they would pay for daring to touch my omega.

Violet

No brain damage. Only a mild concussion. And, most importantly, a prescription bottle full of heat blocker and some birth control.

The doctor said there was no guarantee it would end this bull shit completely but would definitely cut down some of the worst of it. My body hurt enough. I sure as hell didn't need the cramping on top of it.

Andrei had stayed in the room, his hand wrapped around mine the entire time the doctor and nurses tended to me and gave me the results of the tests they'd run. And I clung to him as tightly as his fingers were wrapped around mine.

His presence eased the anxiety and almost erased the fear that some psycho would rush into the room and drag me away again. When he'd stepped back in after I'd spoken with Wilder, he'd carried hints of his pack. I wanted to take the fragrances and wrap them around myself like a cape or a shield.

"When can I leave?" I asked.

Even with the pack and Wilder, I didn't like being so exposed, so vulnerable. And I was currently wearing yet another hospital gown.

I preferred the oversized t-shirt I'd woken in back at the safe house. It smelled like my guys.

Not mine. They weren't mine. They were tasked to protect me, to protect the precious omega. I was a job to them.

Was I, though? Because they sure as hell behaved like possessive alphas any time Wilder got too close.

"The nurse is getting your discharge papers together and then we can head out," Andrei said.

I turned to look at Wilder. "Are you coming back?"

Andrei's hand tensed around mine.

"Do you want me there?" Wilder asked.

I looked around at Andrei, Wilder, and Mac. "Will it cause a problem if I say yes?"

I could pretend I wanted another body between me and the enemy. But Wilder calmed me in a different way than the pack. His essence was soothing, like balm on a burn.

"I need to get supplies of my own. I have nothing at the safe house." Wilder turned to Andrei. "Should I get some things for her?"

The muscles in Andrei's shoulders were tense and a muscle jumped in his jaw when he nodded his head in jerky movements. "She'll need some clothes. Toiletries." He turned his eyes to me. "Do you want to make a list?"

"Can someone get stuff from my apartment? And maybe make sure I still have an apartment?"

"Not a good idea," Mac said.

I turned a frown on him as he leaned against the wall, his thick arms crossed over his chest. "Why not?"

"Because someone can be followed back to you. For now, the only people who know where you're staying are trusted members of ORE. That reduces any risks to your safety. If one of us goes to your apartment, there's a chance they could be followed back to the safe house. We would sacrifice our lives to keep you safe, but that won't do any good if we're outnumbered and killed."

Bile turned in my stomach. Sacrifice their lives for me? Why the hell would they do that?

But they already had. One of the teams had lost two of their own members while trying to free the omegas from the compound. I hated that I was responsible for that.

Nope. Not doing that. I was not responsible for any of the deaths. I was a victim, too. I didn't choose to perfume. I didn't choose to be an omega. And I sure as hell didn't choose to be taken.

"So you're just going to, what? Buy me clothes?" I asked, looking from one guy to the next.

"Yeah," Mac said, his brows raising and a hint of *duh* in his tone.

With a frown, I shook my head. "I'll just wear...whatever."

A sound escaped Mac that was part growl, part purr. And everything south of my belly button tightened at the same time my muscles relaxed.

"Get her clothes. Toiletries. Girl stuff," Andrei said, his voice deeper as he pulled a card from his wallet. "Do you want to make a list or do you want him to guess?"

"I..." I had been given minutes to actually think about the fact I currently had nothing to my name. I couldn't return home. I couldn't retrieve anything that belonged to me. My mind was turning so quickly I couldn't focus on what exactly I needed. "Do you guys have scent blockers?"

"Why would you need that?" Wilder asked.

When I raised my brows and stared at him a few minutes, my meaning got through to him.

"Oh. Right." Did his cheeks darken?

"I'll find some," Mac said. "What else?"

"I...how should I know what I need? I don't have any clothes. Just get something in my size. Shorts and sweats. T-shirts. Underwear." I wanted to ask for bras, but I could forgo them for a period. Even with bigger boobs, I had always hated them. They were restrictive.

"Size?" Mac asked.

It was my turn to blush. What woman wanted to admit her size in front of…well, anyone.

Andrei noted my silence. With a tilt of his head, he smiled softly down at me. "Is this a girl thing? You don't want us to know your weight and size and age and all that?"

I couldn't hold back the roll of my eyes or the smile. "Fine. Size ten in bottoms. Or large in bottoms and extra-large in tops."

I could squeeze into a large shirt, but then it would stretch across my boobs. I wanted comfort more than style right now. I wanted to… shit, I wanted to find a closet, fill it with blankets, and nestle inside for a while.

The urge to nest was new to me. It had been so strange the first time my heat crashed over me and I'd dragged blankets, comforters, and pillows into my bedroom closet. But it had made me feel safe, had helped the anxiety that came with the discomfort of an omega heat.

"Got it," Mac said.

Then he stood there, staring down at me until I grew uncomfortable.

"Mac," Andrei said without pulling his eyes from my face.

"Right. Stuff. Wait. What if she's discharged before I'm done?"

"We could wait," I offered. "I can go in with you and–"

"No," all three men said in unison.

"We'll wait. We'll get you back to the safe house, then Mac can get the things you'll need. Deal?" Andrei asked.

"Why can't I just go with–"

"The same reason you can't return to your apartment yet. You're still perfuming. It might not be one of the fuckers who took you that we come across, but there will be other alphas in public. And I'm not in the mood to kill someone in the middle of some big box store tonight."

I hadn't realized my scent was still strong. For some silly reason,

I'd hoped everything would slow down the second the heat blocker entered my system.

So…back to the safe house. Back to another locked room. Back to another cell.

At least this time, I wouldn't have to fear my door being opened at any given time and being dragged to the fun room.

CHAPTER 6

ilder

"WHAT THE FUCK ARE YOU DOING?" Andrei growled.

Violet had been carried into the house then Andrei demanded a meeting with me in the yard in front of the cabin.

"What she asked me to do," I answered him.

He was riled up, and the last thing I wanted was to rise to the bait. I wouldn't back down if the fucker wanted to attempt to bully me, but neither did I want to add more stress to Violet by going fisticuffs with the pack's head.

"This isn't your pack."

"And?" I said, my arms crossed over my chest, feet shoulder width apart as I tried to remain loose and relaxed.

I wasn't sure whether Andrei knew I didn't have a pack. It wasn't something that had ever appealed to me. I'd seen the way my family's pack had all but imploded when one of the members had been killed in a car accident. A simple freak accident late at night caused my omega mother to practically grieve to death. Then the two other alphas who'd helped raise me sunk into such depressions they'd forgotten I existed.

Why form a connection with someone so deep and profound if it could destroy everything in its path?

"You will keep your fucking hands to yourself. If you so much as–"

I threw both my hands up and took a step closer to him. "Like you pointed out, I'm not a member of your pack, nor am I a subordinate on your team. I don't follow your lead. I will do what she needs from me. What she wants from me," I said, jabbing a finger at the house. "I'm here because she asked me to be here. And I'll stay as long as she needs me to."

"You will not fucking touch her," he barked.

The alpha bark might have affected his own pack, but did nothing more than cause my hackles to rise.

This was why it was dangerous for a group of alphas to be in such close proximity to an omega in heat. Things could get…dicey. Even as a beta, I found myself a little drunk on her perfume.

"I'm not here to fuck her, if that's what you have in your head." Not that she wasn't fucking beautiful. Not that her sweet scent didn't make me want to breathe in the air around her just to taste it on my tongue.

But I wasn't a predator. I wasn't like the low life scum who took without asking or forced themselves on omegas in their most vulnerable state.

We stood posturing and glaring for a bit. Then I got bored. I was only here because Violet had asked me to stay. That was it. She was an omega, a victim, one of only a few we'd been able to save. If my presence helped her, I would stay as long as she needed.

"We done?" I asked.

Andrei's nostrils flared as he inhaled deeply, releasing the breath in a low trickling growl.

"I'm not sure if you're trying to intimidate me or warn me or what but…" And then it hit me.

Holy shit. This pack wanted the omega. They had found a scent match – not that I believed in that shit. People met, they formed a connection, they fell in love.

Although...okay, yeah. Her scent definitely made me want to seek out a local carnival and dive face first into that cotton candy machine. And she was beautiful, even through the damage to her face and the blood and gore and dirt coating her hair and skin.

But she wasn't mine. She wouldn't be mine. She couldn't. I had no intention of bonding with anyone. Ever.

"Keep your hands to yourself," Andrei warned once more before stalking back up the wooden steps and into the house.

It wasn't lost on me that he didn't slam the door behind him. He'd closed it like a normal person to avoid freaking Violet out.

If she wasn't asleep yet, the pills the doctors had given her would help her drift off soon. Chase had carried her into one of the four bedrooms the cabin boasted. That was when Andrei had beckoned me outside for our little chat.

Turning toward the door, I watched shadows moving around inside. Four bedrooms. One was officially occupied. That left five men to vie for the other three. And I sure as fuck had no intention of snuggling up with any of this pack. It was obvious I wasn't welcome here. And that was fine. The only person who mattered, the only opinion that mattered was Violet's.

The air was cool, but I wasn't quite ready to go in. Not ready for the glares, the growls, and the pheromones that had raged since I'd dared to touch Violet in the backseat of my team's SUV.

She was thin. Like she hadn't been fed nearly enough for far too long. There were purple crescents underlining her eyes from lack of sleep. I didn't blame her. She had probably been terrified to go to sleep for fear they would take advantage of her.

After checking all her injuries when we'd arrived at the safe house, I had been surprised she hadn't complained once about the pain. There had been so much glass embedded in her soft flesh, in her feet, her arms, the backs of her legs. There were cuts in various places from the roll over and a bruise that was quickly turning purple along the side of her face.

Yet still...I found her attractive. Beautiful.

Mine.

Nope. Not mine. Not now. Not ever. As a beta, I could keep my shit together when around an omega in heat.

As long as I could keep my body and heart on the same track as my brain, I would be fine.

But as I neared the house and detected the hint of her sweetness, my dick immediately stood at attention.

Keeping my heart on the same track might be easier. But my cock was apparently ignoring my brain.

Chase

Liam paced the floor as I stripped for bed. The two of us would share one of the remaining three rooms. That left Mac in one and Andrei in the other.

I couldn't give a shit where Wilder would sleep. He shouldn't even be here. The fucker should be back with his own pack, his own team.

Violet was our responsibility.

Although...he had helped clean up her wounds. And he'd made sure she went to the hospital to make sure there were no serious injuries. One more set of eyes on her couldn't be a bad thing...right?

"Does she want him? Is that why she asked him to stay?" Liam asked in hushed tones as he continued pacing.

"I don't think sex is on her mind at the moment," I said, sitting on the edge of the bed and watching the man who owned my heart shove his hands through his hair in agitated movements.

I had never seen him look so...lost. Was that the word? Lost? Or maybe obsessed.

I knew the feeling. We had wanted an omega for the pack, but I had been just as happy to be bonded to Liam.

Andrei had marked each of us, leaving crescent scars on our necks when we'd joined the pack. But I had marked Liam separately. We were pack. But he was my mate. He was who I wanted to grow old with. He was also the only person I truly trusted in this world.

And now, there was a broken, terrified woman in the cabin who'd captured the attention of all four of us.

Five of us. Because Wilder didn't say no when she'd asked him to stay. She hadn't begged. No tears had glistened in her eyes. All she'd done was asked him to stay and...*voila*...he was now somewhere inside the cabin until further notice.

A petty part of me hoped he was on the couch. Nah. I hoped he was on the floor. Or maybe in the SUV. We'd made it obvious he wasn't welcome. This was the same safe house we had used on many occasions so every inch of it was covered in our scents.

Liam finally stopped trying to wear a path into the hardwood floor and turned to look at me, propping his hands on his hips. "You feel it, too, don't you?"

I knew what he was asking but wasn't sure I was ready to voice anything yet. She had been through too much to have to worry about four alphas wanting to bring her into our pack. The mere thought of any of us breaking her skin with our teeth made anger hot in my veins. She didn't need any more pain.

She needed...

Fuck. Everything. She deserved the world. What the fuck did we have to offer? A job that could end the lives of any of us at any time? We had enough money to ensure she was comfortable. We could keep her safe.

But we kept fucked up hours. We went into situations like the one she'd been held in on a regular basis. One of the teams had lost two of their members. I felt a bit like an asshole that I didn't know whether any of the other teams were bonded or not or if they simply worked together.

What if that had been one of us? A bullet had grazed my side, barely requiring more than a bandaid. But it could have been far worse. Any of us could have fallen tonight.

I could have lost Liam tonight.

Grief settled hard and fast in my chest as I stared into his beautiful face. I had fallen for him instantly. While he was a few years older than me, he remained sweet and kind to anyone he met. He never used his massive size to intimidate anyone. He put everyone's needs before his own.

And that sweet chocolate cake scent that rolled from him as his mood shifted always made me crave more.

"What? What's wrong?" he asked, dropping his arms and crossing the room in three long strides.

He stopped in front of me. I reached for him, dragging him close so I could wrap my arms around his waist and bury my face in his stomach. I'd wanted to do this since we'd finally climbed into the second SUV. But we'd had other pressing matters that didn't involve reassuring myself that Liam was in one piece.

His fingers threaded through my hair until he tugged hard enough that I had to tilt my head back to look into his face.

"Tell me," he said, his voice soft.

"I could have lost you," I choked out as emotion clogged my throat.

Dropping to his knees in front of me, he moved until he was between my thighs, cupped my face in his warm, calloused hands, and slanted his mouth over mine.

He didn't deepen the kiss. And neither did I. We were content breathing each other in.

I hadn't lost him. I hadn't lost any of my pack.

And now, we had an omega in the next room who would need us all to get our shit together and help her through the next few...well, however long it took to find the fuckers and kill them.

When Liam pulled back, his eyes glistened with unshed tears. "I love you," he whispered, the taste of chocolate frosting landing on my tongue with his breath.

"I love you, too."

The sweetness of the moment was over. The next time we came together, it was with a desperation, our hands hurried and rough as we took turns removing each other's clothing, touching everywhere we could as though inventorying the other for wounds.

Making love to Liam had always made me feel as though my world was perfect, as though all the pieces of a puzzle had finally snapped into place.

But tonight, my mind continuously went to Violet and wondered if she had enough room in her heart for four alphas.

Something jerked me awake. My eyes flew open. I flicked my eyes around the dark room. Liam was pressed against my back, his warm, heavy arm draped over my waist, his cock nestled against me. He hadn't moved. At least not enough to snap me to full attention.

A scream rent through the air a split second before a crash echoed in the air.

Liam was out of the bed the second I was, our feet hitting the ground at a full sprint. We were both still buck naked, but I didn't give a shit. Something was wrong. Someone was hurting Violet.

I nearly ripped the door from the hinges to get out, to get to Violet. Liam slammed into my back when I skidded to a halt.

Andrei and Mac stood in the open doorway leading to Violet's room. Andrei's hands were held out in front of him, palms out, as he murmured words that didn't make it to my ears over the screams and crashes.

"What the fuck?" Wilder said, his feet thundering across the floor as he, too, skid to a stop outside of her room.

Five men stared into the bedroom as Violet threw anything she could get her hands on across the room. Broken glass and mirror shards twinkled with the light overhead. Wood was splintered everywhere. Her bed was bare, the sheets and blankets tossed everywhere.

"She's going to hurt herself," Wilder muttered low enough only for the rest of us.

I wasn't sure what to do. I had no idea whether she was releasing pent up rage or if she was in the middle of a night terror. If she was acting out from a nightmare, any of us could freak her the fuck out.

But Wilder was right – there was way too much littering the ground now that she could step on and slice her feet even further.

Andrei stepped into the room, his hands held out in front of him as he continued speaking in low, soothing tones.

He could use his alpha tone, use his bark to get her under control, but none of us liked doing that. It felt like manipulation.

"Violet," Andrei said, raising his voice for her to hear him over the sounds coming from her mouth.

Watching her was damned near heartbreaking. I wanted to rush in there and wrap her in my arms, make every memory that was haunting her disappear, bring her peace.

"Omega," Andrei barked when she lifted her hand to throw something through the window.

Her hand halted and her eyes went wide. Fuck. Andrei would beat himself up later for doing this, but we had to protect her, even if from herself.

"Close the door," he said to Mac over his shoulder.

Mac nodded and pulled the door closed, locking Andrei and Violet in the room together.

And for a second, I wondered if I shouldn't be worried for Andrei's safety. Because the look in Violet's eyes was nothing short of murderous.

CHAPTER 7

ndrei

HER EYES WERE WIDE as she stared at me. Her hand stayed poised, but I couldn't figure out what she'd found to throw. The room was only outfitted for temporary stay.

And then my eyes focused. She was ready to throw a bottle of scent blocking shampoo through the only window in the room.

"I shouldn't need this," she said, her voice hoarse from screaming. "I shouldn't need this."

Moving forward slowly, I reached out and waited for her to put the bottle in the palm of my hand. After setting it on the dresser that miraculously remained unscathed, I crossed the room and lifted her into my arms, settling her on the mattress.

"I want you to stay right there," I barked. Fuck. I hated using my alpha power on her. I hated using it on any omegas. It made me feel like I was their master. There was something in their genes that forced them to obey their alpha's command.

Her alpha's command.

I let that thought fade to the back of my mind. I couldn't focus on that. Wouldn't focus on that.

Right now, she needed comfort. She needed...

Fuck. I didn't know what she needed.

Starting with the larger pieces, I picked up broken pieces of wood and tossed them into the corner of the room. My own bare feet got stuck by a piece of mirror but I didn't so much as wince. She would likely blame herself.

"Stay there. I'll be right back."

I couldn't walk around the room barefoot unless I wanted to end up with feet as torn up as hers. And the pack sure as hell wouldn't carry me around.

The pack and Wilder congregated in the living room, their heads whipping around to stare at me when I closed the door behind me with a soft snick.

"Shoes," I said as an explanation of why I was no longer in there with her.

After shoving my feet into a pair of boots, I hurried back to her room. Shirtless, boxers, and combat boots. Quite a look.

"Is it me or is he kind of hot like that?" Liam said a second before I closed the door behind me again.

I shook my head with a soft smile, but my heart cracked a little when I found Violet exactly as I left her. She hadn't moved a muscle like she was frozen in place.

Keeping one eye on her, I moved quickly, cleaning up the larger pieces of broken glass. I hadn't brought a broom in with me so there were still shards everywhere.

"You can't stay in here," I said, hands on my hips as I surveyed the damage. She had damaged the walls, ripped the sheets, dumped half the contents of some of the soapy shit Mac had bought for her.

The bags of clothes he'd brought back were inside the closet untouched, and she still wore my t-shirt from earlier in the night. The fact she hadn't changed into something else made me feel all warm and fuzzy inside and made my dick twitch behind my boxers. She would be completely covered in my scent.

"I'm sorry," she whispered.

Turning my eyes to her face, my fucking heart shattered. A tear rolled over her lashes and trailed down her cheek, followed by another from her other eye.

"There's nothing to be sorry for," I said, crossing the room to sit directly beside her.

Without a word spoken, she leaned into me and I let her. I let her draw from my strength, let my scent warm her, comfort her.

"You can sleep in my room tonight," I told her, keeping my voice as even as possible.

"Where will you sleep?"

"I'll bunk with Mac or sleep on the couch."

"I'll take the couch."

"The fuck you will," I said then winced. "Omegas don't sleep on couches while alphas stretch out on beds."

Before she could argue, I slid one arm behind her back and another under her knees, lifting her and cradling her to my chest. The door swung open before I could reach for it. Mac waited until we stepped out before walking ahead of us and opening the door to the room I had occupied.

"She okay?" Mac asked.

"She has a name," Violet said, a peek at the woman who'd sassed us in the SUV appearing.

Mac chuckled. He ran a hand over her hair when I sat on the side of the bed with her cradled in my arms. "Tell me how we can help," he said.

Her head wagged side to side over and over. "I don't know."

After a few moments, Mac left the room and returned with a shopping bag. After digging around inside, he pulled out a plush, pink blanket and draped it over her bare legs. He dipped his hand inside again and emerged with a squishy stuffed animal shaped like a pig.

"My sister loved these when she was in heat," he explained with a shrug when both Violet and I raised our eyebrows at his gift.

There were a couple more soft blankets in various colors and textures that he laid on the bed. "These are supposed to help calm omegas," he said.

Then took his empty bag and pulled the door shut behind him.

Violet hugged the stuffed pig to her chest and inhaled deeply. "It smells like Mac," she muttered as though to herself.

"Do you want him to clean it?"

She shook her head then nuzzled further into my chest. "No. I like his smell."

I bristled inwardly but didn't say a thing. Mac was part of my pack. I had marked him myself, bonded him to the four of us for life. There was no reason to be jealous.

"You need sleep. Are the blankets okay? Soft enough?"

I had never had to think about things like textures or smells in my room. In fact, I rarely let another living soul in any space I claimed. The fact I hadn't growled when Mac followed us in was nothing short of a miracle.

"They're fine," she said, then yawned.

"Can you tell me what happened? Did you have a nightmare?"

Violet chewed on her lips a few seconds and her sugary sweetness suddenly smelled burned. Anxiety. Anger. Sorrow. He knew it would take her a while to overcome the things she'd suffered as well as the things she'd witnessed.

"Do I have to talk about it now?" she asked.

She was waiting for me to use my alpha power to force her into talking. And I sure as fuck wouldn't do that. "You don't have to do anything you don't want."

Standing, I turned and lowered her onto the mattress, making sure the special blankets Mac purchased were within reach before pulling the comforter up to her chin.

"Do you need any more pain killers?"

"They make me feel sick."

"How's…everything else?"

She huffed a laugh. "Am I horny? Do my insides feel like a hot poker is digging around? Yes and yes."

I wasn't sure how to react to her questions or answers. So I stood there like an idiot, shoving my hands into the pockets of my sweats.

"We're all right on the other side of this door. If you...please don't break anything else," I barked. And, yeah, I felt like a dick again. But Wilder was right – she would end up hurting herself. "If you need us, we're right out there. Call for any single one of us and we'll be here in a heartbeat."

Turning, I flipped off the light and opened the door.

"Will you stay?" she whispered in the dark.

Fuck yeah, I would stay. I just wasn't sure it was a good idea. She'd just admitted that her heat was taking hold even with the heat blockers. I would have to reject her if she begged for my knot. That would force her to suffer further and give me the worst case of blue balls of my life.

"Are you sure?" I asked.

"I promise not to take advantage of you," she teased, but her voice was tight.

Steeling myself and lecturing my dick to stay down, I rounded the bed and lowered onto it, staying on top of the bedding instead of climbing in beside her like I wanted to do.

When she rolled over and squeezed herself as close to me as she could get, I lifted my arm so she could snuggle closer, draping it over her shoulders.

"You're safe, little omega. No one will ever hurt you again. I swear on my life."

As her breathing grew slow and steady, I could have sworn I heard the faintest purr rattle from her chest. For now, she was content. For now, my sweet little omega was at peace.

A rattle worked up my own chest, my purr chasing us both into a deep sleep. Hopefully, she would get a few more hours of rest without nightmares waking her.

DREAMS OF VIOLET played through my mind. Her hand ran up my hard cock, her fingers lightly toying with the swell of my knot. Her lips were on my neck as she nuzzled close, her tongue flicking out to taste the point of my pulse.

Eyes flying open, I realized it wasn't a dream. Violet was touching me. Tasting me. Testing me.

Shit.

This was what I had feared; why I hadn't wanted to sleep beside her.

As I laid stiff as a board, her hand slid past the waist band of my sweats until she could wrap her fingers around my girth and give me a long, slow stroke.

A moan escaped my lips before I could stop it.

"I hurt," she whimpered.

That sound was as potent to an alpha as my bark was to an omega. She was in need. It was my job to take care of her in any way she needed. But I had already demanded the pack and Wilder keep their hands and their dicks to themselves. I would be a fucking hypocrite if I rolled her over and slammed my cock into her wet heat.

"Violet," I said, gritting my teeth as I wrapped my fingers gently around her wrist and pulled her hand from my pants. "I can't."

"Please," she begged.

A pain filled whimper came from deep inside her chest as she buried her face in my neck, her breath warm against my skin. Cotton candy and lollipops. And all I wanted to do was taste both on my tongue.

"It hurts so bad."

"What hurts, sweetheart?"

"Everywhere. The blockers aren't helping. My skin feels like it's on fire and everywhere hurts...here," she said, taking my hand and placing it low on her stomach, just above her sex. "It hurst so bad."

Her voice was shaky. Her skin was hot to the touch.

I couldn't fuck her. I just couldn't. But I could at least try to help her.

Rolling onto my side, I ran a finger across her lips. She sucked it into her mouth, her tongue rolling over it, and images of those same lips wrapped around my cock about stole my breath.

A pop sounded when I pulled my finger free and trailed it down her chest over my t-shirt. Stopping at her panty line, I inhaled deeply and dug for the strength to stop myself once I got her past the worst of it.

She gripped my wrist and tugged until my hand settled over her mound. Her underwear was soaked with her slick and my brain turned to mush. Pushing her panties to the side, I slid my finger through her folds as my breathing grew to pants and my heart thundered in my chest.

I'd fucked plenty of people in my life. But I had never felt as though I could come in my boxers simply from touching another person.

Already, precum was soaking the front of my sweats.

Dipping my finger inside of her, I rolled my eyes to her face and tried to see her in the dark room. I wished I could see the faces she made when she was being pleasured. I wanted to see her face when she fell apart, when her inner walls clamped around my finger.

I was trying to be gentle, slow. That wasn't what she needed.

Hands clenched tightly around my wrist, she began to fuck herself with my finger. I added a second and she moaned, a throaty sound at the back of her throat.

No matter how hard I tried to keep my own desires out of the scenario, my bone deep need to dominate in the bedroom continuously tried to push forward.

I needed to taste her. I needed to taste her sweet slick on my tongue.

Fingers still plunging deep inside of her, I scooted down until my face was lined up with her sex, moving my thumb so I could suck her clit between my lips and tease it with my tongue.

Her fingers left my wrist and clenched my hair, holding me in place as she rocked her hips, effectively fucking my mouth and my fingers.

This wasn't enough. This would never be enough.

But it would *have* to be enough for now. The moment she was in her right mind I had every intention of showing her the rougher side of fucking. I wanted to put her over my knee and pinken her ass, watch as she wiggled, make her beg me to shove my knot deep inside of her.

Her breathing became shallow as her hips continued to rock and grind and her hands tugged my face closer. I kept my tongue on her clit, flicking it, sucking it, teasing it with my teeth while I plunged my fingers hard and fast inside of her slick coated cunt.

Violet tensed, a sexy mewl leaving her lips as her pussy clenched around my fingers, coating them and my tongue with her release. I licked and sucked and lapped up every drop like a starved man.

When her muscles relaxed against the mattress, I slowly pulled my fingers from her and sucked them dry, savoring every bit I could.

Within seconds, her breathing had slowed again. She'd immediately fallen to sleep once the pain receded.

Well, fuck. My dick was so hard I could have used it as a battering ram and my balls were tight with the need for release.

Reaching for my phone, I turned it on so I could see her face, pulled my dick from my sweats, and took it into my fist. Maybe this was wrong, staring at her as I jerked off, but I was drowning in her scent, in the taste of her slick, in the taste of her release.

Fantasizing about the day I could bend her over and slam my cock hard into her, I grunted, clenching my teeth as hot cum hit my stomach.

I searched the floor with the light of my phone until I found the shirt I'd discarded before bed, and cleaned myself before lying back down.

That was all I would allow myself. For now.

But soon. Fuck, I hoped *very* soon I would feel her clenching around my cock as I ruined her for any other man, as I erased the memory of any other cock she had ever ridden.

CHAPTER 8

iolet

S<small>OUNDS WERE</small>…<small>DISTORTED</small>. My thoughts were muddy, like I was trying to push the dreams away.

Someone touched my cheek. My forehead. Something cool and wet dabbed at my face.

"Can you open your eyes?"

The voice sounded so far away, yet I could feel the mattress dipped beside me, could feel their touch on my face.

As I pushed the fog away, warm, heady scents wrapped around me like a blanket. Pepper. Leather. Oranges and sweet cream. Mint. Whiskey. Chocolate Cake.

Pack. The pack was here. The guys were here.

Where was here?

"Open your eyes, sweetheart. Look at me."

Wilder?

Peeling my lids open was far more difficult than it should have been. Finally, I was able to look around the room, but it tilted and spun, making my stomach turn.

The next time I tried, the room was darker and Wilder leaned close so I wouldn't have to strain to see him.

"Is this normal?" That was Liam's voice.

"How the fuck would I know?" Mac.

They were all crowded in the room. The cloth was removed. When it touched me again, it was cooler. A cold, wet washcloth was being pressed to my cheeks and forehead.

"Should we take her back to the hospital?" Chase.

"No," I croaked out, my throat feeling like I'd swallowed flames.

As I focused on Wilder's face, the tilting and spinning slowed until I could look around without feeling as though I would puke all over myself.

"What–" I tried to clear my throat, but it resulted in a fit of coughing.

"It's her cycle. She's feverish." That was Wilder again.

"How can we help her?" Liam asked.

No one spoke. The only way to help an omega through her heat cycle was with a knot. And the last thing I wanted was for five men to start pawing at me.

Every bit of my skin felt tight, sensitive. Overly sensitive. Every touch felt equal parts tingling and irritating through my nerve endings.

Lifting a hand, I reached for…I didn't know. I knew what my body needed, but there was no way my mind could…

"Oh shit," I breathed out.

Fingers. A tongue. Touching Andrei's cock.

Searching the sea of faces, I found him leaning against the wall to my right, his eyes on mine. I'd woken in the middle of the night feeling as if I were being torn in half. I had touched him. I had wallowed in his scent, rubbed my face along his cheek and throat.

And then I'd begged him to…

But he hadn't. He'd only helped ease the pain without seeking any pleasure for himself.

Part of me wondered if I should have felt ashamed. But the other part, the part that knew I had no choice in how my body reacted, how my hormones took over during my cycles, pushed that shame away.

Andrei had helped me the best he could without letting his own alpha urges take over.

With a smile, I dipped my head at him with a silent thank you. I didn't know whether the others knew, whether they'd smelled me on him when he'd left the room, but no one said a word about it.

"You're a fucking beta. Isn't your scent supposed to calm her?" Liam said to Wilder.

"Wilder," I croaked out.

"Yeah, sweetheart," he answered, still touching the cool cloth to my face.

Grabbing his arm, I tugged until he was forced to either pull away from me or lower himself beside me.

"You sure?"

"Not sex," I told him. Of course I knew that would help. But…no. Not after the compound, after hearing men and women screaming, after seeing the bodies…

He nodded as though he understood and stretched out on the bed beside me, turning me so his front was to my back.

That helped. His scent didn't affect me the same way as Andrei's or even Mac's. I didn't feel the need to beg him to take me.

Instead, his scent and his energy soothed away a bit of the discomfort.

"Chase?" I asked, raising my brows at his concerned face.

"Anything, sweetheart."

He laid down next to me, turning so he was facing me, clasping my hands in his.

But it wasn't close enough. I needed to feel the warmth of his body against mine.

"More."

His sweet smile appeared, highlighting twin dimples I hadn't noticed before.

Maneuvering himself, he turned until he was the little spoon, his back pressed to my front, reached back to grab my arm, and draped it over his waist.

He toyed with my fingers as we laid there, me sandwiched between two huge men, an alpha and a beta.

"I'm not sure whether I'm turned on or jealous," I heard Liam tease.

"Shut up, dumb ass," Mac said. But there was no anger in his tone.

My eyes closed as their murmurs started up again. The pain and fever felt as though they were slowly draining from me as I stayed wedged between Chase and Wilder, peppermint and oranges easing me into a dreamlike state.

"We need to make some phone calls. How the fuck do none of us know how to help her?" Andrei said, his voice soft.

"Because we've never had an omega," Mac answered.

"We're grown ass men. Not teenage boys feeling tits for the first time," Andrei said. This time, there was definitely anger in his voice as his words came out in a growl.

They weren't mad at me. They were angry with themselves.

I wanted to tell them not to blame themselves; I didn't even know what I needed. I didn't know how they could help. I had perfumed later in life and had hidden myself away during each cycle, using toys or my fingers to ease some of the pain.

But it had never been anything like what I was experiencing now. I had no idea whether it was from the crap they'd shot into our systems or the fact I was surrounded by alphas who made me want to swim in their scents until I was drowning in them.

Wilder's arm tightened around my waist, his entire body lining mine. Chase laid still, his only movement the soft swipe of his thumb along each of my fingers as though memorizing them.

Anything else the men not in bed with me said faded away as I fell to sleep, dreams of chocolate cake and peppermint and so many other yummy treats chasing away the nightmares.

MAC

. . .

Leaning against the wall just outside the bedroom, one ear was tuned in to Andrei as he put in a call to headquarters. The other was on any sound that might come from behind the closed door.

She'd asked for Wilder first. Wilder wasn't part of the pack. He wasn't one of us. Jealousy surged through me as I'd watched him climb into the bed and turned her so he could wrap himself around her.

But as I'd watched color return to her cheeks, I had to admit I was glad he was there. He was helping her. He'd helped her a few times already.

Then she'd asked for Chase. Not me. Not Liam. Not Andrei. But at least he was part of our bond. He was pack.

So what did that mean? It was obvious this little omega was meant for us, but then there was Wilder…

Fuck. If I'd known how fucked in the head the presence of a scent match omega would cause me, I might have fought against the urge to find one.

We'd all wanted an omega in our pack for years. It was like we all knew there was a missing piece to our fucked up puzzle. And Violet had all the right corners and edges to complete our group.

"They were all dosed with something to induce artificial heat," I heard Andrei explain over the phone.

So many deaths within a span of a few hours. So many omegas lost. Those fuckers had executed them as they'd tried to escape. So what the fuck was the point of taking them to begin with?

One of the male omegas had been swollen with a pup and they'd shot him. Had they simply taken the omegas for some twisted sex slaves? Or were they intentionally trying to impregnate them? And what was the point of that? What was their end game?

I hated mother fuckers like those back at the compound. Hated mother fuckers who took without asking, who treated the most fragile of society as their own personal playthings, as tools, as toys.

"The doctor prescribed her some heat blockers but it hasn't kicked in yet."

Pushing from the wall, I paced to the kitchen and opened various cabinets. I wasn't sure exactly what I was looking for, but I was pretty sure it wasn't in there.

"He's not pack," Liam said, a pout on his face.

"Yeah. We've already determined that," I said, resisting the urge to slam the cabinet door closed.

"Are we sure we can trust him with her?"

"Chase is in there. He'll keep an eye on him," I said.

Liam flopped onto the dark plaid couch and turned his attention to the closed door.

It had been almost an hour since we'd left the room and let her get more sleep. Andrei had stayed with her overnight and said she struggled a lot in her sleep, crying out, throwing her hands out as though she was fighting someone in her nightmares.

It would be a while for the cuts and bruises to heal. I couldn't fathom how long it would take for her inner wounds to heal. And those would most definitely leave scars.

"Mac got her clothes and shit. Scent blocking stuff."

That she'd thrown around the room last night. I would have to check to see what would need to be replaced.

"Some blankets, yeah. And this…what was that? A stuffed pig or something," Andrei said, turning to me with raised brows.

The stuff animal was marketed specifically for omegas. The texture and softness were supposed to be soothing while the lack of any type of scent was supposed to be a reprieve when their senses were overloaded. I don't know why I chose a pig instead of one of the other animals. I just thought it was cute. Whatever.

"Copy," Andrei said. "Did Wilder check in, let you know he was still with us?"

He was silent again as he listened to our commander over the line.

Part of me hoped our boss demanded Wilder return to base, rejoin his team. But…he was helping Violet. I would sacrifice just about anything if it meant she was comfortable. If she was happy. And…I wanted to see her smile. She obviously had a dark sense of humor; I'd noted that when she'd chastised us for talking about her like she wasn't there.

But I wanted to see more. I wanted to see her healthy. I couldn't wait until all her exterior wounds healed. I couldn't wait to see her on her feet, walking around, demanding things from us.

But would she? She didn't behave like a typical omega. Andrei told us she'd perfumed late in life, that her family had kicked her out the moment she was a legal adult because they'd believed her to be a beta.

What kind of fucked up parents discarded their own daughter like that?

If she'd presented later, she might not have a clue that she could literally quirk her finger and any one of us would come running. She could ask for the moon and I would lasso the son of a bitch and gift it to her on a silver platter.

All she'd asked was for Chase and Wilder to cuddle her. Although…

Andrei had smelled strongly of Violet this morning. I was sure a lot of it had to do with sleeping beside her all night, but could there have been more?

No way would he have fucked her. I'd known him long enough to know that went against everything he believed. He would rather cut off his own balls than take advantage of an omega in such a vulnerable state.

That was a question I would ask when there were no witnesses. Or maybe I wouldn't. I wasn't sure I wanted to know the answer. Wasn't sure how I would feel if I found out Andrei…

But if she was ours, if she could heal from this and accept us as her pack, wouldn't we all feel her, touch her, taste her at some point?

Fuck…I hoped so.

But only when she was ready. And if that took months, or even years, I was more than ready to wait. This was the first time I'd encountered an omega and knew almost immediately that she belonged in my life. In our life. In our pack. In our home.

"Copy. I'll let him know. And I'll relay the information to my team."

Andrei ended the call and turned to face me and Liam.

"Well?" Liam asked impatiently.

Liam was the idiot of the group. Not because he lacked intelligence, but because everything always seemed like it was a game to him. He preferred to joke and play and treated every mission like a fucking video game that he could conquer.

"What all did you get when you went shopping?" Andrei asked me.

I racked my brain, trying to remember everything. "The scent blocking crap she asked for. The blankets. The stuffed animal. Clothes. Underwear. Toothbrush and toothpaste. A hairbrush. Uhhh…" Fuck. What else had I bought?

I'd noticed a lot of things scattered around the room when she'd gone into a rage and destroyed the room we'd assigned to her. We would have to get it cleaned up, sweep up all the glass, and find some new bedding before anyone could sleep in there.

She could always sleep in my bed. Or nestled between Liam and Chase. And Andrei hadn't seemed to have a problem with her taking over his bed, although he'd stayed with her last night. She'd practically begged him to stay with her.

Even with all our assurances, she acted as though she expected the enemy to appear from around every corner to drag her back to the compound.

The compound that should be leveled by now. Enough hours had passed that ORE should have sent in several teams to collect the dead omegas, the fallen ORE team members, and kill any enemy who was left. Then set off explosives to reduce the building to nothing more than rubble.

I wished I could have been there. I wished I could have been the one to pull the trigger and end the life of any single person who'd had a hand in what Violet and the others had gone through.

"Any word on more survivors?" I asked.

There had only been five left between three teams. But there had been quite a few who'd run on their own, not waiting for us to get them out safely.

A lot of fucking good that would have done. My team had only pulled two to safety and only one remained of those two. Sweet, quiet Amora had been killed in that rollover, her neck snapped like a twig as she'd been tossed around the cab.

Why the fuck hadn't we insisted both women buckle in? Yeah, they were safer from the bullets flying through the air huddled on the floorboard, but Amora had still been killed.

So close. She'd been so close to freedom. So close to returning to her life.

"Not yet. The teams are searching the woods, trying to follow any trails to see if they actually got away or if they, too, were shot down by the perps," Andrei answered.

It wasn't the answer I wanted. But it was all we had to go on for now.

"What else did he say?" Liam asked. "Do we need to find more crap?"

"Soft stuff. Blankets. Pillows. She needs a nest."

I turned my attention to Liam and raised my brows. This cabin was perfect for a group of alphas. We didn't have personal dens in case we went into rut, but we weren't here often enough or long enough to worry about that kind of shit.

"What kind of nest?" Liam asked. "How do we build a nest?"

"Fuck if I know," Andrei said, pushing his hands through his shaggy hair before smoothing them down his beard. "Did you get pillows or just the blankets?"

"No pillows," I said.

"I'll go get her more shit," Liam offered. "What colors?"

Well, shit. A group of guys trying to shop for an omega who had no idea what she needed. We didn't know fuck all about her, didn't know her favorite color, favorite food. Nothing. All we knew was we all had the same goal – to make her as comfortable as possible while she healed and suffered through a forced heat cycle.

CHAPTER 9

iolet

It had been three days since my escape from the compound. And all three nights, I'd begged at least one of the guys to sleep in the same room with me. Actually, I'd begged them to sleep beside me, pressing their warmth against me, soothing my frayed nerves with their warm and spicy scents.

Today was the first day I was able to take a real shower instead of scrubbing at myself with a soapy washcloth. Although none of them would allow me to be alone in the bathroom. Liam currently sat on the toilet seat, rattling off the things he'd purchased and asking repeatedly if the scent blocking shampoo and soaps they'd bought for me were okay.

"I'm fine, Liam. You can go hang out with the guys," I said through the closed curtain.

It was so weird to be standing naked under the spray and have a man sitting out there waiting for me.

I'd had to throw modesty out the window when I finally got the green light to shower, though. I'd had to be carried to the bathroom because of my damaged feet. Then I'd needed help removing my shirt because of my aching muscles and joints, then needed help removing bandages I couldn't reach.

Wilder lectured me to get in, wash, and immediately get out and not to linger too long. I'd answered him with my middle finger over Liam's shoulder as he'd hefted me in his arms and stepped into the bathroom.

"Nope. Not falling on my watch," Liam said.

Rinsing off, I turned the knobs to end the spray, then reached around the curtain, holding my hand out and wiggling my fingers.

Liam chuckled softly as he pushed a soft towel into my hands.

As I ran it down my face, I stopped and inhaled deeply. It smelled of the pack. But Wilder's fruity scent was missing.

The towel wasn't threadbare like those at my apartment. It felt new, like it had never been used, yet was saturated with every single member of the pack who'd saved my life.

Okay. I couldn't stay in here all day. As the cool air met the water on my skin, chill bumps raised. Drying as quickly as possible, I wrapped it around my torso and tucked the end between my breasts before pulling the curtain open.

Liam was looking at his phone. He glanced up at me, down at his phone, then his eyes jerked back to me. His gaze made a slow perusal from my bruised and battered face down my throat, hesitating where my breasts spilled over the top a little. Then he resumed his appraisal of my barely covered body, ending on my bare toes.

"Nail polish," he said, jabbing a finger toward my feet.

"What?" I looked down. There was no polish on my toe nails.

"We need to get you nail polish. I'll paint them for you. Pamper you a little."

"I'm pretty sure I don't want anyone touching my feet for a while."

Even standing long enough to wash the nastiness from my hair caused a burning ache in the soles of my feet. But a bath was nixed the moment I mentioned it.

Liam lifted his hands, offering me a pile of pastel pinks and purples with a hint of glitter coming somewhere from the center.

"What?"

"Clothes. Mac bought them that first night."

"Are you going to stand there and watch me dress?"

It was meant as a tease. But the moment I said the words, heat rushed my body and my body flushed with need. At that moment, I would have preferred he jerked the towel from my body and trailed his lips and tongue over every inch of my body until I smelled like rich chocolate cake, until I could taste it on my lips.

"I mean, I would be happy to..."

Reaching forward, I snatched the pile of clothing from his hands and twirled my finger, indicating for him to turn his back.

Those dimples appeared a second before he turned and waited as I sat on the edge of the tub and struggled to pull on the panties then the super soft sweatpants. Standing outside the tub, I pulled the pants up my legs and over my ass.

But when it was time to pull on my shirt, I struggled.

With a sigh, I raised one arm to cover my boobs and cleared my throat. "I need help," I admitted begrudgingly.

I had taken care of myself for so long and now I needed these guys for...well, practically everything.

Liam was still grinning like a fool when he turned. Even when his eyes dropped to where my boobs were barely covered, that grin stayed in place.

"You have amazing tits," he said, reaching for the shirt and shaking it out. "Hope that doesn't offend you."

Any other time? Yeah. It probably would have pissed me off to have a guy, especially an alpha, commenting on my boobs when my life felt like it was spinning off its axis. But I had fantasized about having Liam's lips and tongue on me mere seconds ago.

When he held the shirt up to slip over my head, I halted his hands and gawked at the shirt Mac had picked out.

As I stared at the pink shirt with a sparkly cartoon unicorn poised as though in flight, a giggle bubbled up in my chest. The giggle turned into full laughter as I pictured big, macho Mac carrying this shirt through the store and setting it on the conveyor belt.

"Seriously?" I said through laughter as Liam shrugged and pulled the neck hole over my head.

"We didn't know what you like. Most female omegas are into girly shit. Sparkly stuff. Soft stuff."

The shirt was definitely soft. But I had never considered myself girly by any stretch of the imagination. At least not in the pastel, sparkly unicorn way.

"Are all the clothes he bought like this?" I asked when he helped me push my arms through the sleeves.

"I'm afraid so. Well, they don't all have unicorns, but I saw a lot of pastel crap in those bags."

The blankets and pillows Liam had bought were soft colors but not so pre-teen. And they were all so soft, so squishy. And they smelled heavily of my pack.

Shit. No. Not *my* pack. *The* pack.

The blankets all smelled as though each had left their scent on them intentionally. I was happy for it. Whether I refused to be knotted simply because a psychotic alpha with some kind of power trip drugged me didn't mean everything about these guys couldn't bring me comfort.

Liam inspected me from head to toe again. "Want me to wrap your boo boos?"

Wrinkling my nose, I shook my head. "Do I have to? They pull on my skin."

His broad shoulders rose and fell. "Ask Doc Wilder out there. He's the one with all the medical orders."

One of his arms wrapped around my back then he bent and slid the other behind my knees, lifting me easily from the ground and taking my weight off my feet.

His nostrils flared, but he didn't say a word as he carried me toward the door. Before we joined the others, I took the opportunity to bury my face in his neck and inhale deeply, dragging the sweet chocolate yumminess into me until I could taste it on my tongue as though I'd just shoveled half a cake into my mouth.

A soft purr rattled from Liam's chest as he pulled the door open and stepped into the hallway. Masculine voices and the smell of bacon floated on the air.

Wilder sat on the coffee table, a variety of medical supplies spread out beside him. "Set her down so I can check out her feet," he said.

Liam's purr cut off as he carried me to the couch and set me gently onto the cushion directly in front of Wilder.

Wilder's hands were careful as he lifted the first foot and touched the skin around the gashes. They were tender but not as painful as before.

"They're healing, but you still need to stay off them as much as possible," he said then spread some kind of ointment along the cuts, his fingertips feather light. "I want to keep your feet unwrapped until they're completely dry."

"Yes sir," I said with a mock salute.

It was easy to be around Wilder. His scent called to me but in a completely different way than the other guys. His felt like how I imagined a brother would feel…if mine hadn't turned their backs on me the same day as my parents.

At least the other four guys were no longer growling every time Wilder touched me or looked in my direction.

"How is…everything else?" Wilder asked with a raised brow.

"Better today." After waking with a raging fever a couple days ago, then sleeping for hours with the two guys snuggling me, I hadn't had any more issues.

Eh. That wasn't completely true. I was horny. All the time. But it wasn't to the point that I lost my mind or begged someone to touch me. Just the nearness of the guys kept the fever at bay. And the fears.

"How long do you think we'll be here?" I asked when Wilder shifted me so I was lying down with my feet propped on the couch.

Andrei carried a cup of coffee and a plate filled with bacon, eggs, and buttered toast to me, handing it to me before lowering onto the spot where Wilder had just been.

"My commander is still seeking the leader of that particular compound. They've been able to identify a few of the players, but there are a lot of them who are still out there, a lot we didn't kill."

And there was that fear again.

I picked up a piece of bacon and started breaking off pieces and dropping them onto my eggs. I was hungry but worried I might expel anything I put in my stomach after learning there was still a threat looming right over my head.

And once again, I found myself cursing my stupid perfume and my stupid hormones. If I'd stayed a beta, I would have been able to live a normal life.

If I'd presented earlier, I might still have my family. But did I really want people like that in my life? They'd tossed me out like last night's dinner because I didn't fit into the mold they'd chosen for me. If I ever saw them again, I might take a picture of their expressions when they found out I bloomed late and wanted nothing to do with them.

"If you're all here with me all the time, who's out there saving other omegas?" I asked.

"There are plenty of teams on the ORE," Wilder said.

"Speaking of, isn't your team missing you about now?" Liam said with a shit-eating grin.

None of them had bothered hiding the fact they didn't want the outsider in the cabin. More specifically, they didn't want him around me. Without a single word, without a knot, without a bonding bite, they had chosen me as their omega.

And I couldn't find a hint of anger over that.

I wanted them, too. I just...wasn't sure I was ready for anything more than survival for now. Even if I craved each of them every time their essence surrounded me like a blanket.

Andrei

. . .

Violet was perfuming as I sat in front of her and didn't appear to be aware of it. We were learning how to care for an omega while she was learning how to navigate her new life, her new designation. She'd gone a while before being discovered, but I couldn't imagine how she'd suffered alone.

I didn't want to imagine it. I didn't want to think of her in pain, discomfort. Hell, I didn't want to think of her so much as stubbing a toe.

Since when did I become such a fucking sap?

Easy answer – the moment her cotton candy sweetness seeped into my skin, into my cells, into my bone marrow and made itself home.

I hadn't touched her or tasted her other than to comfort her since that first night. When she'd started coming around from her fever, the memory seemed to creep into her consciousness. She'd turned her eyes to me and nodded, as though to thank me. For helping her? Or for my discretion?

Either way, I was more than happy to help. And that dickhead part of me had wished she'd asked again. No way would I ever be content with only the one taste. I'd walked around with a boner since that night.

I hadn't missed the way the pack sniffed the air as I passed, nor the looks they exchanged. But no one asked. And I didn't offer up any information.

My phone dinged in my back pocket. Pulling it free, I groaned. "Commander wants one of us to come in, see if we can help identify a few of the dead players. Go through some pics to try to pick out those we didn't kill."

"Not it," Liam said.

"Wilder can go," Mac said, his arms crossed over his chest as he leaned against the wall near the kitchen.

"He is going. But we need to go in, too."

"We're not leaving her here alone," Mac said.

"*Her* has a name," Violet said as she picked at her food.

Liam and Chase huffed a soft laugh. That had been one of her go to comments any time we talked about her as a job.

A smile teased my lips. Pressing them into a line, I tried to keep my face neutral and professional. "We're not leaving Violet alone," I said, looking pointedly at her. "Mac and Liam will stay behind. Chase, Wilder, and I will head into headquarters. If any of you need us to grab something while we're out, speak up."

"Pizza," Violet said before anyone else could respond.

"Frozen or carry out?"

"Yes," she answered, finally taking a real bite of her toast.

"Anything else?" I asked.

It was obvious she wasn't overly comfortable with all the attention, that she wasn't used to having others wait on her hand and foot. But, for one thing, she was unable to walk on her damaged feet. It was more than an honor to carry her from room to room.

And fuck, that was what we were built for. An alpha's job was to cater to his omega, to cater to her every whim. I'd fantasized about having an omega in our home for years, and had always wondered whether that need would be as prevalent as I'd heard.

Yep. It was. And it was beyond wanting to fuck her. Beyond wanting to hear her moans as I pumped into her.

I wanted her to smile like she was now. I wanted her happy. I wanted to be covered in sugary, sticky sweetness. I wanted to carry her scent on my skin and on my tongue.

"I'm sure there is but I can't think of anything off the top of my head."

"Have one of them text me if something comes to mind," I said.

"Get ready. We leave in ten," I said to Chase and Wilder. Both of whom looked less than pleased that they were leaving the cabin.

No. They were pissed they were leaving Violet, even for a few hours.

Leaning forward, I pressed my cheek to Violet's, marking her with my scent, before leaning back and pressing my lips to her forehead.

When I pulled back, she was looking into my eyes. "Are you this sweet with every omega you save?"

Suddenly, my tongue refused to cooperate as I stared into her pretty caramelly brown eyes.

"No?"

"That sounded more like a question than an answer," she said. There was a smile on her lips but it didn't reach her eyes.

Was she concerned about the attention, or did she need a confirmation of sorts?

"No. I mean, yes. I'm always gentle with omegas. But no...I've never..." I raised one brow instead of blurting out 'I've never finger fucked and ate out an omega who was in my bed when I was supposed to be protecting her.'

"I like you, too," she whispered then winked.

Once Wilder and Chase were ready, they grabbed their go bags and passed by the couch. Wilder squeezed her shoulder lightly. But Chase...Chase surprised the fuck out of me when he lowered and nuzzled his cheek against hers the way I had. He was leaving his scent on her, as well.

Was she aware of what we were doing? That we were claiming her in the only way we would allow ourselves for now?

"Call me if there are any problems," I said to Mac.

"What the fuck kind of problems could there be?"

"I could be a maniac," Violet said as she bit off another piece of bacon then used the remainder to point at Mac. "I could be a monster and beat you up."

Mac's lips twitched at the corners as he shook his head. "I'll take my chances."

Violet was half the size of Mac. Hell, she was nearly half the size of every one of us. How her parents couldn't tell merely by her petite size that she wasn't a beta...

Fuck that. Why her parents would give a shit what her designation was would remain a mystery to me. And probably should remain a mystery. Because I couldn't think of a single excuse they could give that wouldn't make me want to hurt them in every way possible.

CHAPTER 10

iolet

ANDREI, Chase, and Wilder had been gone an hour already. But it felt longer.

There was only a small analog TV in the cabin. No cable. No streaming services. Only a DVD player plugged into the ancient model.

"You guys couldn't have upgraded to something…bigger?" I asked.

I had urged Liam and Mac to join me on the couch as the fear began to creep back in. I knew they wouldn't let anything happen to me, but it felt like I was alone anytime one of them wasn't touching me, even when it was something as simple as a hand on my knee or a press of their leg against mine.

"We don't tend to spend much time here," Mac answered, his eyes glued to the screen.

It was an older nineties movie complete with the saxophone filled soundtrack.

Mac was on my left. Liam on my right. Leaning to the side, I rested my head on Mac's shoulder and sighed when amber and whiskey feathered over my skin and made me hum in approval.

Stretching further, I laid my legs on Liam's lap and sighed when he gently massaged my calves, careful of any knicks, cuts, or bruises.

"I look like Frankenstein," I muttered as I stared down at my bare legs.

"Frankenstein's monster," Mac muttered.

"What?" I tilted my head back so I could look into his face.

"It was Frankenstein's monster. Dr. Frankenstein built the monster." He lowered his face to look into my eyes…

And we both froze. The warm whiskey exploded from him, sucking me in, making me drunk. Only without the spins or future hangover.

No. This was the belly warming, inhibition dropping kind of drunk.

His eyes dipped to my lips, and my body instantly warmed. *Kiss me. Kiss me*, I pleaded in my head.

Whatever he saw in my face gave him the encouragement – or maybe push – he needed. Lowering his head, he barely grazed his lips against mine before pulling back.

His tongue darted out, tasting me on his lips. A growl mixed with a purr as he dipped down again, kissing me deeper, sliding his tongue into my mouth for a better taste.

Liam's fingers continued to massage my calves but slowly climbed up my thighs. *Yes. Please yes.*

The more they touched me, the more I wanted them to touch me. Everywhere. I wanted their hands on every part of me. My heat had waned, so this was all me.

Or rather it was the connection I craved with this pack.

When I'd woken and realized I had begged Andrei to touch me, I hadn't felt an ounce of regret.

And now, with one alpha kissing me and the other tentatively working his fingers further up my thigh, there was none of that awkward hesitation I often felt during the first time with a man.

Wrapping one arm around Mac's neck, I spread my legs, giving

Liam permission to explore further. If he stopped, if either of them stopped...

Mac pulled away, his lips kiss swollen, and stared into my eyes. "Are you sure?"

"Make it better," I begged.

The pain wasn't nearly as it had been during the forced heat, but my body was bordering on feverish again. I just wanted to feel good for the first time in weeks.

His mouth crashed down on mine, his kiss desperate. When he pulled away again, he situated me so I was draped over his lap, my back on his thighs, and cupped my chin in his big hand.

As his tongue invaded my mouth, Liam slowly began to pull my sweats down my legs. My panties stayed in place.

"Violet, I need to know this is okay. I need to know this isn't your heat speaking," Liam said, his breath warm on my thighs.

As much as I didn't want to, I pulled my mouth from Mac's and looked down my body at Liam.

The words were on the tip of my tongue. But what if I said them and I had been wrong about what I'd felt for these guys, about how they appeared to feel for me? What if all of this was simply because they had saved me?

No. That didn't feel like the truth.

How I felt in Mac's arms with Liam searching my face was the truth.

"Mine," I whispered, lowering my hand to run my fingers down his cheek. "My pack."

With a growl, he lowered his head, pushed my panties to the side, and closed his mouth over my clit.

As I tossed my head back on a moan, Mac captured my mouth again, one of his hands finding my breast to fondle it through the soft t-shirt. His fingers were gentle but firm as they pinched and rolled a nipple between them, tugging lightly until I squirmed.

Liam's tongue made long swipes through my folds from my clit to my opening and back until I was nearly panting with need. Pressure and heat built low in my belly until I was ready to beg for release, beg for him to enter me, beg for him to knot me.

Not yet. Not yet. Not yet.

I had to remind myself that not only was my mind not quite ready for that but my body was still battered and sore. Once I felt one of them swelling inside of me, locking us together, I might not be able to stop. I might have to feel them over and over until I no longer knew where I ended and they began.

Mac abandoned my mouth and kissed and nipped a path down my throat, his teeth grazing my pulse point before returning to taste my lips, to taste me.

The sensations were so much, too much. Not enough. I needed more. More. *More*.

A whimper worked from my chest. An omega crying out to its alpha.

One finger slid inside my slick wet pussy. Then a second. Liam bent his fingers, rubbing the exact right spot as he licked and sucked my clit.

My body tensed and shook as wave after wave of ecstasy swamped me, rolled over me, dragged me under until I could barely breathe.

Mac swallowed my cries, fucking my mouth with his tongue until the aftershocks began to fade.

Liam pulled his fingers from me and feathered the softest kisses along my thighs, my mound, up to my belly button, his lips wet with my slick dampening my skin.

I could feel Mac hard beneath me, but he didn't make a move to touch me any further, didn't bark at me to present. In fact, he pulled his lips from mine and removed his hand from my breast and stared into my eyes.

"You are so fucking beautiful," he whispered, as though I wasn't staring up at him with a bruised and swollen face.

But...I believed his words. I believed he could see through my injuries. He wasn't simply saying he thought I was pretty. He was seeing straight to my heart, straight to my soul.

. . .

As the night grew on, I had started falling asleep on the couch. But I didn't want to sleep alone. I didn't want to lie in Andrei's bed without someone else sleeping beside me. The nightmares stayed away when one of them was with me.

Mac offered his bed, but Liam growled and lifted me into his arms, carrying me to his bed. His reasoning was Chase would be there later to crawl into bed and snuggle me from the other side when the three returned. If three of them returned.

I wanted Wilder there, too, damn it.

I wasn't sure how long I'd slept. But the mattress dipped and shook, dragging me awake.

Peeling my lids back, I watched as Liam rolled on top of Chase, his lips devouring Chase's. His hips were moving as though he were…

Were these two lovers? I knew they were all bonded, but I hadn't realized Chase and Liam were mates.

Oh no. Would Chase hate me now? I thought he had looked at me with the same lust in his eyes as the others. And he was so sweet and gentle, holding me when I needed it.

I wasn't sure how I would feel if I bonded with these guys only to find out they were out there screwing other people.

This was the moment I should squeeze my eyes shut and try to ignore the soft moans coming from Chase's mouth. Or I should excuse myself and crawl to the couch.

I couldn't make myself do either.

Like a freaking voyeur, I watched them make love, watched through the dim light coming from the bathroom as Liam pulled back to look into Chase's eyes with so much affection, so much adoration.

They were absolutely in love. They were absolutely mates. And I'd begged Liam to eat me out.

Well, technically, I'd begged Mac to help. And I hadn't exactly had to force Liam to do anything. He'd been the one to touch me first.

As my eyes roamed down to where their bodies connected under the blankets, I missed the moment when they both realized I was watching.

"I'm sorry," I whispered in the dark.

"For what?" Liam asked.

"We…" I looked from Chase to Liam.

Had he not told Chase?

"I can taste you on him, sweetheart. It's okay."

"But you're…you two love each other."

"And you're ours, too."

Another moment that should have made me bristle. I had been the first to claim them, though, right? I had only said it to Liam, but I'd meant it about all of them. I had claimed them as my pack.

What would Andrei think when he found out? Would he remind me I was simply part of his job? Would he reject me? Pawn me off on another team?

"Come here," Liam whispered.

His hips still slowly rolled below the comforter. Chase reached his hand out, taking mine and bringing it to his lips.

"Does this bother you?" Chase asked softly.

I frowned.

"Does it bother you that I'm fucking Chase with your taste still on my tongue?" Liam asked with a sexy smirk in his usual playful and flirty tone.

Holy hell. When he put it that way, my entire body felt as though it would go up in flames. My instinct to leave the room might have been the right one. Because I was sticking to my guns about not fucking these guys.

Or at least I was going to try really hard to stick to those guns.

"Do you want to be ours?" Chase asked.

He was so freaking sweet. So quiet and gentle. He held my hand against his cheek as Liam continued making love to him.

"Is that weird? We don't know each other."

"I knew you were mine before I saw your face," Liam admitted.

Chase smiled up into Liam's eyes with a nod. "Same."

"Andrei is going to lose his mind when he finds out," Liam said.

The warm feeling in my chest and deep in my body faded slightly. Was I right? Was I seeing things that weren't there?

"He's wanted an omega in our pack from the beginning. He wants you. Anyone with eyes can see that," Chase said.

Yet he hadn't made a move. I'd had to shove his hand into my panties that night. Not that he'd needed much encouragement after that.

"Come here," Liam said again, rolling so I was pressed against Chase's back as he continued to push into him, Chase's legs wrapped around his waist.

It was so erotic. Yet romantic. I felt honored that they were not only allowing me to watch but had invited me to be there with them in this intimate moment. I kissed Chase's shoulder. Liam reached over and cupped the back of my head, lifting me for an awkward kiss.

And then the bed moved harder as Liam's thrusts became harder, faster.

He released the back of my head and cupped one of my breasts, pinching the nipple.

"Kiss her," he told Chase.

I gripped Chase's face and turned it toward me, slipping my tongue between his lips with no hesitation.

Liam lasted only moments after that. "So perfect," he said through clenched teeth as he finished.

CHAPTER 11

ndrei

MAC and I sat at the round, wooden table at the far side of the kitchen, mugs of steaming coffee in front of us. Liam, Chase, and Violet were all still asleep.

I had opened the door last night to check in and had been nearly overcome with her cotton candy perfume and a shit load of green tea, peppermint, and chocolate cake.

A growl had bubbled up my chest at the thought of either of them touching her. But she was currently playing big spoon behind Chase with his muscled arm draped over Liam.

Part of me didn't want to know what happened in that room last night. The other part of me was jealous that they might have felt her slick soaked pussy before me.

But the greatest part was pissed. They better not have taken advantage of her. As far as I could tell, her cycle wasn't giving her as many problems, but Mac had told me what had happened last night, that she'd begged them for help, and that Liam had used only his fingers and tongue to ease the symptoms of whatever the traffickers had given her in that compound.

How the hell could I say shit when I'd done the exact same thing the first night we arrived in the cabin?

"She's going to be mad Wilder didn't come back," Mac said before sipping his coffee.

"She'll understand. He has a job. He's not pack. He has his own team. The only reason he'd been allowed to stay as long as he had was because of Violet," I said.

Turning my head, I glanced down the hall toward the closed bedroom door for the tenth time since sitting at the table. It had been far too many hours since I'd seen her face or heard her voice. The entire time we were walking the remains of the compound, then sitting on our asses at headquarters and studying photos of possible perps, my mind was on the little omega back here.

Mac followed my line of sight. "They didn't fuck her," he muttered, bringing the mug to his lips. When he pulled it away, I could feel his eyes on me.

"What?" I asked.

"She laid claim last night."

My brows slammed together. "What the fuck do you mean she laid claim?"

"We both made sure she was aware of what she was doing. You know we wouldn't..." He set his mug down. "When Liam checked in again, she said *Mine. My Pack*. Those exact words."

For a few seconds, all I could do was blink. Then my heart rate kicked into overdrive until I wondered if this was how it felt to have a heart attack.

Raising a shaking hand, I laid it over my chest and turned to look at the closed door again.

"Are you sure? You heard her say those words."

The faintest smile ghosted the corners of Mac's lips. "I'm positive, brother. She feels it, too. We're not imagining shit. She's ours. Our omega. Out of every single person in that compound, we saved the one who's perfect for us. This whole thing...it feels like fate or some shit."

I huffed a humorless laugh. "Since when has fate ever been good to us?"

Mac jerked his head toward the door. "They found each other. We each found our pack. And we found her. I'd say we're pretty lucky."

Luck wasn't something I ever put much stock in. In fact, the whole fate thing scared the shit out of me, too. All four of us would put ourselves in front of a bullet for Violet. But we would eventually have to return to our job. We would have to go back to saving other omegas.

And she would be left alone, unprotected. That was the shit that terrified me.

We couldn't keep her in some padded panic room during our shifts. Especially since we never knew how long those shifts could be. Or if we would return from them in one piece...or at all.

Our job was dangerous for various reasons. While our faces weren't overly known, our names were. Members of ORE didn't exactly remain anonymous any more than the police or fire firefighters. Since we were responsible for shutting down dozens if not hundreds of outfits like the one who'd held Violet, we had accrued our share of enemies. The type of enemy who would strike at us in the most painful way.

What could be more painful than losing a member of your pack? Losing your omega.

"Is the nest done?" I asked, trying to distract myself from the thought of losing the first person who made me want to change everything about my life.

Maybe not everything. But this job...my job could end up causing her to lose one of us or becoming a target herself. There were other ways we could protect omegas without getting shot at every time.

"It's the best I could do. I'm not sure a walk-in closet is the ideal nest. But it'll do until we can get her home and build her a real one."

Home. The thought of finally going home and having her there permanently warmed my heart and freaked me out.

"She might not need it. The second the commander gives us the green light, we'll see if we can't get her to move in immediately," Mac said. "She said something about her apartment. You think she still has one?"

"Don't they have to give a month or more before evicting someone?" I asked.

"How the hell should I know?"

"Yes," a sweet and sleepy voice croaked from the hallway.

She was walking on her own, one slow shuffling step at a time. She wasn't supposed to put any weight on her feet for at least another week.

I shoved my chair back, but Mac beat me to it, rushing to her side and lifting her into his arms. He deposited her in one of the empty chairs then immediately poured her a cup of coffee and started rummaging through the fridge for something to make for breakfast.

"Can we have pancakes today? Or waffles? Something sweet."

Her back was to Mac, but I saw the uptick of his lips he tried and failed to hide. Of course she wanted something sweet. She'd slept beside a man who smelled heavily of chocolate cake with thick, sweet chocolate icing.

"Anything you want, sweetheart," Mac said.

He pulled down a box of powdered pancake mix and set it on the counter. There wasn't a waffle maker in the cabin so he would have to make her pancakes. I just hoped we had syrup. Otherwise, one of us would have to leave her again to go shopping.

"It's usually something like sixty days warning before they toss your stuff onto the curb," she said around a yawn. And I couldn't help but wonder if she was speaking from experience.

She was staring at me now. "Did those hurt?" she asked.

I frowned at her and glanced down at my arms bared by the t-shirt I'd pulled on this morning. I'd been asked dozens of times through the years how much each of them had hurt.

"No. The piercings."

I raised my brows and shrugged. "The ears, not really. The nose hurt when it was healing. The nipples–"

"Your nipples are pierced?"

We'd slept side by side that first night. But she'd been lost both physically and emotionally. I wasn't surprised she hadn't noticed.

Grabbing the bottom hem of my shirt, I lifted it until both rings were revealed.

Violet leaned forward and stretched a hand forward. Her fingertip barely grazed the hoop through my right nipple and all the blood sunk from my brain and went straight to my dick.

Apparently, that little movement had affected her as much because her perfume practically exploded from her.

"I've never seen a nipple piercing in real life," she said softly.

Something hit the ground in the kitchen and snapped me and Violet out of the moment. I glanced over her shoulder to see Mac staring wide eyed at the back of Violet's head. His eyes moved to mine and he mouthed 'fuck me.'

Yep. I felt the same way. That little moment, her tentative and almost shy touch and the explosion of her omega perfume had taken the two alphas in the room by surprise.

Violet followed my line of sight. Mac quickly recovered and bent to pick up the tub of butter he'd dropped, smiling at her as though nothing was out of the ordinary.

There was no way Mac's dick wasn't as hard as mine. An omega scent was like a drug to any alpha. This omega? *Our* omega? She was air, and water, and life.

The sweet cotton candy and lollipop smell had faded, but it was still in the air and on my tongue. It was a part of me now as much as it was her.

"You wanna wake up Liam and Chase–"

"No," Violet said. A soft pink hue colored her cheeks and she dropped her eyes to her hands for a second. "They were up kind of late."

Well, I'd been right about at least part of my assumption. The mated pair had fucked. But Violet had been in the room. Had she seen it? Had she watched?

"Did it bother you?" I asked, reaching for her hand and twining my fingers through hers.

"What?"

I jerked my head toward the door.

Her blush grew darker. "No."

She was blushing so hard she was nearing tomato red. It hadn't bothered her. As her scent grew stronger, I realized…it had turned her on. There wasn't a doubt in my mind that this woman, this little omega was created specifically to be with me. To be with us. To bond with us. To be the most important part of our pack.

And, hopefully, to one day carry our pup. And I couldn't make myself care whose pup she carried. As long as we stayed a family.

Violet

I HAD OVERHEARD Mac and Andrei talking about my future with them, about moving into their pack house. But when I'd joined them in the kitchen, neither of them brought it up again. Neither of them asked me whether I wanted to be a part of the pack, whether I wanted to move into their pack house.

I knew as a fact now that I hadn't imagined the connection I'd felt with each of them. So were they simply tiptoeing around my feelings, fearing another meltdown?

There was no way I could promise them it wouldn't happen again. My fear stayed in the back of my mind as long as one of them was within touching distance. But what would happen when real life returned? When the threat was over and we left this place?

As I cut into my second pancake, the door to Liam's and Chase's door creaked out. They both shuffled out, their hair sticking up all over the place, their eyes heavy with sleep.

"Morning," I said around a mouthful of syrupy sweetness. It reminded me of Chase's kiss. Of Liam's smile.

My body began to grow warm again as memories of last night

pushed to the forefront. The moment all four heads lifted and turned toward me I knew my perfume had just filled the room.

"So, um…" I started, not sure exactly what I was planning to say but wanting to get my mind off seeing Liam and Chase making love, of feeling Liam's fingers and tongue on my pussy while Mac rolled my nipples between his fingers and kissed me.

Of the fantasy of swiping my tongue across those rings through Andrei's nipples.

"Yes?" Liam said, that teasing smile I was quickly growing fond of wide on his face.

"Any news last night?" That was a good question. And would definitely cool my raging libido faster than a cool shower.

Chase growled softly, the sound barely vibrating from his chest.

Andrei scooted his chair closer and stole a piece of bacon from my plate.

"Hey! Get your own," I said, stabbing at his retreating hand with my fork.

"We might be in the clear," he said before shoving the entire strip between his lips.

"Really? It's over?"

He shook his head as he chewed. "I said *might*. The powers that be are under the impression this was a rogue outfit. Not organized by anyone with power."

"Why do they think that?"

"Well, for one, the dead omegas," Andrei said, and my chest squeezed.

Amora. Sweet Amora with her terror filled eyes as we'd huddled on the back floorboard of the SUV. We had truly believed we were out, we were safe.

"Hey," Andrei said, taking my hand into his and scooting until our knees touched. "You're okay. You're safe."

I frowned at him. My breathing had grown to pants and my heart raced behind my ribs. In that short period of time, terror had begun to drag me down, the memories of Amora's lifeless face had become superimposed over the beautifully rugged faces of the men who were quickly burrowing their way into my heart.

With a nod, I turned my hands over to squeeze both of his, staring into his eyes and focusing on his leather and pepper smell to ground myself.

Wait...

"Where's Wilder?"

Shouldn't he have been awake by now? Although, he'd slept on the couch since we'd arrived.

"He rejoined his team," Chase answered as he filled his plate with pancakes, eggs, and bacon.

Well, that made me a little sad. I liked him. I was comfortable around him. And I didn't feel the need to refrain from climbing onto his lap and riding him like a bull every time he looked at me.

"Was I right in assuming he's a beta?"

"Wilder's a beta," Liam confirmed around a mouthful.

And there was my answer. That was why I was so at peace around him, why my perfume didn't affect him as strongly, why I hadn't thought about begging him to help me through the short heat cycle.

"He'll be back," Andrei reassured me.

"Are you guys going to go back to growling at him?" I teased.

"Probably," Mac said then winked at me.

Andrei started to scoot his chair away, but I stopped him with a hand on his forearm. I liked the feeling of his knees pressed against me.

"Is this normal?" I asked.

Four heads raised, four sets of eyes settled on me, and four sets of brows raised.

"Is what normal?" Liam asked.

I looked down to where Andrei was pressed against my knees. "I feel...I need your touch." Tilting my head, I looked around the table. "I know Andrei spilled my secret. I know you guys know I didn't perfume until later. I've pretty much stayed away from alphas as much as possible since then. But I feel like I'm being clingy."

"Not clingy," Chase said with a shake of his head. "You're not clingy. We want to touch you, too."

"It's...how would you describe it?" Liam asked, turning to look at Mac.

"Don't look at me. I bought her sparkly pink shit that she hates. I apparently know fuck all about omegas."

"Hey! I don't hate them. I was just surprised."

"She hated them," Liam said.

I tossed my balled up napkin at him.

"I do not hate them."

"It's normal," Andrei said, ending the teasing before food started flying back and forth across the table. "Omegas are comforted by touch. Especially when they find their mate."

"Mates," Liam corrected with his mouth full.

"We're figuring this all out the same time you are. Mac, uh..." Andrei turned and glanced at Mac before turning back to me. "Mac made you a nest. It's not much. It's in the walk-in closet. There's a bunch of blankets and pillows and stuff in there. In case you need it."

"Aw, Mac. Thank you."

He was clearly the oldest of the group with gray hair hinting through the thick, black of his hair. His cheeks flushed pink as he nodded and pretended to focus on his nearly empty plate.

"When we...when this is over and we can leave here..." Andrei started, but let the question hang in the air.

I didn't want to burst out a yes without knowing exactly what he was asking, especially if it wasn't the question I was hoping for and ended up making a fool out of myself.

Liam looked from Andrei to me then back. "Oh for fuck's sake. She already claimed us. Just ask."

Andrei glared at him for a few seconds until Liam rolled his eyes.

"He wants to ask if you'd be willing to stay in the pack house. With us. As our omega."

It was the question I was hoping he'd ask. But now that the words were out there, I wasn't sure how to feel about them, how to react to them.

Yes. This was my pack. Even after the short time with them, I knew it deep in my bones. I had been in a house full of alphas during my heat and none of them had taken advantage of me. I'd had to beg them for even a hint of release.

Granted, it wasn't a true heat. And they were official team members of Omega Rescue and Extraction. Their job was to protect us, to protect omegas.

But it was more than that. They were gentlemen. They were sweet and tried to anticipate my needs before I knew I had them. Like the makeshift nest they'd built in the closet. Or the soft, fluffy blankets and the squishy pillow Mac had purchased for me that first night.

Just because I had grown up not knowing I was an omega didn't mean I hadn't seen the way alphas coddled and doted on them. My dads were constantly waiting on my mom, bringing her gifts, constantly touching her as they passed, sometimes nothing more than a brush of their fingers across her shoulders, other times pulling her onto their laps as we all lounged in front of the TV on movie nights.

The more I thought about it, the more I realized how often the guys tried to be near me, how often they would bicker over who got the privilege of carrying me from one room to the other. They would practically fight over the right to sleep beside me each night, or sit with me on the couch with my feet on their laps.

And I had discovered I craved their touch. I craved their nearness.

I couldn't imagine I would feel the same way about any alpha I met. I sure as hell didn't want any of those assholes at the compound to touch me.

"You don't have to answer right away. We probably have at least another week here before my commander gives us the green light to move you out of the safe house," Andrei said. He pushed a hand through his shaggy hair, dragging it away from his face.

He seemed to have a hard time meeting my eyes now.

Liam didn't have that problem. He stared at me with a smirk, those dimples barely winking at me from his now whisker covered cheeks.

Andrei's beard was thick and soft. But the other guys had kept pretty smooth shaven since we'd arrived. Seeing the stubble on Liam lent him an air of bad boy that made me squeeze my thighs together under the table.

"Yes," I blurted before I could change my mind.

They all stared at me wide-eyed. "Yes?" Chase asked as though he was afraid he hadn't heard me correctly.

"I told you she was pack," Liam said with a soft chuckle.

I wasn't pack yet. No one had left a bonding mark on any part of my body. Yet.

That would come later. When I no longer required one of their big bodies pressed against me to keep away the fear and nightmares of being dragged away again.

CHAPTER 12

iolet

"Can we at least sell some of it online?" I asked as the guys carried my tattered, rundown couch to the dumpster.

Liam wrinkled his nose at me. "Who the hell would buy it?"

"I bought it," I said.

He scoffed and shook his head as he hoisted one end and followed Mac through the front door. "Either you have terrible taste or this thing was cheap."

It had been cheap. Actually, it had been free. I'd had it since I was finally able to settle into an apartment without risk of being evicted within months. When my parents had kicked me out, I'd left the family home with nothing but a duffel bag of my clothes and personal toiletries. I'd had no job, no skills, no college education, nothing.

So, I'd made do with odds and ends I'd found.

There wasn't much to box up to be moved to the pack house. I hadn't even seen the pack house yet, but imagined it was bigger than my one room apartment if it fit four gigantic alphas.

Wilder had volunteered to help move me out today. And for once, none of the guys growled at his presence.

"You still shouldn't be on your feet so much," he lectured as he passed.

"Oh, please," I scoffed as I shoved the last of my clothing into a bag. There wasn't much. I could never be considered a fashion icon with my worn jeans and graphic tees and threadbare sweatshirts.

But they were mine. Some I'd brought with me from my parents. Others I'd bought at thrift stores with my first paycheck after I'd found a job.

There was no way my position hadn't been filled by now. Waitresses tended to simply stop showing up for work all the time. My boss probably thought I'd quit when I did a no call/no show.

There had been no one to call the police when I went missing.

At least my landlords had noticed. They hadn't called the police, but they hadn't attempted to evict me, either, and were so sweet when I asked to break my lease early to move in with the pack.

"My feet are fine."

Lie. They ached. But not nearly as badly as they had in the beginning.

It had been two weeks since I'd been taken from that place. My bruises were fading to yellowish green, the swelling had gone down, and my stitches had all been removed. There was still a little discomfort in some places, but I was starting to feel like myself again.

It had been a week since I'd fooled around with Liam and Mac. A week since I'd witnessed Liam and Chase make love.

A week since any of them had touched me any more than holding my hand or pressing their bodies against mine.

Yeah, my induced heat was long gone, but my body was constantly revved, like I had never truly known lust until I'd met this pack. I wanted someone to touch me other than the chaste kisses they placed on my forehead, or the sweet caresses they ran along my arm or shoulder.

There was time. If I was going to make a place in this pack, if I was going to form a true connection with them, I had to give them time to feel comfortable with me being in their lives and in their home.

But...didn't alphas crave their omegas? Wasn't it ingrained in them to breed with their omega every chance they got?

Stop being a perv.

The fact I'd had to beg for release made me somewhat antsy. Somewhat. I knew the four of them were waiting for me. It wasn't so much that they were trying to find a way to make me fit into their lives as they were waiting for me to heal from the wounds I'd suffered – physically, mentally, and emotionally.

Sure, the fear still rose from time to time. But I trusted them when they said they wouldn't let anything happen to me. That they would never let another asshole drag me away to some hell hole. And that it was okay to leave the safe house and resume a semblance of normal life.

I had no idea how that would look. I'd simply been doing my best to survive for so long that I wasn't sure what a normal life would look like as a member of a pack.

And I sure as hell didn't want to mimic my family's pack. My dads doted on my mom, but they were...possessive and aggressive. There were times my brothers and I practically had to beg for attention from our mom. And a majority of those times we were sent to another area of the house or outside so they could have our mom to themselves.

My hair was pushed off my shoulder and a soft pair of lips grazed along my throat. Leather surrounded me and warmed me from head to toe. Sometimes, when Andrei did things like this, I felt as though he were teasing me, giving me just enough to keep me on the edge, to see if I would beg him again.

"You need any help in here?" he asked against my neck, his breath warming the place where his lips abandoned.

"I'm about done," I said. My voice sounded breathy in my own ears as I leaned my head back against his shoulder.

His arms wrapped around me and his lips began a torturous path from my collarbone to nip at my earlobe. "I can't wait to have you home." A soft purr rattled against my back as he started rocking us side to side as though we were dancing to our own music.

Nerves tickled my belly as he nuzzled my shoulder and neck more.

"I can't wait to have you in my bed," he said softly, the words wrapped in pure alpha growl.

Those butterflies turned to a hive of bees buzzing in my belly the same time heat pooled low in my belly until slick dampened my panties.

For a week, I'd been trying to drop hints that I wanted...something. More than a cuddle buddy. More than sweet kisses. I wanted to feel their hands on me. Their lips. Their tongues.

I squeezed my thighs together at the memory of Liam's wicked tongue working me into a frenzy as Mac had tasted my mouth.

I had yet to feel any of them deep inside of me.

Were they waiting for me to come out and say *hey, I could really use a dick?*

Or more than one.

Never in my life had I felt like I was a walking time bomb, like at any point I would grab one of guys, rip off their clothes, and have my way with them.

Maybe that was what they were waiting for. I might have been horny, but I wasn't sure I was confident enough to make the first move. Other than when I was in pain and squirming and begging a complete stranger to make me come.

"Did..." My thoughts grew hazy as Andrei's tongue lapped out to taste the point of my pulse on my throat.

"Hm?" he asked, his breath warming the damp spot on my skin.

"That night. The first night. Was that okay?"

He pulled away and turned me so he could look into my face.

"What do you mean?"

My face flushed as I lowered my eyes to his chest. Now that I knew they were there, I could see the faint outline of the rings through each of his nipples and felt an overwhelming urge to smooth his shirt up so I could tease them with my mouth.

"That night. When I woke up. And...you know..."

"When I fucked you with my fingers and tongue?" he asked, one brow raised.

Something was different about Andrei. There was a shift since the moment I'd agreed to move into the house with the pack. His alpha characteristics were more obvious. He was commanding, but in a hot way, not a creepy asshole way.

"Yeah. That. Did it make you uncomfortable that I practically shoved your hand into my panties?"

His chuckle was deep, his smile just shy of predatory. "No. It didn't make me uncomfortable. I hated that you were hurting and would have done anything–" He brows drew together a brief second. "Almost anything to help you. But there is no way any of us would have taken advantage of your cycle to get ourselves off."

He bent close and put his lips close to my ear.

"Can I tell you a secret?" he asked.

My voice no longer cooperated, so I nodded.

"I jerked off after you fell back to sleep. I stared at your beautiful face and rubbed my dick until I came on my stomach."

Slick immediately soaked my panties.

"Is that why none of you have…"

"Fucked you?"

A whimper escaped my throat. "Yeah."

"Our job was to protect you, regardless of our feelings for you. When we're home, when you're comfortable, when you're all healed up, all you have to do is say the word and we'll do anything you want. Don't be afraid to ask for anything you want. And I don't mean just sex."

He winked down at me and smirked, that sexy crooked smile making me want to slam the door shut, shove him onto the used mattress I found on some site, and ride him until my legs shook.

"There's a room for you, but it's pretty bare. You'll need to let us know what you need to make it yours. And there's a nest, but it's pretty bare, too. Just a few pillows from the cabin. You'll need a lot more than that before your next heat. Or in case you just need a rest or break or whatever."

"I don't have any money. I barely made—"

He silenced me with his lips, earning a frustrated growl from me.

When he pulled back, he cupped my jaw in both hands and bent so we were eye to eye.

"Let us take care of you. That's our job. If there's anything else about the house you want changed, say the word. Four alphas don't exactly know how to decorate, so it looks more like a bachelor pad than a home."

I snorted a laugh. "You see my place. I'm not exactly an interior designer."

It was actually more because I never had the money for things like art or pretty bedding. Necessities only. And now Andrei was making it sound like I would be some pampered omega who just spent her alphas' money on pretty things.

"If you two are going to get naked, I'm watching," Liam teased from the doorway.

Andrei gave him a half-hearted growl, but wrapped his arm around my shoulders to guide me out of my bedroom for the last time.

"She really needs to be off her feet," Wilder said.

"I'm fine," I told him.

"She stopped letting us carry her around a couple days ago," Chase said.

"You guys are going to spoil me."

"That's the plan," Liam said.

"Let us do our job," Mac said as he passed, carrying the last of my belongings to the waiting SUV.

"Your job isn't to treat me like a porcelain doll."

"It kind of is," Wilder said with a shrug. "They'll go crazy if you don't let them pamper you. Just saying you might as well learn to enjoy it."

A frown pulled my brows together as I looked from one face to the next. I had been on my own for too long to simply release the control and hand it to someone else.

This was something they would have to take slowly. They would have to be patient with me and accept the fact there were times I wouldn't want them doing everything for me when I was perfectly capable of doing them myself.

Mac

WE WEREN'T EVEN HOME YET, HADN'T settled her into the room that would be hers, and already I could tell there would be a shit load of power struggles.

She wasn't used to being an omega. We might not have spent a lot of time with one, but it was ingrained in us to take care of them. It was in our molecular build to pamper our omega, to give her everything her heart desired.

The second the doctor gave her permission to put more weight on her feet, she refused to let any of us carry her anymore. Did she not realize it was as much for us as it was for her? It felt so good to have her cradled in my arms, to feel her arms around my neck, to be surrounded by her sweet smell.

Less than an hour and the pack house would be full of cotton candy and sweet, sticky lollipop.

Glancing in the rearview, I bit back a growl. She was riding with Wilder and Andrei while Chase and Liam rode with me. She hadn't lied when she'd said there wasn't much to collect from her apartment. But at least she had her own clothes.

She'd denied hating what I'd picked for her on that first shopping trip, but what I'd seen in her tiny closet and her drawers were nothing like the sparkly shit I'd bought. Though her clothes definitely needed to be upgraded.

It wasn't that I didn't like her lowkey, down to earth style, but half her shirts looked like they were barely hanging on by a thread. And the holes in the knees of her jeans didn't look like the fashionable kind, but rather like she'd worn them for years without replacing them.

No chance was I volunteering for another shopping trip, not unless she accompanied me this time.

I did, however, plan to head out as soon as we got her settled in so I could look for a gift. It couldn't quite be considered a courting gift since we hadn't had a chance to properly court her. And I didn't want to wait until her next heat to shower her with presents.

Already, I could hear her protests over any money spent on her, but she'd have to get used to it. We had waited a long fucking time for her to come into our lives. My omega would have everything. It would take some coaxing, but we'd get her to make her bedroom her own, decorate it however she wanted, fill it with anything she could dream of.

"Why does that fucker always have to be around?" Liam grumbled from the backseat.

"She hasn't seen him in a while," Chase said, turning to glance over his shoulder. "If our omega wants her beta buddy around, then he can come around."

"Hope he isn't expecting a key to the fucking house."

Mac huffed a laugh. Hell no, Wilder wasn't getting a key to the house. But Chase was right. We couldn't deny her anything. She liked Wilder. He soothed her in a way only a beta could. And she didn't appear to be sexually attracted to him. As long as he kept his hands and his dick to himself, there would be no problems.

I wished I was in the car with Violet when we pulled up to the house. I wanted to gauge her reaction. I wanted to see what she thought of how we lived and watch her face for any tells. She could say one thing with her mouth, but in the weeks we'd spent with her, I'd learned to read her micro expressions. I could tell when she was fibbing, when she was uncomfortable with a subject, when she was hungry…

When she was horny.

She was no longer our official assignment. We no longer had to worry about our commander stepping in and removing her from our custody. We could now spend the time necessary to meld her into our pack, to cover her in our scents. I could finally sink my cock into her, knot her, feel her pulsing around my dick.

Andrei and Liam had been the only two fuckers who'd had the opportunity to feel her wet heat, to taste her on their tongues. But I was a patient man. I would wait until she was ready.

And then I'd wreck her. I would make her come over and over until she could no longer stand, then I'd hand feed her and hold her while she slept.

Fuck. My dick was hard as stone at the mere thought. We finally had our omega. And she was everything I wanted and more than I knew I needed.

CHAPTER 13

iolet

THE GUYS WERE busy carrying my meager belongings into the house, but all I could do was stand outside and gape. This was not what I expected. At all.

Well, maybe a little. It was a log cabin, similar to the safe house where we'd stayed, but this was nothing like that small place.

There were two stories plus dormer windows. Did that make it three stories? Or two and a half? The house sprawled from one side to the other.

I had been warned it was a bachelor pad, yet there was pretty landscaping along the front and leading down both sides of the fairy tale type sidewalk that led up to a covered deck that wrapped around until I could no longer see it. There were Adirondack chairs, wicker couches with soft looking cushions, and fans that spun overhead.

It was like a whole other living area right there on the deck.

The house was isolated, tucked far back from the main road and only visible after driving nearly a quarter mile up the pristine, smooth asphalt driveway.

"You said this was a bachelor's pad," I said to Andrei when he stepped back outside.

He turned to look at the house as though just noticing it. "You haven't been inside."

"Well, unless it's all gross and nasty inside, I'm pretty sure you exaggerated. Or lied. Or…whatever. Because this place is gorgeous."

I wouldn't have thought members of ORE made nearly enough money to afford a place like this. Apparently, I had assumed wrong.

His warm, muscular arm wrapped around my shoulders and urged me up the steps and into the house. Inside was no less beautiful, but was definitely more on the masculine side. The inner walls were log, as well. The place smelled of the cedar or pine that had been used to build the place, but there was still the strong hits of pepper and leather, chocolate cake, green tea and peppermint, and whiskey.

This was one hundred percent the home of alphas. Andrei had said to make any changes I wanted. I had no idea where I would start.

I didn't hate it. At all. But it was all male. All macho alpha. Not a touch of softness or femininity anywhere.

"Where is everyone else?" I asked as I surveyed the space around me.

The front door opened onto a large living room with a high, peeked ceiling. There was a huge, wrap around leather couch that was deep enough to snuggle with one of my guys while watching a movie.

"Oh! Do you at least have streaming services here?" We had watched the same five DVDs over and over when we weren't playing games or cards.

"They took your stuff up to your room," he said, answering the first question. "And yes, we have a shit load of streaming services here. Not that we get to use them all that often. We're out on jobs a lot."

It was a reminder that they'd been unable to protect other omegas because they'd spent all that time with me. I had to constantly remind myself there were other teams with the ORE who could rescue omegas from shitty and dangerous situations.

But another fear presented itself. And I hated how selfish that fear was. My guys would have to return to work and I would be left alone in this big house far from any witnesses.

They wouldn't have brought me here if they didn't think it was safe, though, right?

Andrei placed a hand on my lower back and led me further into the house. "That way is the kitchen. It's usually pretty well stocked with junk food. Let me know if there's anything we need to get. Favorite ice cream, that kind of thing."

His hand left my back, smoothed down my arm, and wrapped around my hand. Tugging me toward the stairs before I could get a full look at the kitchen, he chuckled. "You'll have plenty of time to explore. I promise. This is your home now. There are no rooms off limits."

"Not to you," Mac said at the top of the staircase. "We don't…" He cleared his throat and looked over his shoulder toward the hall at his back.

"Mac is a little possessive of his space," Liam offered as he appeared behind Mac. "But not to you," he said quickly, holding his hands out.

"You're welcome in my room anytime you want. I just don't want these assholes in there."

"It's an alpha thing," Liam fake whispered as Andrei and I grew close.

Chase stepped behind Liam and wrapped an arm around his waist, bringing him closer. They hadn't shared any forms of display at the safe house when not behind the closed door of the room they'd shared. It was obvious they were more comfortable being themselves in their own home.

It hadn't been because they were shielding me. It was because they were on the job. I was no longer the job. I was their omega. They were my pack, my alphas.

Sort of.

Was there some kind of waiting period before one of them latched their teeth onto my neck to bond me to the pack? And who would do the marking? All of them? Andrei?

Mac was the oldest. But it seemed as though Andrei led the team. I had so many questions that I probably should have asked before we'd moved my entire life into their house.

"This is my room," Andrei said, pushing the door open to the first door on the right. I craned my neck to look inside, but he tugged me along before I saw more than the large bed with deep burgundy bedding. "There'll be plenty of time to explore that room later," he whispered in my ear.

I shivered, then turned narrowed eyes on him. "I swear you keep doing that on purpose."

His brows waggled up and down as he urged me forward. "Your smell gets even sweeter when you're turned on. I can taste it on the air."

He licked his lips as though to prove his point.

And did nothing for the heat spreading through my limbs.

The next door he opened was on the left. "This is Mac's. You'll be the only person other than him that gets to see past the frame."

Mac grunted in response.

Further down, Liam and Chase stood outside of a door on the right. "This is our room," Liam said. Chase smiled down at me, his sweet face shy as his gray eyes darted from my face to Liam's and back.

"You're across the hall from us," Chase said, pointing at the last door in the row.

The door stood open and Andrei urged me to step in. My things sat in boxes, a lamp on the nightstand beside the bed, my two duffel bags full of clothes atop the dresser.

But other than that, Andrei was right – it was bare and lacked any personality. I had no idea how I would dress it up, but it needed something that reflected me so it would feel more like my new home and not another room I was borrowing or another rented space that I feared I would be kicked out of when I couldn't make enough in tips to cover the rent.

There was a king size bed centered along the wall that adjoined to Mac's room. The dresser sat across the room opposite the bed. Two nightstands with only my thrift store find lamp sitting on one of them. That was it. No art. No bedding to cover the mattress. No rug on the dark stained hardwood flooring.

"Okay. I see what you mean about bare," I said to Andrei over my shoulder.

"We have sheets and stuff to get you through the night. But we'll head out in the morning to get whatever else you need."

"I don't need anything," I said. "I'm used to working with what I have on hand."

"Yeah, well. You're ours now. And we're going to spend our money however we want," Liam pouted.

I wasn't sure I had ever seen such a big man pout before, but he managed to make it both cute and sexy.

"It's an awful big bed for one person," I teased.

"Oh, you won't be sleeping alone," Liam said before anyone else could chime in. "I officially volunteer to help you break in the mattress."

I frowned at him. "It's new?"

The looks on the guys' faces was nothing short of confused. "Why would we give you a used bed? That's nasty," Liam said.

"Don't be an ass," Mac said, coming up behind Liam to cuff him against the back of his head.

The mattress the guys had tossed into the dumpster back at the duplex had been used when I got it. I cleaned it the best I could, but… yeah. Someone had used it before me and there was nothing I could do about it.

I hadn't always lived like that. My family pack had been fairly well off and lived in a house similar to the size of this one. My dads all worked in finance in one form or another. They drove new cars and gifted my brothers with new cars.

Me? Nope. I had bought my first car on my own when I was booted onto the streets.

A petty part of me wanted to walk around and take selfies of the way I lived now so I could send them to my family, rub in their faces that not only was I an omega, but had found a pack of amazing alphas who cared about me. I wanted them to know my life was amazing without them.

Biting my lip, I was so tempted to ask them for a car. They had, after all, said they would give me anything. What a test that would be.

For now, I didn't have a vehicle at all and would need one of them to either drive me where I needed or let me borrow one of theirs.

I couldn't ask them to buy me a damn car. But maybe they were right about letting them take care of me. After so long, it would feel so nice to feel as though someone actually gave a shit about me. This pack cared about me.

And…I was their omega. Wasn't it customary to allow our alphas to treat us like royalty?

My nose curled at my own thoughts. Yeah. That was going to take a while to accept. But we could start with the small stuff like new bedding that was my style.

As long as each of them took turns covering the sheets in their scents.

Chase

She was here. Violet was in our home. Her sweet scent rolled and changed as she walked around the place, exploring the fairly large home. It got amazingly sweet on my tongue when someone touched her. There was a hint of burned sugar when she was scared or nervous.

Right now, it had leveled out as she craned her neck to look up at the peaked ceiling made of exposed beams.

Andrei hadn't shown her the nest yet. She looked a bit overwhelmed. But she looked like she belonged in this place.

I tried to see the house through her eyes, the exposed log walls, the masculine art hanging on walls, the deep brown leather couch that fit all of us comfortably.

First thing I wanted to do when she was settled in for the day was dog pile onto the couch and wrap myself around her. I wanted to bury my face in her hair, in the crook of her neck, and inhale her until I was drowning in cotton candy and the stickiness of the sweetest lollipop.

"Are you hungry?" I asked her as she stepped into the kitchen and made a beeline for the glass French doors that led onto the back deck.

She glanced over her shoulder at me and I swear the clouds parted and created a halo of sunlight around her. Her bruises were fading and showcasing the true beauty of her face. Her hair was so dark, almost as dark as Mac's and Andrei's. Her eyes, normally a caramel color, looked like honey with the sunlight in them. Her lips were so soft and full and begging to be kissed.

My eyes roamed down her body from her elegant neckline, to her narrow shoulders, to the side view of one of her heavy and full breasts. She'd put on a few pounds since we'd taken her to the safe house. Her hips were rounding out. Her ass looked as though it begged for my hands to cup it and squeeze both cheeks.

"Not really." She smiled softly at me. "How the hell do you guys afford this place? Does ORE really pay that well?"

I rubbed the back of my neck and shifted my weight from foot to foot. I was fine conversing with Liam. We'd spent years getting to know each other. Having Violet in our house, knowing we could have a lifetime together if she asked to be bonded made me more nervous than the first time I'd slept with Liam.

Hell. It made me more nervous than the night I'd lost my virginity at seventeen.

It wasn't the thought of bonding her that made me nervous. It was the fear of her spending time with us and then deciding we weren't what she was looking for that terrified me.

"I, uh...my parents left me an inheritance. I bought this place for the pack. I didn't really have any use for all that money."

Her eyes popped wide, her lips parted, and she turned to face me.

"Are you one of those top secret, undercover millionaires or something?"

I felt the heat rush my cheeks and I dropped my eyes to my shuffling feet. "Kind of."

She stared at me a few more seconds before she finally blinked. "So...you don't need to work?"

"I love what I do. I love what we do. I don't plan on stopping until I'm too old to chase after the bad guys."

Her expression softened and a smile pulled up the corners of her lips. Affection filled her face as she crossed the room, wrapped her arms around my waist, and rested her head against my chest.

I only hesitated a heartbeat before hugging her closely to me, resting my cheek on the top of her head and breathing her in.

"You're so freaking sweet," she muttered, nuzzling her cheek against me. And if I wasn't mistaken, I heard her inhale deeply as though she was dragging my scent into her lungs just like I was with her.

"So when we say to let us buy you anything you want..."

Her body shook lightly then she pulled just her top half away to look into my face. "It's because you can afford it?"

"Yeah," I said as my cheeks flamed hotter.

"You're blushing," she whispered.

"Yeah," I said again like a dork.

Her eyes dropped to my lips before raising to my eyes. "You haven't kissed me since that night. You've barely touched me."

There was a touch of insecurity in her pretty eyes. "I didn't want to rush you. I know this is a lot. We all want you to be able to set the pace of our...relationship after everything you've been through."

A tentative smile twitched on her lips. She raised on her toes, grabbed me by the back of my neck, and dragged my face down to hers. It was soft at first, an exploration as her tongue pushed into my mouth.

And then it turned hungry as her scent turned sweeter. Running my hands up her back, I cupped her face and tilted my head so I could deepen the kiss. I couldn't get enough, wasn't close enough.

Releasing her face with one hand, I pressed it to her back and pulled her closer until our hips were lined and I knew damn well she could feel what her presence did to my body.

Her fingers lifted to tangle in my hair, her nails scraping against my scalp, and I feared I was going to blow my load in my jeans right there in the kitchen before I touched any other part of her body.

My hands smoothed from her back and cheek down her shoulders, moved to the front to cup her tits in my hands before reaching for her thighs and coaxing them around my waist. Carrying her to the island, I sat her down and settled between her thighs, pushing as close as I could get.

Violet rocked her hips along my length, moaning softly into my mouth. I wanted her. I wanted her so fucking badly. But the first time I felt Violet's wet heat wrapped around my cock would be in a bed, not on the counter in the kitchen where anyone could walk in on us.

There would come a day when it would become common, normal to catch each other making love to our omega. When she went into heat, we would all end up spending days easing her pain, pampering her…

Knotting her.

The mere thought made my dick twitch in my pants.

"That's so fucking hot," Liam said as he entered the kitchen.

Violet pulled away with a gasp and pressed her face against my chest like a teenager who'd been caught making out with her first boyfriend.

"Please. Don't stop on my account."

The jerk leaned a hip against the counter and grinned. Sad thing was, he wasn't kidding. He'd already told me more than once that he had fantasies of watching me please our omega while he stroked himself.

"You could at least take her to your bedroom," Mac grumbled as he entered the kitchen and began rummaging through the pantry.

"We weren't…we were just kissing," Violet said, a pretty pink hue coloring her cheeks.

Mac passed us and smoothed a hand over her hair, leaning to

whisper in her ear, "You're free to be yourself here. You're safe. You're home. Let your alphas take care of you."

She shivered at his words. Damn it. I wanted to be the one to make her shudder like that. But I wasn't flirtatious like Liam. I wasn't a dominant bad boy like Andrei. And I didn't have the gruff sexiness like Mac.

Her hands smoothed up my shirt until they hooked around my neck to pull my face down for one more peck before she wiggled and made it obvious she was ready to get off the counter instead of putting on a pornographic display for the pack.

Assholes. Just a few more minutes. I just wanted to taste her for a few more minutes. Play with her full tits, feel her core rub along my hard cock…

Instead, I would either have to walk around with a boner or duck into my bedroom to jerk off.

Nah. I would rather wait until I had the real thing. I would wait as long as Violet needed. I was the youngest of the four of us and had yet to knot anyone. I'd had betas beg for it during sex but always feared I would hurt them. And pain during sex was Andrei's deal, not mine.

When Violet was ready, I would give her anything she needed, anything she wanted.

When she was ready, I would latch onto her flesh and make her mine.

I couldn't wait to feel her presence in our pack bond.

CHAPTER 14

iolet

"This is plenty, guys." I giggled as they each dropped something new into the overflowing cart.

Chase held the side of the cart and guided it toward the sensory section of the store that was specifically labeled for omega comfort.

"Any colors you hate?" he asked as he ran his fingers over the selection.

"Mac bought me blankets. I think Liam did, too."

"We need to get your nest finished. And not just for your heat. It's your space. It needs to be perfect."

The room had been painted a crisp white, and only contained a few pillows when I'd first moved into my bedroom. Not that anyone let me sleep alone in it last night. All four of the Alphas had squeezed in around me when I went to bed.

And all four refused to allow Wilder to stay the night.

That was fine. He had a life of his own. And now that I was no longer being targeted, he needed to rejoin his team to save the world. Or at least save as many omegas as possible.

I liked the bedding they'd used on my bed last night. It smelled heavily of Chase and Liam, as though the five of us had been wrapped in their arms all night.

Mac and Andrei had grumbled and bickered over who got to spoon me while the other slept on the outer side, meaning one of them would end up butted up against either Chase or Liam. In the end, I'd ended up sleeping with Mac's lap as my pillow, Andrei draped over my back, Liam pressed against my front side with his hands wrapped around mine, and Chase spooned behind him.

Yet, with all of us in that bed, there had still been plenty of room. Not that any of us utilized it. Not that any of us bothered to put any breathing room between one another.

I hadn't realized until they had each started to hold me, to touch me, to caress me in gentle ways how touch starved I really was.

"Just touch them. See which ones feel best. Then pick the colors you want," Chase said, moving behind me and wrapping his arms around my waist while resting his chin on my shoulder when I hesitated. "Let me take care of you."

Let *him* take care of me. He didn't say *us* for once. He wanted to spend money on me. He wanted to treat me like his bonded omega, even if I didn't yet carry their marks.

"This is weird for me," I said, turning to look at him over my shoulder.

He pulled back a little so we weren't cross eyed as we stared at each other.

"Because you took care of yourself for so long," he said rather than asked.

"Yeah. I don't trust...I'm scared I'll get used to getting spoiled and then–"

He kissed the words away before I could speak them, something that had always annoyed me in movies.

But Chase wasn't trying to silence me or keep from speaking my mind. He was doing his best to reassure me while in public.

"There will be no *and then*. We're yours, Lil' Bit. *I'm* yours."

Of the four, Chase was the quieter of the group, sweet, bordering on shy. He was also super affectionate when he was given the space and time with me.

Lil' Bit. I didn't know why, but I loved that nickname from him. Sweet, like his green tea scent when he was aroused.

"Just a few," I said, giving in to his sweet plea.

A grin stretched wide on his gorgeous face. He nuzzled his cheek against mine for a second before stepping past me and guiding the cart to the long rows of omega comfort items.

The cart was already stuffed with several sets of sheets, an oversized downy duvet and cover in a pretty sage color, and fluffy, soft towels in a similar sage green.

Liam pushed a cart with a long, thick roll that would unwind into a fluffy rug to cover a majority of my bedroom floor. There were also bathroom items like bath mats, and a few extra scent blockers for the days when I couldn't handle the overload of all the pheromones flooding the house.

Pillows were spilling over the sides of both carts, constantly being picked up as one toppled over the side.

"We need another cart," Liam declared.

Opening my mouth to argue, I snapped it shut when Chase raised a brow and leveled a look on me. Fine. I would let them do this. I would let them succumb to their alpha urges to care for their omega. I would let Chase spend some of his inheritance on me, as long as he wasn't causing any financial strain on himself or the pack.

Would they be amenable to me getting a job once we were settled into our lives together?

And was there anything in the area that hired people with no marketable skills? I don't know that I would have ever admitted it to anyone, but I had no desire to return to waiting tables. It wasn't that I thought I was too good for it, but I had made so little money and the thought of counting my tips at the end awakened the anxiety I carried for so long over whether I would fill my fridge, keep my electric on, or put gas in the tank of my crappy car that broke down more often than not.

It wasn't a secret that a majority of omegas didn't work. Their alphas took care of them. Or their families. It was...iffy for them to be among the public. Even dangerous. Especially if they perfumed around unbonded or rutting alphas.

As I watched each guy seek out more stuff to shove into the third cart, I had a fleeting thought – would it really be so bad to be taken care of for once? I wanted to believe them. I wanted to believe they meant it when they said I was theirs, that they belonged to me.

I wanted to believe I finally had a family who loved me. Even if we were brought together for the same reason that ripped my biological family away from me.

"What about this one?" Chase asked, running his hand over a blanket as soft as bunny fur in a warm taupe color. I liked muted colors, warm earthy tones. But I still thought it was cute that Mac had loaded up a pile of clothing and blankets in pinks and purples and covered in glitter.

"It's pretty," I said, running my hand beside his. His fingers were warm as they grazed along mine and sent tingles up my arm.

He grabbed two and tossed it into the cart we manned.

"She needs more than two," Liam scoffed with an exaggerated roll of his eyes.

"There are dozens of blankets in this aisle. I'm sure I can find a decent assortment."

Both Chase and Liam blinked at me, a look of surprise on their faces that I'd decided to stop fighting them on this.

If nothing else, I could look at it as my new pack helping me fill my baser needs for comfort. Just like they did when they held me when my anxiety or fear spiked.

"Hey," Andrei called from a couple aisles over. "Send Vi to aisle fifteen."

"Vi can hear you," I called back.

Leaving Liam and Chase to argue over whether or not I needed a blanket in every texture and color, I hurried to where Andrei was inspecting what looked like one of those papasan chairs people used in the nineties. But instead of wicker, the whole thing reminded me of a big cushioned cradle, something I could sink into when the heat pains started up and I couldn't get comfortable.

"What do you think of this? The frame is sturdy in case you need one of us in there with you and it comes in different fabrics and colors," Andrei said, barely ghosting me with a glance before opening a catalog to show me the selection.

Okay. Now this was getting too much. "Don't you think all the pillows and blankets will be fine in the nest?"

"This isn't just for the nest. You can put it in your bedroom or the living room or wherever. I want you to make the house yours. And black leather couches don't exactly scream beautiful omega."

A blush warmed my cheeks when he winked down at me. Out of the four, he was the roughest around the edges with all his tattoos and piercings. I noticed the way people did double takes when he walked past or the way they would change aisles when he stood in one. He was intimidating.

Not to me. He'd shown me nothing but kindness since the moment we'd met.

"We could get two. One for the living area and one for your bedroom. That way, you can curl up in it when you need to."

I reached for the price tag hanging from the side, but he playfully swatted my hand away.

He crowded me until my back hit the shelving and then leaned in, trapping me in a cage of his arms. "I'm trying real hard to keep my alpha instincts in check," he murmured softly, his voice deep and growly, his breath warming my lips. "I appreciate the fact you're not used to having someone take care of you. But let us do this. I won't ask you to sit around with your feet up while we hand feed you grapes. But…we didn't exactly get to court you properly. Consider all this one big courting gift."

"This is too much even for a courting gift," I said with a breathy laugh. It was the most I could muster with Andrei so close, his yummy leather and peppery scent wrapping around me and caressing against every inch of my body like fingers.

His face dipped and his nose nuzzled the sensitive spot just below my ear. I shivered as my heart began to race.

As though realizing we were in public, he immediately straightened and put space between us, returning his attention to the big lounge egg as though he hadn't just set my body on fire.

"Two of them," he said to himself with a nod.

All I could do was stand there like a dork, slick dampening my panties as my sex throbbed with need.

There was no way I was going to wait for any of these guys to make a move. I needed to be touched in more ways than the cuddles and chaste brushes of their fingers along my body. I wanted more of what Chase and I shared in the kitchen. Only I didn't want clothes separating us and I wanted to be in a bedroom.

Or the nest. There would be room for all of us in the nest. I could love on all four of my alphas with no restrictions.

And that was what I wanted. It was more than simply fucking. That raw need would come during my heat cycle, of course, the need to be filled as often as possible would override any thought, any need including eating or drinking. I might be new to the omega life, but I knew enough to know part of having a good alpha was trusting that they would care for us during the time when our primal, baser side took over.

No. What I wanted now was a physical connection, physical intimacy with the men who had not only saved my life, but were quickly embedding themselves into every crack and crevice of my heart.

ANDREI

I HAD ONLY MEANT to prove a point, show her how much we all wanted to be with her, show her how much she meant to us. And then her scent had awakened my alpha side until I had to fight the urge to dry hump her in the middle of the aisle.

Fuck, she smelled good. Tasted good. Not that I'd had my mouth on her since that first night.

We'd all been doing our best to give her time to acclimate to being a part of our pack. As much as I wanted to bend her over, slap her ass until it was pink, and slam my dick into her until she begged for more, it would have to be on her timing, not mine.

Then there was another pressing issue. How would she react to my dominant side after what she'd gone through? I would rather cut off a nut than scare her.

Although Violet was pretty good at speaking up for herself. While she didn't like talking about her time in captivity, she had told us about her escape attempts, about fighting the guards when they would drag her from her room until they started sedating her to get her back and forth without a struggle.

She was a strong woman. If I hadn't witnessed her perfume, I might have wondered if she was a beta with alpha instincts.

"Can you think of anything else you need?" Chase asked, appearing at the end of the aisle.

Violet blinked slowly then turned her head toward him. She looked drunk. And I couldn't help the boost to my alpha ego. I'd done that without touching her. I'd done that with my presence, with my scent, with my nearness.

Unfortunately, I had also awakened my own damn libido. My dick was so hard it was uncomfortable and would end up with a permanent imprint from my zipper.

Mac pushed one of the carts forward, passing by all of us without glancing in our direction. What was he up to?

"This really is enough," she said with a chuckle.

"Pajamas. And a robe. Soft stuff. Even if you don't sleep in it, you'll need it when your cycle hits," Chase offered.

"She'll be naked when her heat comes," I muttered under my breath.

But she'd caught it. Her cheeks flashed bright pink and sugary sweetness wafted from her until I could taste cotton candy on my tongue.

"I have pajamas," she protested, a shy yet excited smile on her face as Chase wrapped his hand around hers and dragged her toward the sleepwear.

There was a whole section specifically for omegas with various soft fabrics and textures.

I grabbed an order tag for the lounge, then leaned my forearms against one of the carts, following behind Chase and Liam as they continued to talk her into a full selection of fleece, flannel, and others. She finally acquiesced and bought two sleep sets that consisted of tank tops and thin pants, and a robe that looked as soft as a cloud.

An image of my fingers opening that robe, of peeling it from her naked body like opening a gift did nothing to ease my raging boner.

Three carts loaded to the brim plus tickets to have the lounges delivered to the house and we were ready to check out. Mac was behaving oddly. Or more oddly than normal. Secretive, even.

But there was a hint of a smile on his lips. He was definitely up to something. If that asshole had found a gift for Violet, I needed to make sure the next one I got her was even better. No way would I let the oldest of our group one-up me.

As the cashier dragged each item across the register, beeps filled the air. And Violet's eyes grew wide.

"Nope," Liam said, wrapping an arm around her shoulders and guiding her away so she couldn't see the total.

All four of us made decent money with our jobs, but Chase was determined to pay for this entire trip from his inheritance. After he'd built the pack house, the money simply sat in different accounts and investments, accruing interest and wealth. Wealth that Chase had planned on spending on his omega.

Our omega. He might be paying for this trip, but I was definitely going to get to know every single thing I could about her, to discover her favorite everything so I could buy her one of each. Favorite ice cream? Three tubs in the freezer. Favorite color? A whole room would be decorated accordingly.

My alpha instincts might have bordered on dominant, possessive, and a little on the rougher side, but I would dote on my little omega until she grew used to it, until she realized how special she was, until she realized her importance in our lives.

CHAPTER 15

iolet

THE GUYS HAD SPENT two days redoing my entire bedroom and finishing my nest, filling it with the dozens of blankets and pillows. The two ridiculously large egg lounge things Andrei had ordered were delivered the day after our shopping trip. One sat in a corner of my room near a bookshelf. The other was in the living room beside the leather couches.

It looked so odd, yet so perfect. The masculinity of the leather matched my alphas while the plush seating in a pale, smokey blue was feminine without being girly. Within the first few days of living in the pack house, hints of me, hints of my presence were appearing all over the large place.

Already, this place felt like home. And I knew it had everything to do with my alphas rather than the location. I was as comfortable and at peace in the cabin – even when I didn't know whether I was still being targeted – because they were with me.

I hadn't seen Wilder since I'd officially moved in and was starting to miss him. He was the first friend I'd made since going into hiding after my first perfume. Not that I'd had a load of friends to begin with. Or…you know, any friends. I moved around and changed jobs so much it was hard to form true connections.

Now, I laid in the humongous bed with Chase spooning behind me and Liam lined along my front until I could barely move. Not that I wanted to.

I had never understood the need omegas had to be touched, to be held, to be near their omegas. I always wondered if they were lazy, if that was the reason they were often seen cradled against someone's side or sprawled across their lap.

I understood now. It wasn't so much that I didn't want to get out of bed, to move. It was that I didn't want to leave the warmth and peace the guys brought me.

Chase's arm was draped over my waist. His hard cock was pressed against my ass, practically nestled between my cheeks. I still had a while before my real heat came to life, but that did nothing to lessen my need. None of them had made love to me. Andrei had helped me through a wave of pain the first night we'd arrived at the cabin. Liam had made love to me with his mouth.

But that was as far as any of them had taken it.

I was tired of waiting.

Taking a chance, I wiggled a little, pushing myself back against Chase. Liam's breathing was still slow and steady, a light snore rattling from his open mouth that sounded so much like a purr.

Chase's arm tightened around me and hugged me tighter until I was pulled away from Liam a few inches.

His face nuzzled into my hair until his lips pressed against the back of my neck. A sigh left my lips at the soft contact until his teeth grazed along my skin, soothed by his tongue.

I was tired of waiting. So fucking tired of waiting.

Sliding a hand between us, I pushed past the elastic waistband of his boxers and reached for him, circling his thick cock with my fingers. His waist bucked forward at my touch and a purr rattled up from his chest, vibrating against my back.

As I stroked him slowly, his hand moved from my waist to cup one of my breasts, lightly pinching my nipple through the thin material of my brand new tank top. It then smoothed down my stomach and dipped below my pants, his fingers sliding through my folds until they found my clit.

Biting my lip, I tried to stay silent as the tip of his index fingers slowly circled the swollen bud, then slid further back until he dipped inside of me.

Slick dampened my panties, coating his finger as he slowly pumped into me.

More. I need more.

Without waiting for him, I pulled my hand free from his boxers, back still to him, and shoved at the hip I could reach so I could push his boxers down, trying to remove the barrier between us. The mattress shook as he chuckled and maneuvered to shove them down his legs, then helped me to pull my sleep pants far enough down for him to slide his dick between my thighs.

The sensation of his velvet covered steel sliding along my sex, growing wet with my slick, made flutters pulse low in my stomach until I thought I would come before he was sheathed inside of me.

More.

Before I could make another move, he gripped my thigh and raised it, opening me for him. The flared head of his cock pressed against my core and I bit back a moan. "Mate," he whispered against my neck as he pushed into me slowly, sliding in with ease.

My eyes rolled closed as he pushed until his knot added resistance. Chase started a slow rhythm, pumping his hips so his cock rubbed all the right places inside of me.

A hand cupped my breast, my tank pulled down to expose it. Peeling my lids open, I watched as Liam lowered his head to suck the pebbled bud between his lips and grazed it with his teeth before soothing the sting with the flat of his tongue.

Liam pulled back and helped me roll until I was straddling Chase with my back still facing him, my breasts and exposed sex facing Liam.

"So beautiful," he murmured, his eyes drinking us in. "Your knot is so fucking swollen," he said to Chase before lowering his head. His tongue made a path from my clit down to Chase's knot, to his balls where he stopped to suck them into his mouth.

Chase moaned, his hands going to my hips where they tightened until his fingers gripped me almost to the point of pain. Almost.

"More," I said, finally voicing what I'd repeated in my mind.

Liam's tongue swiped back up, focusing on my clit as Chase held me still and began to pump into me harder, faster.

"Oh shit," I breathed out. "Fuck." I threw my head back and squeezed my eyes shut as the two pushed me to the precipice then shoved me over.

My pussy squeezed around Chase's cock as ripple after ripple of pleasure darted through me.

Liam gripped my hips just above Chase's hands. "Show your alpha how much you like his dick," he said, leaning forward to kiss me, my taste on his lips, before pushing me down until Chase's knot stretched my opening then locked us together, my slick and Chase's cum pooling in the cradle of his groin.

Chase moaned my name as heat rushed though me in spurts, his cock jumping with each jet of release.

"Mmm," Liam hummed, cupping Chase's balls and fondling them as he finished inside of me. "So beautiful," he repeated.

Chase rolled us back to our sides, his knot locked inside of me. Were I in heat, his knot would have retreated faster. It was easier to breed your omega more often. But since this was nothing more than lust, than carnal need, he might very well be locked inside of me for thirty minutes or more.

The problem with that was the longer he stayed flared inside of me, the more I wanted.

"You smell that," Liam said with a smile as he knelt over us. "Our omega wants more."

"You realize how weird it is for me that you guys can all tell when I'm horny because of my smell."

"Consider it a gift. You don't even have to ask. We just know."

"Then why am I the one who keeps making the first move?" I asked with a raised brow.

"We were trying to let you get settled. But, honey, trust me when I say we're ready whenever you are. I have never wanted anyone as much as I want you."

Chase cleared his throat dramatically behind me then chuckled.

"Okay. I have only wanted one other person as badly as I want you."

A thought rose in my head. Or rather a fantasy. The three of us playing together. The problem was I wouldn't be able to see a damn thing since Chase was locked in behind me. Would it be terrible to ask for some tall floor mirrors so I could see my bed from different angles.

A hand appeared over my shoulder as Chase reached for his mate.

He'd called me his mate. Chase had claimed us both. I shouldn't have been jealous. I had claimed all four of them, declared all four of them as mine. I wanted all of them but wasn't sure I could share them with anyone outside of the pack.

"Where are Mac and Andrei?" I asked. They weren't in the bed when I'd woken this morning.

"I don't know if you want all four of us already," Liam teased.

With a roll of my eyes, I shook my head. "I–" But I couldn't finish the sentence. Couldn't voice the fantasy I wanted to play out without being interrupted by the other two alphas.

"They're checking the surveillance equipment and speaking with a woman who reported a stalker. They'll be back later," Chase answered.

His breath warmed my skin, his green tea and peppermint flaring when I pushed my hips back and squeezed my inner muscles around his knot.

Liam's eyes were back to roaming me, roaming where Chase was embedded deep inside of me, locking gazes with his love at my back.

His cock was hard and jutted forward when he pushed onto his knees. "My omega wants more?" he whispered, threading his fingers through my hair.

As he scooted forward, I immediately opened my lips when he offered himself like a gift.

His fingers tightened in my hair and he began to pump into my mouth. From my position, he would have to do the work. I only had so much leverage.

That, apparently, didn't bother the flirty alpha. Soft moans escaped his lips as I stared up into his eyes while he fucked my mouth slowly. One hand left my hair and reached over my head, presumably to touch Chase.

As Chase's hips began to push forward again, slick began to soak my thighs. How was I so close to coming again when he could barely rut into me with his knot locked in place and no contact with my clit?

Liam's eyes rolled down to my face. He pulled his cock from my mouth and lowered to taste my lips. When he stared into my eyes, I could see the question in his eyes.

"Make love to our mate," I whispered against his lips.

He bent and kissed me, his tongue dancing against mine.

The mattress shook and dipped as Liam moved until he was cradled behind Chase. "I love you," I heard them mutter to each other a second before Liam moaned and Chase was pushed further into me.

I needed a mirror. I needed to see. All I could do was listen as the two moaned in unison, enjoy the feeling of Chase's knot being shoved into me. He reached between us until his fingers found my clit and fondled me, stroking to the same rhythm as Liam pumping into him from behind.

Chase wouldn't be able to take Liam's knot. Alphas' bodies weren't meant for that. But that didn't mean they enjoyed each other any less. I had gotten off before Liam had shoved me down onto Chase's knot.

Liam's hand stretched across Chase to reach for me. In an awkward move, I turned my upper body with my lower body still clamped around Chase, and sighed as he massaged my breast, tweaking the nipple, rolling it between his fingers. I still couldn't fully see everything from this angle, but I could see Liam's hips pumping, could see the muscles in his ass bunching, could feel Chase's heavy breathing as he neared orgasm from having his prostrate stroked by

Liam's long, thick dick and his knot deep inside my cunt, rubbing my inner walls.

"Holy shit," I breathed out as both men continued to stroke and fondle me while Liam fucked the love of his life. "I'm going to come again," I groaned as the pressure built and built.

"Fuuuck," Liam growled, pushing hard into Chase as Chase pinched my clit. "Come for your alphas, Violet. Squeeze Chase's knot."

That was it. That was all I could take. Explosions rocked through me, fireworks exploded behind my closed lids, and my body tingled from head to toe.

That was, by far, the hottest, yet most romantic sex I'd ever had in my life.

And for the first time in my life, I found myself looking forward to my next heat when we would all be locked in the nest together. Would Mac and Andrei participate with Liam and Chase, or would their full attention be on me?

The latter was just fine. All of the above would be good. And from this moment on, I would no longer wait for one of them to decide when I was ready. I would simply go after what I wanted.

And what I wanted soon was to discover how Andrei's nipple rings would feel on my tongue. I wanted to taste his peppery scent deep in my throat. I wanted to feel his fingers wrapped in my hair and see if he was as dominant as I assumed.

"Again already?" Liam teased as my perfume exploded from me as new fantasies began to grow.

My stomach growled just as I began to wiggle my hips against Chase for more.

The guys laughed. We would have to wait for Chase's knot to deflate so he could remove himself from me. Then I needed to eat.

But after…we had all day to explore each other.

CHAPTER 16

ac

A GROWL RATTLED nonstop from my chest the entire trip home. The only thing keeping me from slamming my fist through the windshield was the fact I was the one driving. If I crashed us into a tree, we wouldn't return to our omega.

"Have any others been located?" Andrei said into his phone.

There had been several omegas found dead surrounding the compound even after ORE had searched it and razed it to the ground. Teams had been sent out, trackers hired in hopes of at least learning a direction of where any who might have escaped had headed.

What they'd found were omegas who'd been executed. Not just killed, but shot in the head as though they'd been forced to kneel and wait for their death.

The four omegas team three had rescued were currently being moved from their homes and back into protective custody. We had gained permission to keep Violet in our house instead of moving her back to a safe house. Our home was armed for bear, and alarms were on every entry or exit point including windows in the basement.

The property line also had wildlife cameras and censors that would trigger if anything larger than a deer happened to wander through the woods or up the driveway. Our home was impenetrable. And the four of us were not only highly trained, but her fucking alphas. No one could keep her as safe as we could.

"Copy. We'll go radio silent until further notice."

Andrei ended the call and practically threw his cell onto the dash.

Violet had only recently started to return to a semblance of normal life. She hadn't returned to her apartment, but it felt as though she had always belonged in our home. It had only been days, but it was hard to imagine her not in our house, her scent not coating every surface.

How would she react when she found out she was once again on lockdown? She had literally left the house once since she'd been rescued from the compound. We would keep her safe, but I hated the thought of fear returning to her eyes or the way her sweet scent would take on the burned sugar smell.

"How many?" I asked as the growl continued to rattle loudly.

"All of them. As far as the commander could tell, the only omegas who got out of there alive are the four with team three and Violet."

Fuck. That meant dozens of dead omegas. Dozens of the rare gems of the world. Who the fuck…why the fuck…

I couldn't finish a thought. The only thing I could focus on was getting back to my omega, to my mate.

We weren't bonded. We couldn't feel her the way we could each other. Both Andrei and I knew the moment the three had…enjoyed each other this morning. But we couldn't feel our sweet Violet. I couldn't wait for the day when I could feel the happiness I'd felt from Chase, or the lust and satisfaction I'd felt from Liam through the inner thread that tied me to Violet.

"Can you drive faster?" Andrei grumbled.

"Not unless you want me to fly off the fucking road."

The back roads to our house were filled with switchbacks and blind hills. One wrong turn and we could end up at the bottom of the deep hill, head long into a tree, or even crashing into the odd car.

After what felt like an eternity later, I finally pulled the SUV into the garage, watching the rearview mirror until the electric door slid shut behind us.

Andrei was out of his seat and practically running for the door before I got my seatbelt off.

One step inside the house confirmed what I'd felt through our bond link. Heady scents of arousal, of Violet's sweet slick, of strong hits of Chase's peppermint green tea and Liam's chocolate cake was practically dizzying as I stepped into the mudroom and made my way through the house until I found everyone in the living room.

"What?" Violet asked, her wide eyes going from Andrei to me and then back again. She could tell we were strung tighter than a fucking guitar. "What happened? Are you okay?"

She was wedged between Chase and Liam, her lips pink and kiss swollen. Both alphas went from relaxed and content to tense within a split second and a surge of anxiety rippled over our connection.

"They found the omegas who tried to escape that night," Andrei said without preamble.

"That's great! Why do you both look..." Her words trailed off and she blinked a few times as she came to the conclusion without being told facts. "They're dead."

Andrei nodded.

"All of them?"

"All but you and the four team three evacuated."

Her blinking became rapid as her eyes grew glassy with unshed tears. Her chest rose and fell quickly as she began to practically pant.

"I think...am I hyperventilating?" she asked as a tear escaped over her lashes and trailed down her cheek.

Fuck. This was one of those rare times I wished Wilder was here. Every single one of us would hold her as long as she needed. We would lend her our strength, purr for her, wrap her in our scents. But it wouldn't be nearly as calming as quickly as a beta's scent to a stressed omega.

Chase wrapped an arm around her shoulders and pulled her tightly to his side. He wrapped his other arm around her until he was practically hugging her to his body.

"Breathe with me, Lil' Bit. Slowly in…hold it. Slowly out," he said, showing her with his own breaths what he wanted her to do.

Her eyes stayed locked on Andrei as she nodded and followed Chase's instructions.

"You're safe," I said, unable to handle seeing her like this. I wanted to find every mother fucker who'd had any hand in her abduction and the murders of the omegas and slaughter them. I wanted to find them and kill them slowly and painfully, drawing it out so they would know the fear and pain they'd inflicted on so many others.

Her eyes turned to me. Lifting an arm, she held out a hand to me. I didn't hesitate to reach for her, to grab her hand in mind and kneel at her feet beside Andrei's knees. She had four alphas who would destroy anyone and anything to protect her. We would risk our own lives to keep her safe.

"I got you a present," I said, hoping to distract her from the moment.

It was probably best to let her process what she'd learned, but I hated the fear and sorrow filled look in her pretty eyes.

"A present?" she asked with a sniffle. Her brows drew together as her attention strayed to the egg cup thing Andrei had picked out for her then to the throws and pillows littering the couches. "You guys got me a whole lot of presents," she said.

Raising her hand to my lips, I feathered kisses to each knuckle before squeezing once and releasing her. I raced to my bedroom and grabbed the bag I'd hidden inside my closet. I had planned to wait until her next heat. Or at least until after I was finally able to bury myself inside of her.

But now was probably a better time to see her smile.

Or at least I hoped it would make her smile.

Retaking my place at her feet, I held the bag up to her. She extricated herself from Chase's side, the crease still between her brows, and peeked inside. After rifling through the gift paper the attendant had helped me with at the store, she pulled a long cardigan from deep inside the bag.

I had paid attention to the colors she'd chosen when she'd shopped for comfort items. I'd purchased the sweater in a soft blue that reminded me of the sky just after the sun rose above the trees.

"Thank you?" she said, confusion in her tone.

With a chuckle, I grabbed the tag with the instructions and showed her. "As each of us cuddle with you while you're wearing this, it'll trap our scents. Even if you wash it, you'll still be able to carry us with you anywhere you go. It's…the lady said omegas love these things."

Her eyes moved side to side as she read the tag then raised to my face, widening as a sad smile quirked up her lips.

"I love it," she said. This time, the tears that spilled over her cheeks were a combination of pain and joy. The smile she gave me was watery as she practically lunged at me and wrapped her arms around my neck, pressing her nose into my neck instead of resting her cheek against my shoulder.

She stayed like that for several minutes, simply using me for comfort. And I could have held her all night long.

When she finally pulled away, she swiped at her tears then grimaced. "I got tears on your neck," she said, reaching forward to dry the spot.

I stopped her hand. It was just another way for me to bathe in her scent. "Leave it." Kissing her palm, I released her so she could return to Chase's side.

With a deep inhale, she released the breath in a rush. "So what's the plan? I don't want to leave here."

"We don't have to leave," Andrei said, lowering to take the place where I'd been kneeling and putting his hands on her knees. "Our house is as safe if not safer than any location owned by Omega Rescue and Extraction. And as unknown as the safe house locations."

"We're officially on duty. With you. Here," I said.

A wry smile slowly stretched across her lips. "Was this some kind of ploy to get paid time off with your omega?"

She was trying. She was doing her best to make light of the situation to avoid sinking into fear, to avoid focusing on the fact she was one of the few who'd survived that breeding compound.

"I wish we were that clever," Andrei said.

Her eyes moved from one of us to the next. "Okay. I need to hear all of it. I need to hear the plan."

"That is the plan. We're currently on lockdown here. We're treating the pack house as a safe house," I said.

Andrei explained to her about the cameras, the alarms, and even the sensors around the property. He explained to her that there were loaded weapons in every room, even if they were completely out of sight.

"I think she needs to learn to shoot," Liam suggested.

"Absolutely," I agreed.

Her brows popped up on her forehead and her eyes went wide. "As in shoot a gun?"

Several smartass comments floated through my head, but I kept them to myself. "Yes. As in shooting a gun. We will keep you safe. But it can't hurt to learn to protect yourself. This will all be over soon. ORE will find the fuckers responsible. You will be able to leave the house and the property again. Being familiar with a gun, knowing how to handle it and shoot it safely would make all four of us feel better about you going anywhere without us."

Liam snorted. "Not happening," he muttered under his breath.

Violet raised one brow and shot him a glare. "I was on my own since I was eighteen. Yeah. I got snatched. Once. It won't happen again. And I don't want to have a bodyguard with me twenty-four/seven." She nodded. "When can we start…uh…gun training?"

Violet

After such an amazing morning – and afternoon – the bubble of happiness was popped the moment Mac and Andrei stepped through the door. I'd been so excited that they were finally home. I'd been practically on the edge of the couch as I watched for them to step through the door of the mudroom.

Until I'd seen the hard look on Andrei's face.

Five of us. There had only been five survivors from the compound. At least this time, I wasn't sequestered away in a cabin in the middle of the woods. I was in the pack house, surrounded by them, everything holding hints of their deliciously addictive scents.

The sweater Mac had gifted me was currently lying on the bed while I took a hot bubble bath. I planned on wrapping up in that and snuggling with my guys so it would be covered in their essence. Hell, I might wear it to bed if we were all going to snuggle together again tonight.

As I laid my head back and enjoyed the fragrant steam rising from the water, the bathroom door squeaked as it was pushed open.

Turning my head, I gave Andrei a lazy smile.

"Smells like you had a good day," he said with a jerk of his head toward my bedroom.

Heat rushed from my chest, up my neck, and straight to my cheeks. Among other places.

"A very good day," I teased.

As he stepped in and closed the door behind him, I noted the large mirror attached to the back that stretched from the top to the floor.

"Can we get deliveries here? Or are we staying completely off the grid?" I asked as I remembered that I wanted a mirror in my bedroom so I could see everything next time I shared time with Liam and Chase.

"I would rather not have anyone uninvited here until the culprits are located," he said.

His voice held that raspy growl he'd had back at the store and my pussy throbbed to the beat of my heart as he slowly stalked toward me.

How the hell did such a nerve-wracking sentence rub all my erogenous zones simply from the growl in his voice?

Lowering to his knees, his eyes trailed across the surface of the bubbles as though he could see my naked body below.

"Did you please your alpha?" he asked.

I clenched my thighs under the water at his question. Then I decided it was time to enjoy myself with my alphas, to enjoy my time with them...in case my time with them was limited.

"I pleased them both," I said.

My voice was husky, breathy in my own ears.

His eyes dropped to the water then to my eyes. "Are you done with your bath?"

With a nod, I whimpered when he reached into the suds and hit the lever to drain the tub. He lifted me and settled me into his lap, back facing him. He hadn't bothered drying me. I was soaking his shirt and pants.

"What–" I started to protest.

But my words were cut off when he maneuvered us until we were facing the mirror as if he had read my mind about the mirror. This wasn't exactly what I had in mind, though. I wanted to see Liam and Chase fucking while they fucked me.

When his knees slipped between mine and opened me wide, exposing my pussy in the mirror, I had a brief moment of shyness where I felt the need to cover.

"No," he said, stilling my hands and holding my thighs wide. "Before I touch you, I need you to tell me a word."

He smoothed a hand down my stomach until his fingers slid through my folds. Suds clung to my skin, slipping down my wet, glistening skin as he began to torture me by smoothing down each of my lips without touching my clit.

"A word?" I asked on a need filled whimper.

He answered with a growl. "A word. I need a word for when you need me to stop. When it's too much."

All I could do was blink and focus on breathing as he continued to tease me. "I don't..." I gasped when he pinched my clit between his fingers then returned to teasing. "I don't understand."

His tongue lapped at my earlobe. The hollow below my ear. Then his teeth grazed a path down my throat before he clamped down hard enough to bruise but not hard enough to break the skin.

I sucked in a breath as the pain sent zings of pleasure to my now slick coated cunt. Watching his finger in the mirror, I tried to make sense of his words.

"I can be gentle if that's what you want. If that's what you need. But if you're willing to let me show you a different side of pleasure, I need a word. Tell me a word so I'll know if I've gone too far. Because stop won't work."

The smile in the mirror was nothing short of predatory as he watched my face. I had a hard time focusing on his reflection or his words when he was teasing me, periodically pinching my clit hard enough to make me gasp and attempt to escape the way he held me open so I could straddle his damn lap.

"A safe word," I said on a moan when he finally dipped a finger into my opening.

He nodded and waited. He didn't pump his finger into me, didn't move while he waited. This man was going to kill me.

"Clover," I finally said as his scent burst from him and made me mewl and whimper and move in an attempt to find relief.

CHAPTER 17

 iolet

THERE WAS something about Andrei from the moment he'd stepped into that room at the compound that screamed dominant. He was all alpha, even if he was kind and gentle with me from the beginning.

"Do you want me to be gentle?" he asked, sliding his finger into me deeper until only his second knuckle was inside.

"No. I want to forget everything. Even for a little while."

That was all he needed.

With my knees spread wide, he began to finger fuck me fast and hard. When he was satisfied with my slick, a second finger joined the first. His other arm came around so he could stroke and pluck at my clit while his fingers made wet sounds inside my cunt.

As my eyes rolled shut, Andrei tsked at me. "Eyes on me," he barked, that low, growly voice sending me over the edge. "That's right. Squeeze my fingers like you're going to squeeze my cock."

My mouth opened on a silent scream as wave after wave of orgasm crashed over me until I thought I would be swept away.

"Keep those pretty eyes open," he said.

I watched as he pulled his fingers free and put them in his mouth, sucking my release from his fingers.

"As sweet as I remember."

He stood so fast I squeaked in surprise. There wasn't much warning before he carried me into the bedroom and deposited me onto the bed and stripped from his clothes.

His cock sprang free as he shoved his wet jeans down his legs, the thick length bobbing and begging to be tasted. As the flared head glistened with precum, I had the urge to lick it away.

When I moved to reach for him, he grabbed my arm and turned me quickly, shoving my chest onto the bed. I was practically on my toes as he kept my upper half pinned to the mattress, my ass and pussy on full display for him. "Do you remember the word?" he whispered in my ear.

As I nodded, the soft down comforter rubbed against my cheek. "Clover."

"If I hurt you, if I scare you, if it's too much, use that word. I will stop whatever I'm doing immediately."

His feet kicked my legs wider until my thigh muscles were strained. Excitement skittered through me, causing more slick to coat my pussy and thighs.

The head of Andrei's cock began to slide through my folds, moving from my clit to my puckered asshole. I had never had anyone back there and wasn't sure I was ready without a little more foreplay. Or at least another orgasm.

But he didn't push in, simply continued to rub himself against me.

"Do you want my cock?" he asked.

"Yes."

"Beg for it," he said.

My cunt began to throb with need. "Please, Andrei. Please fuck me. Please give me your knot."

He tsked again. "You'll get my knot when you've satisfied your alpha."

With that, he shoved forward hard and fast, not bothering to give my body time to adjust to his size. I screamed out at the intrusion, but it wasn't from pain. For a moment, I feared the others would burst through the door thinking I was in danger.

When the doorknob didn't so much as turn, I assumed Andrei had warned them that he needed time alone with his omega. If they'd spent enough time with him, they had probably heard him fuck plenty of women – and men? – through the years.

He might have been the one in charge in that moment, but I would make sure I pleased my alpha so well he would forget about anyone else he might have fucked.

Andrei filled me, his swollen knot straining against my opening, stretching me, teasing my clit, but he never pushed himself the rest of the way in. Nor was he moving. He simply stayed in place, his hands gripping my ass.

"Do you want more?" he asked.

He leaned over my back, his hard chest pressing against me, pressing me further into the mattress. His teeth trailed over the place where he'd latched on earlier sending little tingles of pleasure throughout me.

"Yes. Please. I need more, Andrei. I need more, alpha. Please fuck me."

With a growl, one hand held my head against the mattress while the other trailed up my back until a stinging slap hit my ass.

A guttural moan escaped my lips. I'd been spanked in the past. But that had been nothing compared to how I felt in that moment, how his big hand against my ass felt.

He was keeping my face pressed to the mattress. I couldn't move if I wanted to. Andrei was in full control and could do anything he wanted to my body.

And I loved every second of it.

"Whose pussy is this?" he asked.

"Yours, alpha. I'm yours."

Hand still holding my face against the mattress, he pulled back and slammed into me. Then he started a rhythm that had his hips slapping against my ass, the clapping sound filling the room.

Almost there. Almost there.

Until he pulled completely free of me.

"You don't come until I say so," he said, bending over my back to growl into my ear.

A long, begging whine escaped my lips, followed by a yelp when he moved away from me and flipped me onto my back so quickly I bounced on the mattress.

"Scoot back." I obeyed immediately. "Open," he said. I parted my thighs. "Hold that pussy open for me," he barked. He literally used his alpha bark to compel me to do as he wanted.

It wasn't needed. At that moment, I would have literally done anything he asked as long as he eased the pressure building in my body.

"So pretty," he cooed, lowering his face until it was level with my pussy and giving it a long swipe with his warm tongue.

A slap sounded as his hand hit my sex hard enough to sting. But before I could dwell on the pain, he soothed away that pain with his fingers and tongue, thrusting two fingers into me as he practically devoured my clit.

"You're fucking drenched for me," he said, pulling his fingers free and wiping them clean across my breasts. "Are they virgin?"

In my lust drunk haze, I just blinked up at him.

He pushed my full breasts together and squeezed. "Has anyone ever been between your tits before?"

I shook my head and licked my lips, tempted to beg him to be the first.

He had other ideas. "I will fuck your beautiful tits, but for now, I think I'm ready to feel you clench my dick. Are you ready for my knot? Are you ready to coat my dick?"

"Yes, alpha. Please," I begged.

He climbed up between my thighs, pushing my knees back until they were practically touching my chest, then slammed into the hilt, his knot once again stretching my entrance.

"You don't get my knot until I hear you scream my name."

He fucked me relentlessly, leaning forward to wrap a hand lightly around my throat as he took me hard and fast. The moment the first ripples of orgasm started, he smiled wickedly at me.

"Good girl. Come on my dick. I want to smell like your pussy for the rest of the day. I want the pack to know how hard my omega came for me."

Throwing my head back, I screamed Andrei's name as I came. He pushed forward hard, shoving his knot into me, stretching me until I thought I would go blind. But he didn't stop pumping his hips. He used his knot to bring me again, one hand around my throat, the other pulling and plucking at my nipples.

When he tensed and growled through clenched teeth, I sucked in a deep breath as his dick twitched inside of me and I was filled with so much heat.

The sound of our combined release made a squelching sound as he rutted into me, trying to shove his knot deeper.

"Fuck," he ground out, finally dropping on top of me, holding his weight on his elbows. "I've wanted to do that for weeks."

"So have I," I said, sucking in breath after breath.

Andrei lifted his head and looked down at me. "Why didn't you say anything?"

I awkwardly lifted one shoulder in a shrug. "I thought alphas were supposed to be in charge and all that."

He huffed a deep chuckle as he dropped his forehead to my shoulder. "Sweetheart. When are you going to learn? You're an omega. You have all the power. You are literally in charge of all four of us and can ask for anything your heart desires. I can promise you none of us would have said no if you'd simply asked to be fucked."

"I learned that lesson this morning."

He raised his head and looked into my eyes again. "You pleased both your alphas this morning?"

Heat rushed my cheeks. "Do you really want to hear the details of me being with other men?"

"Oh, honey. Those aren't just any men. Those are my packmates. I want every gory detail."

And so, I told him everything. Including my fantasy of all five of us together during my heat.

My fantasies set him off again. The moment his knot loosened enough for him to pull from me, he flipped me onto my stomach and took me hard and fast again.

And then a third time before we finally left the room in search of dinner and I could barely walk without my legs giving out from beneath me.

Mac

It had been three days since Andrei and Violet had emerged from her bedroom, both swimming in each other's scents. When Andrei moved past me, my entire being was filled with the feeling of summer carnivals and the craving for sticky sweetness and cotton candy.

I'd locked down the bond between us to prevent feeling his lust when I couldn't partake in Violet's sweetness.

Three days of the five of us sleeping in a tangle of arms and legs. Three days of keeping my fucking hands – and dick – to myself.

She'd initiated her first time with Chase. I'd heard her beg Andrei through the walls of her bedroom.

I would be patient and wait for her to come to me. Although it might very well fucking kill me.

The fact she slept with the cardigan wrapped tightly around her every night definitely made me happy. She was ensuring every single one of us was represented so that she could use our scents for comfort whenever she needed.

A bruise had appeared on her shoulder where it met her neck as though Andrei had latched onto her with his teeth. But he hadn't broken the skin. He hadn't bonded her. None of us would push that on her until she was ready.

At least I hoped we would all be able to control our urge to make her our permanent omega.

She was in our house, had chosen to move into the pack house rather than returning to her apartment. And now she was stuck here until further notice. Not that any of us minded. Because we were stuck with her. It was our job to keep her safe. It just so happened every single one of us had formed a deep attachment to her and were falling head over heels for her. At least I knew I was.

I wasn't forward like Liam. I didn't have the gentle sweetness like Chase. I wasn't a possessive, dominant alpha like Andrei. At my age, I'd learned patience, and not by choice.

Peeking at her from the corner of my eye, I bit back a groan when her pink tongue lapped at the sugar on her bottom lip from the cinnamon roll she was eating for breakfast.

We tended to keep the kitchen fairly well stocked. Since we never knew how long each assignment would last, we were never sure how much time we would have to do grocery shopping or meal prep. It was best to keep easy to make or microwavable meals on hand.

I wanted more for my omega. I wanted to be able to cook her a big ass meal. She'd put on some weight since she'd been released from captivity, but I had a thing for big asses and round hips. There was nothing sexier than a woman with curves. The kind of curves I could grip while driving into her.

From the sounds that had come from the bedroom when she'd been with Andrei, she didn't seem to mind hard and fast. Not that I was into the whole pain thing. I might like it a little on the rougher side, but nothing that ran close to Andrei's tastes.

No. Even at my age, I still tended to lose myself when I was knot deep in a beautiful woman and couldn't help but wonder if I would lose my fucking mind when I finally had Violet's slicked pussy wrapped around my cock and clenching it with her release.

These thoughts were doing nothing for my fucking boner. I needed to change my train of thought, get my mind on something mundane so I could stop obsessing over the sounds she would make or the look on her face when I watched her fall apart.

Nah. Not watched her fall apart. *Made* her fall apart. I wanted to use my fingers, tongue, and dick to make her scream as she fell over the edge then shove my knot into her until we both felt boneless.

Pushing from the table, I carried my dirty plate and empty coffee mug to the sink, rinsed them both, then placed them in the dishwasher. I could have sworn I felt Violet's eyes on me as I moved through the kitchen and headed to the office the four of us shared, although we each had our own desks. Liam was a slob, his worktop always littered with paperwork. I never understood how the dude could find anything.

Andrei kept his desk a lot like mine, clear and organized. Chase rarely used his desk, simply set his laptop on whatever surface, including his knee, if he had any work to do from home.

"Where you going?" Liam called after me.

"Office. I wanna check into some things," I answered as I continued out of the kitchen.

There wasn't a whole lot I could do, but at least I could try to do some research, see if I couldn't find a pattern, maybe narrow down a few leads as to who was running the compound and if they were responsible for any other such outfits.

Flopping into the leather chair, I rolled it closer and brought my computer to life. I was the only one of the four of us who still preferred the whole monitor and computer deal over a laptop of some form. I never saw a reason to carry my work from one room to another, and I sure as hell didn't need it when on missions.

Once the system was warmed up, I started searching news articles and logged in to a few of my favorite sites. Click after click, I found similar stories happening in nearly every state. Problem was, there were so many variations. Some of the compounds imprisoned only omegas. Others held females of different designations.

There was even one that had captured and held alphas. What the fuck purpose was there for that? As sick as it was, I could somewhat understand capturing omegas. Since their heats could be forced, they would be amenable to a form of nonconsensual consent. They would beg for release even though they would fight tooth and nail when their hormones weren't overriding logical thought.

But alphas? They couldn't be impregnated. While I supposed a rut could be forced on them the same way they medically induced heat in omegas, what purpose could that possibly serve?

Finger on the mouse, I clicked through story after story, but was still having a hell of a time finding a pattern. Unless the fact there was no obvious pattern was the pattern. The only thing any of these stories had in common was the fact the people found were all being held in similar compounds. They were held in similar housing buildings. There was an infirmary at each hell hole. And each had a location that sounded like what Violet had heard the guards refer to as the *fun room*.

Leaning forward, I pulled up a few stories and minimized them so I could click through quickly. Eyes squinted, I searched each and every face shown, whether suspects, victims, or law enforcement.

There. The face wasn't fully in focus, but I swore it was the same man in each picture. And the fucker was in uniform. That normally wouldn't have raised any flags, but these stories were from various counties throughout the state. That didn't rectify the similar stories in the rest of the states, but it might be some kind of lead here.

"Andrei," I called out, eyes still riveted to the screen. I needed another set of eyes to make sure I wasn't seeing shit.

"Finish eating," I heard him tell I assumed Violet and could imagine the eye roll he received in response.

Heavy steps heralded Andrei's approach. "What's up?" he asked from the doorway.

Jerking my head, I waited as he glanced over his shoulder then moved to stand beside me.

"Flip through these stories, focusing on the pictures, and tell me if anything stands out."

Andrei propped his hands on the desk and leaned in, clicking through the stories, zooming in on the pics. I knew the moment he'd come to the same conclusion.

Straightening, he released a slew of epithets that would make a sailor blush.

"All here?" he asked, his eyes still glued to the screen.

"All here."

Once again, he clicked through the more than a dozen articles, zooming in on the same face that had caught my attention. "Is there a way to save just his face?"

"It's blurry as fuck. Not much to go on."

"But it's something," he said, straightening again and crossing his arms over his chest. "Save that shit. Email it to the commander. Get the department in the loop."

Andrei was a few years younger than me and, technically, team lead. But it still chapped my ass when he ordered me.

Fighting to keep from bristling, I nodded and went to isolating and saving images then emailed them to the commander with a request to have them analyzed by the tech geeks of our department. Maybe they could use some form of face analysis software to get an identity.

Or maybe we would end up exactly where we were now.

At least with Violet in the house, we knew she was safe. What fucked with my head was the possibility that we might not be able to catch this son of a bitch until he struck again and made a mistake.

Fuck.

CHAPTER 18

iolet

THE GUYS HAD BEEN ACTING weird since breakfast. At no point did anyone leave me alone in a room, as though they were afraid I would disappear if there wasn't at least one set of eyes on me.

"Is anyone going to tell me what's going on?" I asked as Andrei leaned down and whispered into Chase's ear.

Liam looked to Mac. Mac looked to Andrei. It looked like they were having some silent, telepathic conversation.

"Okay, now you're pissing me off. Is it about me? Or did something else happen?"

"We might have a lead," Mac answered.

I turned my attention to him as my heart began to trip hammer in my chest. "You know who took me? Took us? You know who started that compound?"

He shook his head, raised a hand to scratch his eyebrow with his thumbnail. "We don't have an identity yet. Just a lead."

I waited for him to elaborate. When he didn't, my already frayed nerves felt as though a cheese grater had been taken to them. "And? What does that mean? Why all the secrets and whispering?"

They were treating me like some fragile damsel in distress. After the bullshit I'd dealt with weeks ago, finding out they might have a lead wasn't exactly something that would have shown up on my anxiety meter.

"He might be in law enforcement."

Oh. That was why they were being so sneaky. Because the people we all depended on to keep us safe were the ones destroying lives, figuratively and literally.

"How…" My voice came out in a squeak. After clearing my throat, I tried again. "How do you know he's in law enforcement?"

No one spoke.

"Nope. You're not keeping me in the dark. I get that there are aspects of your job you can't share, but this involves me."

"Maybe she'll recognize him," Liam said.

"Or maybe she'll have a panic attack," Chase said.

I frowned at him. "At what point have I come across as a broken victim to you?"

Liam smiled, pride bright in his eyes.

Chase looked as though he wished he could shove his foot not just into his mouth but down his throat. "You haven't. And we don't see you that way–"

"Don't say we. You said that shit," Liam said.

"But you went through a lot. And now you're at risk again. I just don't want you to be scared like you were at the cabin."

"I wasn't scared at the cabin," I argued. A few brows raised. "Okay, I was at first. And who can blame me? But I'm not scared here. I trust you guys. And you said the property is secure. Tell me everything. Show me the guy you suspect."

"That's my girl," Liam muttered, that mischievous grin that I'd come to adore highlighting his sweet dimples.

Mac pushed to his feet and left the room. When he came back, he carried a manilla envelope and handed it to me, lowering to the cushion directly beside me and sitting so closely our thighs touched.

I raised my face to look into his eyes. His expression was neutral, but there was something in his eyes I couldn't quite identify. Anger? Fear?

Personally, I felt both those things to my core. I was holding a folder that was at least a half inch thick of pictures of crime scenes.

A new fear unlocked. "Are there pictures of victims in here?" I asked, looking Mac directly in the eye.

His head wagged side to side slowly, but he didn't say a single word.

I knew looking at pictures of compounds similar to the one where I had been held might stir up that old fear, but I also knew I was safe. What I couldn't handle was seeing dead people, dead omegas, people who'd been executed for no other reason than because of the way they'd been born.

Pressing my thigh harder against Mac's, I relaxed the tiniest bit when he lifted his arm and draped it over my shoulders, pulling me to his chest as I opened the folder and stared down at the first picture.

They were stills that had been copied from the computer, blown up, and printed. The images were grainy and out of focus. One after another, I flipped through them, until I got to the eighth pic.

This was clearer. Still not anything that could be used for a mug shot, but I absolutely one hundred percent recognized him.

Pulling it free, I started at the beginning again and compared the pic to all of them from start to end.

"You know him," Mac said. It wasn't a question.

When I tilted my head up at him, his brows were knitted tightly together.

"Your scent turns a little...burned smelling when your fear or anxiety spikes," he said as though my mind could make heads or tails of what he was telling me.

Yeah. I knew him. I recognized him. But I'd never seen him in a police uniform. I'd only ever seen him dressed in a similar fashion as the guards. He had been one of those who'd dragged me from my room in the beginning. He'd been the one who'd instructed his buddy to dose me so I would stop fighting them.

Nodding, I closed the folder but held onto the clearest one. I couldn't stop staring at it. The man's face was turned toward the camera, but he was looking past the photographer. What was he looking at? Dead omegas? Was he inwardly celebrating that he'd gotten away? Was he hoping any that had attempted to escape were dead so they couldn't identify him?

Shit. I could identify him.

"That's why they were killing everyone that tried to run. So he couldn't be identified," I said, my voice sounding far away or like someone had stuffed cotton in my ears.

"We came to the same conclusion," Mac said, his deep voice vibrating against my back that rested against his chest.

Or was that the growl that rumbled through him?

"And he'll keep hunting us until there are no more witnesses."

Shit. Chase might have been right about seeing the pics causing a panic attack. Because at the moment, my heart felt as though it would burst through my ribs. Surely, everyone in the room could hear how loudly it was pounding.

I was safe. I was wrapped in Mac's arms. Andrei was only a few feet from me. Liam and Chase were sitting across from me, their eyes glued to my face.

"How can I help?" I asked instead of allowing the fear to take over.

No way would I sit by and let this asshole hurt more people, not if I could do something to stop him.

"For now, nothing. Not until we're able to figure out who he is. We sent the pics into headquarters to see if–"

"But what if he works with you guys? What if he's a member of Omega Rescue and Extraction? He could have been on one of the teams that came in that night. What if he was the one shooting–"

Mac grabbed my shoulders and turned me so quickly I gasped. "Stop." An alpha bark that made the words stop in my throat before I could continue voicing my fears and my thoughts ended up in a weird tailspin. "He's not a member of ORE. Every single one of us went through so many background checks and psychological testing it would be damned near impossible to slip through."

"But–"

"No," he said, once again cutting me off. "This is why Chase was worried about showing you. I can see everything spinning in that beautiful head of yours. He might or might not be a member of law enforcement. All we know is he has access to a uniform. We don't know his identity, but I promise I'll tell you the second we know anything. And then you can help us lock the fucker up for life."

My breathing was rapid but his words were…not comforting. That wasn't what was causing my system to slow. It was his scent. It was his alpha pushing against my omega, letting me know I was safe.

In the time since my first perfume had changed my designation, I'd worried about an alpha having any power over me. But now? I welcomed it. Mac's mere presence, his big, warm hands on my shoulders, his warm amber and whiskey essence soothed away all the prickly edges of the fear that had done its best to wrap around me and scrape away the peace I had found with this pack.

With my pack.

Bond or no, they were mine as much as I was theirs. The bond was nothing more than a formality. Something we had plenty of time to complete.

Or did we?

If this jackass was eliminating any witnesses to his crimes, my time with the pack could very well be cut short.

Leaning forward, I pressed my lips to Mac's, just a whisper of a kiss against his mouth. One of his hands tightened around my shoulder but he didn't wrap himself around me and hold me closer like the others. He waited patiently as I sipped at his lips, as I tasted his mouth.

When I pulled back, a soft rumbling purr filled the air and his expression was softer, his eyes filled with affection and warmth.

"You're safe. We'll catch the fucker," he said, his gaze never wavering.

And I believed him. At least for the moment. If the person behind the abductions and murders was adamant about eliminating witnesses, it was only a matter of time before he tracked me down along with the four others.

Until then, I would do as we'd discussed and learn to shoot a gun. I wanted to protect my alphas as much as I wanted to protect myself. Because I knew if the situation arose, they would each put themselves in front of a bullet to save me. And I refused to allow them to sacrifice themselves. Not for me.

Mac

For once, when I had Violet in my arms, the last thing on my mind was having her naked and beneath me writhing, panting, begging for more.

No. The only thing on my mind was the fact she'd come to the exact same conclusion as the four of us – she was officially a target as were the four other survivors.

To what lengths would the man go to remove the threat of discovery? Would she ever be safe? Obviously not, not as long as that mother fucker was walking the streets.

I had shut her down when she'd voiced her concern that the perp could be a member of ORE. But I'd already had the same concern. As had Andrei.

The only fucked up thing about that was the fact it wasn't exactly difficult to find the address to the pack house if he was an employee.

As long as the alarms and cameras were up and running, we could head off anyone who might attempt to invade the property.

If it were up to me, there would be no trial. No jail cell. If it were up to me, I would take the fucker into a field and put a bullet between his eyes.

Problem with that was there seemed to be a never-ending supply of monsters just like him. There was a reason police departments, the military, and the ORE were necessary. There would always be criminals, there would always be predators.

The room was silent as we all waited for Violet to process the new information. She stared down at the picture in her hand so long I started to wonder if she was mentally shutting down.

When she barely moved, I couldn't take it anymore. I snatched the picture from her fingers and stretched my arm, waiting for Andrei to take it and slip it back into the folder.

"We need a pack night," Liam declared.

"Isn't every night a pack night?" Violet said softly.

She hadn't pulled away from me, still snuggled against my chest, but she was tense, that burned sugar smell still rolling from her in waves as though pushed into the air with each heartbeat.

"We'll pile the coffee table with snacks and drinks and turn on some stupid toilet humor movies."

"Action," Violet said.

"Really?"

She finally moved, as though whatever had frozen her in her spot had released its invisible hold on her. "Mindless action. Something improbable. You know…the shit where they jump from one building to the next, avoid the gunfire from a hundred gunmen, that kind of thing."

Personally, I didn't think anything with gunfire was a good idea, not after she'd experienced the real thing, but I wouldn't be the one to reject her request.

"What does everyone want?" Liam said, jumping to his feet before anyone even agreed with his plan.

"Chocolate," Violet said, pulling from my arms and rubbing her hands down her face. "Lots of chocolate."

"Do we have chocolate?" Liam asked.

Chase stood and joined Liam in the kitchen. Cabinet doors opened and closed as the two sought goodies for the night.

The couches were deep, but I had the urge to have the entire pack as close as we were when we held her at night.

"Help me move this," I said to Andrei.

He frowned for a second, then caught on to my idea. With Violet still sitting on one end of the couch, we turned it and combined the two until it resembled the biggest theater seat in the world.

"Blankets," Andrei said with a snap of his fingers.

He darted from the room and returned minutes later carrying as many blankets and pillows from the nest as his arms could hold.

A smile stretched on Violet's face as she watched us practically rearrange the living room for movie night.

She had to know. She had to know this was our alpha need to comfort our omega. She had to know it was the best we could give her for now. And she had to know we would tear the state apart piece by piece until we found the fucker and ended his terror on omegas.

CHAPTER 19

iolet

"Yeah, right," Liam said, tossing a piece of popcorn at the TV.

"You're cleaning that up, asshole," Andrei said, his eyes glued to the movie.

"All I'm saying is there is no way he wouldn't have broken his legs on that landing."

I'm not sure what possessed me to request an action movie. I had lived one. But the real thing was nothing like what I was watching on the ridiculously large TV screen. There was no fear, no stress, and no anxiety, even with the manufactured booms and pops from the explosions and gunfire filling the room from the various speakers situated around the room. It really felt like the action was happening all around us, like we were in a movie theater instead of all cozied up and snuggling on the makeshift bed.

Liam was cradled behind Chase, who rested his cheek on my stomach. I was positioned between Andrei's legs, one of his knees raised, an arm loosely draped over my shoulder. Mac was sitting on my left, his shoulder against mine, his fingers twined through mine as he drew lazy circles on the back of my hand. Every once in a while, he would bring our hands to his lips to feather kisses across my knuckles as though he couldn't get enough of my touch. Or maybe it was my scent.

I didn't mind. It felt as though I was literally wrapped in a cocoon with all of them so close. And a part of me couldn't wait for my first heat with the pack so we could spend days together, feasting on each other, spending hours locked together.

A couple on screen held hands as they raced away from the bad guys, ducking into a building and checking each other for bullet holes.

"See? How many people were aiming their guns at them and neither of them have so much as a scratch," Liam said, once again critiquing the realism.

"Why do you think I said I wanted mindless action? No thinking involved. Just…entertainment," I said before spooning the last of my ice cream into my mouth.

Liam and Chase had not disappointed on the snacks nor had they scrimped on the variety of chocolate. Most of it would end up getting put away, but there was no way I would pass on the heaping bowl of rocky road ice cream.

"I'm going to get fat if you guys keep feeding me the way you do," I teased. I swore someone was always offering me food. And very rarely was it anything that could be considered on the healthy food pyramid.

"Mac hopes so," Liam said.

I turned my head to look into Mac's face. "Oh, really?"

His cheeks darkened with a blush as he shrugged. "I like big tits and a big ass."

I had the former but it would take more time to get the latter. I'd lost weight during my time in captivity.

"You saying you wouldn't find me attractive if I was skinny? Or had small boobs?"

"Pft." Mac made a dismissive sound. "I would want you if you wore a damn paper bag over your head and looked like Quasimodo."

A laugh burst from my lips as the other three alphas chuckled.

"What? I'm serious. I guess you can say I'm one of those people who are more attracted to the person inside than the external looks. It doesn't hurt that you're gorgeous and have tits that will fill both hands."

"Her tits are off limits," Andrei said, his eyes still on the screen.

My cheeks burst into flames at the memory of him asking me if my breasts were virgin, when he'd asked me if anyone had ever fucked them before. That night had been…intense. Then, afterward, he'd cleaned me of our release and held me until I fell asleep.

Mac winked down at me, but the pink didn't leave his cheeks.

Leaning my head, I dropped it onto Mac's shoulder. I was officially surrounded by my pack. By my alphas.

"Why haven't any of you marked me?" I asked.

It was like the oxygen had been sucked from the room for as quiet as it had gotten. Andrei was statue still behind me, Mac's chest began to rise and fall with heavy breathing, and Liam slowly turned his head to look at me.

"You want to be bonded to us?" Liam asked.

"You don't want me bonded to you?"

Well, shit. Had I misread everything? No way. They had each declared me their omega. Why would they not want to complete a bond?

"I don't need a bonding ceremony if that's what you're worried about." *Please let that be the only reason they are waiting.*

I wasn't sure how the whole thing worked, but I'd seen the marks on the shoulders of omegas and betas. And I knew that mark enabled the pack to feel each other, to sense the emotions of each of their pack.

"Oh my god," I whispered as embarrassment rose up fast and hot.

Three set of eyes were on me and Andrei tightened his hold. "What's wrong?" Andrei asked, his breath ruffling my hair.

"Could you…did you guys know when I…"

Liam threw his head back and guffawed loud. "Did we know when you fucked one of us? Yep."

"Oh no," I groaned, dropping my face into my hands as that heat in my cheeks grew until I thought I might burst into flames.

Chase's touch was gentle as he pulled my hands from my face then lifted it with fingertips under my chin. "That's not a bad thing," he said softly, his sweet face full of what looked so much like love.

"You guys literally knew every time I…"

"Fucked one of your alphas?" Andrei asked over my shoulder.

"Andrei!" I whisper-screamed.

Yep. My face was going to go up in flames. Along with the rest of my body. Because not only was I blushing to the point of feeling sunburnt, but my body was warming at the memory of each time these delectable men had their hands on me.

His rumbling laughter shook us both as his arms squeezed me tightly against his chest.

"When you're bonded to us, you'll feel us, as well," Andrei whispered in my ear, his stubble scraping the shell of my ear before he nuzzled his cheek against me, scent marking me and sending tingling throughout my body.

That tingling mixed with giddy joy and a touch of nerves. I wanted that. I wanted it more than I was willing to admit. When I'd perfumed, I had feared being claimed by an alpha. I had feared the sense of possession.

But a bond would tie them to me as much as it would me to them. I would feel them deep in my heart and soul.

As much as I couldn't help but wonder why no one had brought it up, why each of them seemed to take their time with me, I wondered if I was ready for something so permanent. The only way to break a bond like that was death.

Andrei still nuzzled his temple and side of his cheek against me, his breath warming my skin.

"Okay…I'm still embarrassed. But thanks for at least not making me feel like a big ol' hussy!"

"I'm pretty sure no one would describe you as big anything," Liam teased. "Unless they were talking about those *tittiiieees*," he said, drawing out the last word like an opera singer.

Of the four, Liam was the most playful and least apologetic about his love of sex. And honestly, his playfulness helped ease that humiliation I'd felt moments ago that much more.

Chase rolled his eyes. Andrei and Mac chuckled softly.

And then we were back to relaxing and watching another movie. They gave me full control of the remote, so I picked an old horror classic.

"Really?" Liam asked, wrinkling his nose at me.

"What? It's an oldie but goodie."

"Liam doesn't like scary movies," Andrei teased.

"Shut up," Liam grumbled, sitting back against the cushions and crossing his arms like a petulant child.

"Aww. Don't worry. If you get scared, I'll check under your bed and in the closet for any monsters."

THE NEXT TIME I opened my eyes, I was surrounded and tangled by warm arms and legs. We had all fallen asleep watching movies, the snacks currently shoved to the end of the pushed together couches.

Sunlight shone through the open curtains and singed right into my eye.

With a groan, I turned my back to the offensive light and snuggled directly into Mac's chest. Andrei was no longer propped up behind me. In fact, after a quick glance around, he was no longer snuggled up with the pack.

Taking a deep hit of Mac's amber and whiskey – and fighting the urge to lick him to keep his taste on my tongue as long as possible – I carefully and slowly began to lift arms from my waist and wiggle away from the three alphas pinning me in.

After a lot of careful gymnastics, I hoisted myself over the side of the couch and padded barefoot through the living room, following the siren call of fresh coffee.

Andrei sat at the table, a mug in front of him, his eyes glued to his laptop. The screen cast blue light on his features, highlighting the circles under his eyes as though he hadn't slept much last night.

"You don't like working in the office?" I asked quietly as I padded forward.

He twitched as though I'd startled him and looked at me over the laptop, closing it before I got too close.

With narrowed eyes, I reached into a cabinet and pulled a mug down for myself, filling it before adding sugar and creamer and sitting beside him.

"No secrets," I said, tilting my head toward whatever he apparently didn't want me to see. "Unless you were watching porn," I teased.

The corners of his lips twitched but he shook his head. "I was going through ORE employee files to see if anyone matched the physical description of those pictures."

"And?"

He sighed heavily and scrubbed both hands up and down his face. Mac was the oldest of the four, but at the moment, Andrei carried a weariness in his eyes that made him appear older.

"I haven't gotten through the full roster yet, but no one matches. So either I haven't gotten to him yet, he's a member of another law enforcement, or, as I suspect, he has access to a uniform."

"Those were different uniforms," I pointed out.

Andrei nodded as he opened his laptop again. "Which is why I don't think he's actual law enforcement. I think he shows up on the scene, blends in with first responders, and makes sure there is no one left who can identify him."

Chills ran down my spine at that. What would he do if he came across a survivor on the scene? Would he pretend to escort them to safety and kill them as soon as they were out of sight? Keep his face turned away so he couldn't be identified then hunt them down later?

"He can't be a high-profile figure of society. I didn't recognize him when he came to my room."

"But he definitely has money. Each of those buildings would take a shit load of money to run. Food, electricity, that kind of shit. And I highly doubt the goons working for him would do it for free." His hand scraped against stubble as he rubbed his jaw. His eyes turned back up to me. "Were they all alphas?"

I shook my head. "I didn't see every guard, but there were at least two betas who came to my room."

His head nodded slowly up and down but a soft growl filled the space between us. He could school his face all he wanted, but he couldn't suppress his alpha instincts.

Reaching across the table, I laid my hand on his forearm and smiled inwardly when he immediately calmed. I still didn't know nearly enough about my new designation, but there were a lot of obvious perks, like bringing peace to my alpha.

My alpha. My alphas. There were four men who I craved more than my next breath, four men who had come into my life during the worst part and had helped erase all those negative thoughts I'd carried about my family's rejection, the fear of what being omega meant, the fear of being taken again, even the stress and nightmares from my time in captivity.

"I'll find him," Andrei said, his eyes still glued to the computer.

Pushing to my feet, I closed the space between us and lowered onto his lap as he opened his arms for me without hesitation.

"Maybe I can help," I said.

Leaning against his chest and sighing when he wrapped his free arm around my waist, I watched intently as he clicked through employee profiles that all included pictures. A rumbling purr vibrated against my chest and I could have sworn the sound was like a vibrator against my sex.

This wasn't the time to be turned on. I was helping Andrei go through pictures in hopes of identifying the man who'd ruined so many lives. But omega biology was screwy.

He hesitated on a profile. "What about him? Same dark hair."

I leaned in closer and studied the man. "No. That's not him."

His sigh was full of frustration as he moved the cursor on the screen and minimized the site.

When his head dropped to my shoulder, I leaned my cheek against his hair. I wanted to comfort him, tell him everything would be okay, that the asshole would be found.

But I didn't want to lie, either. The worst part was that he more than likely wouldn't be found before either more omegas ended up missing or dead. I'd watched enough true crime shows to know serial killers were often caught because they made a mistake. Meaning, they had to repeatedly kill people before they got sloppy and left a trail for the police to follow to their doorstep.

"Are you hungry?" he mumbled against my neck before trailing his lips along the sensitive skin there.

I hummed but wasn't sure whether I was answering his question or reacting to his touch.

Tightening both arms around my waist, he nuzzled his cheek against mine for a few more seconds before placing his hands on my hips and lifting me from his lap just as I'd felt the stirring of his cock.

I had to bite back the frustrated groan at the loss of contact and the missed opportunity to play before the others woke.

As he moved around the kitchen, he held up a pack of bacon and a container of small donuts for me to choose. I wanted crispy bacon and scrambled eggs but it would make too much noise and wake up the guys.

"Donuts," I said with a smile as I lowered into the seat Andrei had vacated. It was still warm from his adorable ass holding it down for…

"How long have you been up?" I asked.

"Haven't really slept."

A frown pulled my brows together. When I made a move to stand so he could have his seat back, he stilled me with a hand on my shoulder then took the one I'd taken when I had first joined him at the table.

When he dropped his head into his hands, my heart clenched. He hadn't slept because he was worried about me. He hadn't slept because his job was to protect omegas. He hadn't slept because he was determined to catch the bastard victimizing people.

Scooting my chair closer, I ran my hand over his hair and rested it on the nape of his neck. "They'll catch him, Andrei. It's not your sole responsibility. You don't need to carry the full weight of this on your shoulders."

He nodded but didn't raise his head or speak.

"Why don't you go to bed? Get a little rest. You look exhausted."

"I am," he said, lifting his head to roll it on his shoulders with a series of cracks. His eyes leveled on me and he studied my face for a few seconds.

"What?" I asked, fighting the urge to fidget under his scrutiny.

"Of all the omegas we've saved, of all the omegas I've met…what the hell did we do to deserve you?" He never cracked a smile, but rather truly seemed amazed by the fact I was there with him, with them.

I pushed my fingers through his hair and leaned in to press a kiss to his lips. "I think I'm the one who got lucky in this scenario."

CHAPTER 20

iam

Violet's door was open. Stepping through, I followed her sweet scent to the bathroom and hesitated outside the door, rapping my knuckles against the wood. I didn't want to catch her on the toilet and embarrass her.

"Come in," she said.

She stood in front of the vanity, running a brush through her long, wet hair. She wore a white, cotton t-shirt and no pants. Through the thin material, I could see the dark panties she wore beneath and my dick immediately stood at attention.

"Fuck, you're gorgeous," I said as my eyes roamed all the way to her bare feet.

A blush touched her cheeks when she turned a smile on me. "Thank you."

Setting the brush down, she turned to face me, and all the blood left my head and settled directly in my groin. Her hair had dampened the front of her shirt and rendered it fucking see through. Her beautiful pink nipples were on display, pebbled from the cool air.

"You okay?" she asked after a few seconds.

"What?"

"I said are you okay?"

I finally tore my eyes from the full tits I had grown obsessed with to find a concerned look on her pretty face.

"Horny as hell," I admitted.

The crease between her brows instantly smoothed and a smile stretched across her face. "I'm convinced you walk around horny all day."

With a shrug, I said, "Well, yeah. Look at you. Do you blame me?"

She actually ducked her chin to look down her body then back up at me. "I'm just wearing a t-shirt. I'm not even wearing makeup."

"Pft." I waved off her ludicrous argument. This woman didn't need anything to be beautiful. She was naturally pretty with the freckles across her nose and the petal pink lips that I could have sworn were made to be wrapped around my cock.

So far, I'd only tasted her and seen her fuck Chase. I knew she'd been with Andrei, too. There was no way any of us could have missed the pleasure that rippled through the bond when our packmate knotted her nor her screams of pleasure when he took her hard and rough.

"I'm getting a little jealous," I teased.

"Of what?"

Stepping forward, I raised a hand and used just the tip of my forefinger to circle the outline of her nipple before pinching the pebbled tip between finger and thumb. Her slight gasp and the headiness of her perfume made my cock twitch in my pants.

"I want to be buried inside that cunt of yours, but you seem to have your preference."

It was a tease. She knew it was a tease. We were all settling into a routine. Andrei had been the first to taste her when he'd helped her through the pain of her medically induced heat. But I'd had her on my tongue simply because her hormones rushed forward.

But I'd yet to feel her clenching around me as she fell apart. And I had every intention of making her come hard before letting myself follow her.

Lifting my other hand, I cupped both her big tits in my hands and massaged them, rolling her nipples between my fingers and smiling when her eyes rolled shut and cotton candy filled my senses and landed on my tongue as her arousal filled the air.

"Do you want me to stop?" I teased.

I knew damn well she didn't. I knew damn well every cell in her body wanted her alpha as much as I wanted her.

"No," she moaned as I rolled one of her nipples then plucked it a little harder.

Her next gasp was swallowed as I crashed my lips over hers, fucking her mouth with my tongue, tasting her and feeling lust drunk.

She wasn't lying. I was always in a perpetual state of arousal. How could I not when I had the love of my life sleeping beside me every night then the most beautiful omega in my home?

Walking her backward, I pushed my hardness against her when we hit the wall. "Do you want me to fuck you against the wall or would you prefer the bed?" I asked against her lips.

"Both?" she answered, as she looked at me heavy lidded, her lips already getting kiss swollen.

"Mm. I think I can manage that."

Lifting her heavy tits in my hands again, I took her mouth, sliding my tongue against hers, tasing the velvety sweetness, sucking in a lungful of her perfume.

The only issue was we were separated by my sweats and her panties.

Reaching under the bottom hem of her shirt, I hooked my fingers in the sides of her panties and shoved them down her legs. Her arousal grew stronger as I trailed my fingers through her slick coated folds.

"Fuck," I growled. I wanted to take my time, but wasn't sure how much longer I could hold out. I wanted to slam my dick in to the hilt, shove my knot until she was stretched, and hold her still as I filled her with my cum.

We had time for that. For now, I wanted to find every secret button on her body that made her squirm, every inch of skin that made her twitch and beg for my dick.

Instead of dropping my sweats to my ankles and thrusting into her, I lowered to my knees, hooked one of her legs over my shoulders, and dove face first into her soaked pussy.

Her fingers tangled in my hair as mewls and moans escaped from her. Her hips rolled and rocked against me as she fucked my face.

"Liam," she breathed out. "I'm…"

"Come on my tongue," I muttered before sucking hard on her clit.

She shuddered, her fingers tightening in my hair, and her release flowed over my tongue. I lapped it up like a starved man, savoring every drop of her sweetness.

Fuck. My intentions had been to wreck her, maybe even make me her favorite of the four. But I was pretty sure I would be the one who lost myself in her. I was pretty sure I was the one who would end up wrecked.

As I stood, I hooked my fingers under her tee and lifted it, exposing her tits and taking one of her nipples between my lips, coating her skin with her slick coating my mouth and chin.

"Liam, please," she whimpered.

That small sound called to my alpha like nothing in the world ever could.

Yanking her shirt over her head, I tossed it over my shoulder, grabbed her waist, and turned her until she was plastered against the door. Gripping her wrists, I raised her hands high above her head and pressed her hands against the wood.

"Leave them there," I ordered. I didn't put any alpha bark behind it, but she complied all the same.

Pressing my hips to her ass, I slid my cock between her thighs, coating my shaft with her slick and smiling as she moaned at the contact.

"Got to make sure my dick is good and soaked before I fuck you," I growled into her ear, and was answered with another throaty moan.

With one hand gripping her hip, I used the other to position the flared head against her sex and slowly fed her one inch at a time, giving her body time to adjust before finally sheathing myself fully in her tight heat.

"Holy shit," I groaned. No wonder Andrei had lost his mind when he'd fucked her. Her pussy was like pure ecstasy.

When her hands started to slide down the door, I moved them back up. "Keep them there or I stop."

"No. Please don't stop," she begged.

Fuck…yes.

Chase and I had had a very satisfying sex life for years. But there was something so different about having my omega beg to be filled, beg to be fucked, beg for pleasure.

I took her slowly at first, dragging my cock along her inner walls and gritting my teeth as she fluttered around me. If she kept that up, I would end up exploding deep inside of her before I had a chance to watch her fall apart again.

Nope. I needed her on the bed. I needed more leverage.

She whimpered again when I pulled from her, but I lifted her in my arms and hurried to the bed, depositing her onto the mattress on her stomach. When she went to spread her legs, I kept them pinned closed with my thighs.

For a second, all I could do was stare down at her ass, stare down at her beautiful body. Using my hands, I spread her cheeks so I could see all of her and wondered if she would ever let me take her ass while Chase took her pussy.

Sliding into her, I leaned over her back and whispered my fantasy into her ear. "Soon, very soon, I'm going to lift you and settle you onto Chase's cock. I'm going to watch you please our man. Then, I going to coat my dick in your slick and fuck your ass until you don't know where Chase begins and I end."

"Yes. Oh fuck yes," she cried out as I began to slam my hips against her ass as the fantasy played in my head with the feeling of her damned near strangling my cock.

"You like the sound of that, don't you? My little omega wants to be filled?"

My words pushed her over the edge, her pussy clenching around me. I kept her cheeks spread and watched as her release coated my dick, coated my knot.

"You want more?" I asked, not letting up as she fluttered with aftershocks.

"Knot. Please. Give me your knot."

Hell yes. I was so close. I wasn't sure how much longer I could have held out.

Lining my front along her back, I wrapped my finger in her hair and tilted her head to the side so I could suck on the bruise Andrei had left on her shoulder and shoved my hips forward hard and fast.

She cried out the same time I grunted loudly as everything tightened then exploded.

"Fuck! I love you," I forced out, unable to hold the words in any longer.

Every twitch of my dick sent jets of cum deep inside of her and I was thankful she'd been put on some form of birth control. I was pretty sure there was no way I could fuck my omega without knotting her, not when she begged like that.

Her lips were parted as she panted, our skin was coated with a sheen of sweat, and my heart thundered behind my ribs.

As many times as I'd dipped my dick in someone, I had never felt the way I did now. I had never felt as though a piece of my fucking soul was now reaching for Violet, like I had found a home inside of her.

CHASE

. . .

THE MOMENT I felt Liam through my bond, I smiled to myself. For all his flirting, for all his teasing, he had yet to make a move on our omega. He had eaten her pussy at the cabin, had fucked me while I'd fucked her.

But there had been something holding him back from finally giving in to his alpha need to connect with our omega.

Fear? Was he afraid I would be jealous? That was stupid. He had literally been there when I'd knotted Violet. He'd gripped her by the hips and helped push her down until her pussy stretched over and around me. It wasn't like he was out whoring with anyone with a hole. He was doing what was completely natural for alphas. The fact the two of us made such a good pair with no power struggle was a mystery in itself.

Probably because I was more reserved than my mate. Where Liam was unafraid to be in your face, I preferred to hide in the shadows, to stay in the background and simply enjoy my life with the pack.

But now that Violet had joined us, I realized we had never been complete. Even with Liam in my life, I'd been missing a piece of me and had never accepted that.

I couldn't wait until she was bonded to the pack, until I could feel the same love and affection I felt coming through Liam's bond.

Mac tensed when the words *I love you* echoed through the walls. That was Liam's voice.

His eyes turned to mine, his brows high.

Still no jealousy. Yes, I was fucking in love with Liam, but I was falling just as hard for Violet.

"You blame him?" I teased.

He grunted. "Wouldn't know," he said before pushing to his feet.

Mac hadn't felt the unbelievable pleasure of having Violet wrapped around him. He hadn't yet tasted her slick on his tongue.

What the hell was he waiting for? She had made it obvious she wanted us. She'd fucking claimed us regardless of the fact she couldn't leave a bonding mark on us. She would have to wait for one of us to complete the pack.

So...what were we waiting for? While Mac was the oldest of the pack, Andrei tended to take the lead both on the job and off. Did we have to wait until Andrei did more than leave a bruise on her shoulder?

And where would I leave my mark? So many places on her body came to mind. It would be so fucking erotic to leave my mark on her thigh so every time I went down on her I would see it there. I could kiss it and suck on it and bring her so close to climax without tongue, dick, or fingers on her clit.

"You good?" Mac asked.

I frowned at him. "Why wouldn't I be?" Couldn't he feel the level of happiness floating through the bond from both Liam and me?

"Because he…" He jerked his head toward Violet's bedroom.

Leaning to the side, I lowered my voice. "Can you honestly say you're not falling for her?"

He grunted but didn't argue. It was obvious she was wrapping all four of us around her finger and it went beyond the need for an alpha to pamper and dote on their omega.

"She doesn't even realize the power she has," Andrei said as he entered the room, a beer in his hand.

It was a little early to be drinking, but being as none of us had anywhere to be for the foreseeable future, I didn't blame him for wanting a beer. Especially after what we all would have experienced through the bond. Liam had damned near lost his mind and now there was the most insane level of dopamine filling my body simply from his joy.

"We should paint the nest walls," I said, my eyes repeatedly darting to the door and waiting for my mates to step through.

And she was as much my mate as Liam, with or without the bond.

"With what? I don't want to leave and risk someone following us home," Andrei said.

"She likes Wilder. She trusts him. Ask him to bring some shit for her," Mac said.

Turning to Andrei, I raised my brows. "They would have no reason to follow him here. He won't carry an omega's scent. Or at least not our omega."

"Still risky."

"She'll go into heat within a few weeks. The nest isn't ready," Chase said.

"Did she say that?" Mac asked, leaning forward to rest his elbows on his knees.

"You know our girl won't ask for a damn thing."

Andrei grunted with a smirk. She'd fought us tooth and nail when we'd simply wanted to make her bedroom her own instead of a stark, plain ass room. Whether she wanted things or not, her omega needed specific items for comfort. She would eventually have to accept that fact and let us do what we did best – spoil her fucking rotten.

I could have sworn I felt Liam's purr through the bonds. He was happy. Content. And it made me feel even stronger for Violet. Because she'd given that to him. She'd brought him that sense of fullness, of joy.

"Why don't you go snuggle with them?" Mac asked.

I turned to glance at him, and he was doing his best to hide his smirk. He'd caught me staring at the door with a sappy smile on my face.

"They need some time alone. We're always crowding her. She needs one on one time with us before we're all crowded in the nest for a week."

My dick twitched in my pants at that thought, at the thought of her ass in the air as she presented for her alphas and begged for our knots. She would be out of her mind with lust and we would be just as lost to her pheromones and unable to deny her anything.

In the years the four of us had been pack, the two had never been in the room when Liam and I had been together. How would they react if the two of us enjoyed ourselves while Mac and Andrei pleased Violet? I couldn't imagine them giving us the stink eye, but I highly doubted they would be amenable to a blow job from the ever persistent Liam, no matter how lost they were to their libidos.

CHAPTER 21

ilder

WALKING into the pack house about knocked me on my ass. The overwhelming scents mingling made me both horny and leery. Violet's pheromones overrode all the spicy scents from the alphas and made me wonder if this was a bad idea.

The four didn't come off as super possessive, but they'd had a habit of growling at me in the beginning when I'd merely attended to her wounds. What would they do now that they'd been to bed with her?

Had they bonded her? If I ever found my omega, I wasn't sure I could wait to tie her to me so I could feel her deep in my heart and soul. I would know whether she was happy, could anticipate her needs before she voiced them, and would know if she was scared or in danger. Unfortunately, my beta bite wouldn't have the same connection as an alpha bite.

Andrei had called me and asked me to pick up some paint along with an extensive list to bring to the pack's house. I hadn't seen Violet since the day she'd moved in with them. It had been nearly two weeks since that day.

The front door opened as I stepped from my vehicle. Mac and Andrei came out and helped me load everything into the house.

"Hey!" Violet said, surprise and happiness on her pretty face.

I wished I could have found her as appealing as the others. She was beautiful, sure. But I didn't possess the same urge as the others to smother her in my scent and scare others away from her.

"What are you – are you serious?!" she said, her eyes wide as the three of us carried in armloads of paint, painting supplies, and other crap I was instructed to bring, including groceries. "Guys!"

She whirled on Liam, who stood at her back, his hands possessively on her hips, before gaping at Mac and Andrei.

"It was his idea," Andrei jerked his head toward Chase.

Violet turned wide eyes on the quiet member of the pack, but he just smiled with a shrug.

"The nest needs to be finished."

"It is finished. There are pillows and blankets covering every inch of the damn floor."

"And it's painted white. You really want that glaring shit during your heat?" Mac said as he passed and carried his load into her bedroom.

I wasn't sure whether I was allowed in that space or not. An omega's room – especially her nest – was oftentimes off limits to outsiders.

"Well…I'm glad you're here. But stop listening to these jerks. They're trying to spoil me."

"No shit," Liam said, pressing a kiss to her temple before stepping away to help unload the last bit from the back of the SUV.

"What did they put you up to?" she asked, closing the space between us and raising her arms to wrap around my neck.

I took a step back and pretended my hands were too full to hug her back. Until her alphas were inside, I wasn't taking the chance of getting my head stomped in by her pack simply because I hugged her back.

Violet followed closely behind me, her sweet smell wrapping around me as her excitement grew. "What is all this?" she asked as I lowered each bag and box to the floor outside the door I assumed led to the nest.

With a lift of my shoulders, I shrugged. "They wanted you to have pretty stuff. Since you guys can't leave, they wanted to make sure your nest is perfect before…you know."

Since when did I have problems mentioning an omega's heat? It was nature, for fuck's sake.

"It's already pretty," she said, swinging the door open and giving me a peek of white walls and piles of blankets and pillows.

Craning my neck, I looked into the room as far as I could without stepping over the threshold. I was nervous enough being in Violet's room; I wasn't about to step foot in the room she would use when her hormones went out of control, when her alpha's pheromones sent her mind and body into a stupor.

"It's…that's not a nest."

A frown creased her dark brows as she turned and looked inside. "Yes, it is."

My attention going back and forth between Violet and her nest, I finally studied her face. "Have you never had a nest?"

I knew she'd perfumed later than most, but surely, she'd utilized a nest during her cycles for comfort.

"I mean," she started, her cheeks turning pink. "I just used my closet. I would throw my pillows and comforter in there, set up my laptop, and stream movies until it was over. And I would…" The blush deepened when she didn't finish her sentence.

She would do what she had to to ease her own discomfort without access to an alpha. She'd used her own hands or one of the *toys* marketed to omegas who were unable to find relief with someone else.

Now I felt a little bad. She'd had no one to guide her through the changes, to help her discover what she needed most during a painful time of her life. Her biology would tell her she needed sexual release, that a knot was a surefire way of ending the discomfort. But there was more to it than that.

She would be feverish, her skin would be oversensitive, her thoughts would be muddied and, without someone there to watch over her, she might forget basic things like hygiene, meals, and water.

A growl rumbled through the room as Andrei entered, his arms full. "No," he said, the word nearly a bark.

"I'm not going in there," I said, holding my hands up and stepping back.

As a beta, these guys shouldn't feel threatened by me. But this little pack was new and they'd yet to bond with Violet. Andrei's alpha was feeling…possessive of his little omega.

With a jerk of my head, I motioned her to join me in the living room, a neutral room. The pack's scent mingled with Violet's in here, but it didn't smell as though they'd…consummated in this particular room.

She climbed over the arm and sat on what looked as though two couches had been pushed together. No way in hell was I joining her there. I was damned good at my job and could hold my own with the best of them, but had no desire to go fisticuffs with four alphas who also happened to work in the same department I did.

"A nest is…" Shit, I felt stupid explaining this to her. "It's like your cocoon. And it's not only for your heat. It should be a space you can retreat to when you're stressed or don't feel well. Haven't you felt the need to curl into a ball and hide under the blankets?"

Her eyes darted to the side as she chewed the inside of her cheek. "Yeah, actually. I just thought…there was a lot going on, so I figured it was all that."

"It's a natural urge to nest for comfort. It should be soothing. Soft. Especially when your heat comes. You notice how something as simple as a pair of jeans feels like sandpaper against your skin during that time?"

Her head nodded as she listened intently. "I usually ended up naked in my closet back at my duplex."

It was my turn to blush as heat rushed my cheeks. Pushing forward, I fought the urge to fidget. "That's where all the blankets and stuff come in. And you—" I leaned forward and lowered my voice. "You really need to let your pack spoil you. Yeah, I get it. You're independent and not used to the attention. But that's how they're built. It's an alpha's job to spoil their omega, to dote on them, to put them on a pedestal."

"It feels weird, though. I mean, it's sweet, but..."

I nodded. "I get it. Trust me. I don't know how I'd feel..." I waved my hand in the air. "It doesn't matter. That shit doesn't happen for betas. All I'm saying is this is the only thing they can do right now to show their...well, their love."

Her cheeks flushed again as a smile stretched across her face. Yep, she was feeling that same warm and fuzzy feeling for her alphas.

"Your pack can't really leave the house without risking your safety until we figure out what's going on." Anger burned through my veins. How many omegas had been killed by the fucker we were hunting? They were rare enough as it was, accounting for maybe twenty-five percent of the population. "So this is how they can dote on you without taking you to nice restaurants or whatever."

Honestly, I wasn't sure what the pack had had in mind before we'd all realized the threat had not been ended. I only assumed they'd want to wine and dine her as much as possible.

"Not only will them buying you stuff and prettying up your nest help their urge to care for you, but it will be better when you go into heat." I frowned. "Have you had any issues since that day?"

Her narrow shoulders rose and fell. "I've been hornier than normal." Her eyes widened and her blush deepened. I kept my face as neutral as possible to keep her at ease. "Sorry. Shouldn't have said that."

"There's nothing wrong with that. Especially if your omega has chosen her pack."

Her head nodded emphatically, but she pressed on. "I've had some minor cramping, but nothing like when they put that crap in my veins."

"It could be residual after effects. Could be your natural heat getting closer. Or, what I suspect, is your body is simply reacting to being around your alphas. Simple biology."

At thirty-three years old, I had yet to find a pack of my own. I had yet to find an alpha who called to me, or even an omega who stirred something deep inside my chest.

Another growl rumbled as Mac passed through the room. "You done with your girl talk? We could use some help."

Violet rolled her eyes and shook her head but couldn't hide her smile. "I assume they're not going to let me help paint, are they?"

"Not a snowball's chance in hell," I teased as I pushed to my feet and winked down at her.

Of the omegas who'd survived the compound, I felt closer to Violet. Might have been because I tended to her wounds in the SUV. Might have been because I'd spent more time with her than the others.

Whatever it was, the small female felt like a sister…albeit a sister from whom I had to keep my distance to avoid four alphas from going into rut and tearing me limb from limb.

Violet

I'd argued that I should be allowed to help with my own nest. But Chase had guided me from the room, straight to the couch where he lifted me and deposited me on the cushions with a bounce. "Stay," he said. He disappeared for a moment and returned with snacks.

Snacks I hadn't seen before.

So not only had they sent Wilder shopping for paint, curtains, more pillows and blankets and more pajamas, they'd sent him to the grocery store. They'd run that poor beta all over the place.

"Can't I at least look?" I'd whined before shoving a cookie into my mouth.

"When we're done. And after the fumes have aired out," Chase said.

"Oh, please. Do you realize how long that will take?"

He pressed his hands to his chest and widened his eyes in a comically horrified expression. "Oh no, wherever will you sleep in the meantime?"

Now, I was half awake on the couch as a movie droned in the background. It was one of my childhood favorites, a musical about an omega with seven mates made sometime in the fifties that was supposed to be set sometime in the eighteen hundreds. My mother used to play it for me regularly and I'd thought back then it was our bonding time.

Now, as I watched one of the seven bringing a bouquet of wildflowers through the door of their log cabin, I wondered if she was trying to teach me how to behave as an adult omega. You know, before she'd decided I was worthless without that designation.

Showed her, I thought to myself as my eyes drifted closed.

Fingers ran softly through my hair, coaxing me toward consciousness as amber and whiskey surrounded me.

"Mmm. That feels good," I murmured, nuzzling against his hand.

Mac and I had had no time alone. He was always sweet, always touched me in some way, but it was rare to receive any physical affection solely from him without one of the others moving in to my other side.

He bent over the back of the couch and pressed his lips to my temple. "You hungry, sweetheart?"

"Mhm."

His lips trailed from my temple across my forehead where he feathered soft kisses, his breath warming my face and stirring things low in my body.

Reaching my arms up, I wrapped my hands around his neck and pulled his face down for an upside down kiss, holding him there for a few seconds before releasing him. "Chase said I can't see my nest until the fumes have aired out," I said, deepening my voice to impersonate my sweet alpha.

Mac's chuckle was deep and gravelly as he grabbed my hips and helped me climb over the sides without tumbling over. "I agree," he said, wrapping an arm around my shoulders and guiding me to the kitchen where Liam and Chase argued softly about whether there were beans in chili or not.

"It's canned. Who cares?" Andrei said. His eyes darted to mine and he smiled softly.

All four were covered in paint. Some even speckled their hair. Hopefully, they'd taken all the stuff out before painting, because by the looks of them, they hadn't exactly been careful as they'd rolled whatever color they'd chosen on the walls.

"Violet," Liam said, turning and pointing at me with a spoon, sauce dripping from the end and splashing on the floor. "Chili. Beans or no beans?"

"Depends on who you ask," I said, really not wanting to get in the middle of a lover's quarrel.

Mac waited until I sat at the rectangular table before pulling out the chair to my left and lowering onto it. Andrei was to my right.

After filling five bowls and setting them on the table, Liam and Chase sat beside each other directly across from me.

So domestic. So sweet. Wait… "Where's Wilder? Isn't he eating?"

"He left a while ago," Liam said around a spoonful of bean filled chili.

With a frown, I turned to Mac. "How long was I asleep?"

His shoulders rose and fell. "Don't know when you feel asleep. But he left about an hour ago; told us to tell you he said bye."

He tucked into his food, but pressed his outer thigh against mine under the table as though he simply needed to touch me. We all had spent hours apart while they'd painted and I'd napped.

The fact I had lazed around while they'd worked their butts off then made us all dinner made me feel weird. Lazy even. But Wilder had tried to talk me into letting my pack do what came naturally to them.

Problem was, it wasn't natural to me. It would take me time to get used to being not only the center of attention, but being coddled and waited on like some spoiled omega.

But wasn't I? Maybe not exactly spoiled, or at least not yet. But wasn't that my future? Especially if that asshole kept killing us off. We were rare. We were even rarer than alphas. We were a small part of society who could carry on the next generation of the population, the only designation who could birth future omegas.

Sure, betas could have children. They could even birth alphas. But they did not have the genes to carry on the omega line.

Glancing down at my belly, I tried to picture it swollen with a child, tried to imagine myself as a mother.

One thing I knew for sure, I would adore my child regardless of their fucking designation in society.

CHAPTER 22

ac

W**HILE** V**IOLET COULD PROBABLY SLEEP** in her own bed with no problems, we were all in agreement she should wait at least a day. It was mild enough outside that we were able to open the windows to the nest and her personal bedroom to circulate in some clean air and get any toxins out.

Personally, I couldn't wait for her to see what we had all done. We'd let Wilder pick the paint color with a few prompts from what she'd picked for herself. She wasn't a dainty kind of girl like I'd originally thought. She didn't like frills, didn't like glittery shit, didn't like pastels and all that.

What was odd to me was the fact that such a vibrant woman preferred muted, neutral colors for her space. Maybe it was the same reason I preferred lighter color in my own bedroom. It soothed the darker parts of me, the parts that wanted to drag her from the bed she shared with Liam and Chase, toss her onto mine, bury my knot deep inside her heat, and latch my teeth into her shoulder.

I wanted her to be mine. Permanently. I wanted to bond her, to feel how she felt. I wanted to be her true alpha. Her first alpha.

It was the main reason I had yet to seek her out, why I had yet to make a move to fuck her. I needed her to come to me when she was ready. And then, I had to use every ounce of control I possessed to take my time getting to know the sounds my pack were already memorizing.

Staring at the dark ceiling, I laid with my hands folded under my head and pondered over the entire fucking situation. Yeah, I was more than happy to be locked in our house with our omega for as long as needed.

But that fucker needed to die. For what he'd done to my omega. For what he'd done to so many omegas.

And what he would continue to do until he was stopped.

He was out there right now, probably hunting for a new crop. If we didn't stop him, he could very well reduce the number of omegas to a dangerous level. And the fucked up part was he wasn't the only one with compounds like the one we'd destroyed.

At least the others were being bred, not killed. Not that being forced to fuck and carry children they might not have wanted was any better. But they still had their lives. And would, hopefully, be rescued by a team of ORE in each state.

"Fuck," I grunted through clenched teeth as I pushed to a sitting position and rested against my headboard.

Why the fuck couldn't anyone identify him? Violet had recognized him as one of those at the compound, but that did nothing to further the investigation. And the last Andrei had heard from headquarters, the facial recognition software was unable to work with such a grainy picture.

Nothing. We had nothing to go on. And my beautiful omega was at risk until I put a bullet in that mother fucker's head.

Sweet cotton candy swept through my room a second before my doorknob squeaked. As the door slowly swung open, Violet was back-lit, her body encased in a pair of soft as silk sleep shorts and a tank top.

"I didn't think you'd be awake," she whispered in the dark.

"Couldn't sleep," I grumbled.

I pulled the bedspread back to make room for her to climb in beside me. Since the day we'd pulled her from that shit hole, she'd been unable to sleep alone. But since she'd been carried off to Liam and Chase's room, I'd figured she would be out cold by now.

"Me neither," she admitted, fidgeting with the hem of her tank.

Jerking my head, I welcomed her into my bed.

I couldn't see her face, but the push of her scent grew as though I'd made her happy. And fuck if that didn't send a little sense of alpha pride rushing through me and straight to my dick.

Violet closed the door behind her softly, then jogged across the room and practically lunged onto the bed, pulling a chuckle from me.

My team alone had rescued so many omegas from different situations. I knew she was still scared of what could happen, still scarred by the events that had unfolded before we'd arrived. But it was obvious as fuck that she refused to be a victim. She wouldn't let those assholes win by collapsing into herself.

Once she was settled against my side, I pulled the blanket over both of us, then turned my head to press a kiss to the top of her head, her forehead, her temple. Really, I was using any excuse I could to leave her covered in my scent.

I was happy she'd fallen so easily into my pack. But fuck…she was constantly covered in my packmates' scents, reminding me I was odd man out.

"What's keeping you up?" she whispered.

Her head nuzzled closer to my chest until it was cradled just under my chin.

"You."

Pulling away, I felt her turn her head toward me. Now I wished I'd left on some kind of light so I could see her face.

"What about me?" she asked.

"How to keep you safe. How to find the cocksucker and kill him."

She hummed but rested her cheek against my chest again.

"What about you?" I asked.

One of her shoulders shifted against me as though she'd shrugged. "I don't know. I guess I slept too much this afternoon. And Liam and Chase fell asleep the second they hit the pillows so it wasn't like we stayed up late…"

I didn't need to see her face to know she'd blushed. I could feel the heat rushing along her arms as though her entire body had flushed when she'd all but admitted she thought they would have worn her out in more fun ways than we'd worn ourselves out painting.

Yet, here I laid wide awake.

Her arm draped across my middle, her fingers lightly grazing along my ribs, causing my muscles to twitch.

"Ohh. Are you ticklish?" she asked, running her short nails along my ribs again.

A very unmanly giggle escaped me as I squirmed away.

"Good to know for future reference," she teased, cuddling back against my side.

Her hands began to slowly caress my abs, my chest, until a purr rumbled from my chest. I could go to sleep like this, with my omega wrapped in my arms, her soft touch better than any lullaby.

Until that light touch grazed across my nipple. I gasped softly. And that was all the encouragement she needed.

Her fingers began to trace over first one then the other, her nails grazing the sensitive skin until my dick was hard as fucking stone.

"Careful, sweetheart," I muttered.

"Do you not want me?"

Oh, hell no. Stretching to the side, I flipped on the lamp on my nightstand and waited while we both blinked against the offensive glare.

Her brows were furrowed as she stared into my face. Her lips weren't kiss swollen. Her chin didn't carry the pink from Andrei's whiskers after they made out. And she didn't carry the scent of my pack any more than she did on a daily basis.

Taking one of her hands in mine, I pressed it to my cock over the blankets. "I'm not sure how you came to that conclusion, but this should tell you how badly I want you."

"Then why…"

"Why haven't I fucked you?" I finished for her.

Her eyes dropped a brief second as that flush returned to her cheeks. "Well…yeah. You barely touch me. You barely kiss me."

"Because the other assholes are always vying for your attention… and because I'm afraid I'll lose all sense of control the moment I feel you wrapped around me."

As she stared into my face, her pupils dilated and her tongue peeked out to moisten her bottom lip.

"Fuck," I growled, cupping her jaw and dragging her mouth to mine.

There were no tentative pecks of our lips, no hesitation. I fucked her mouth with my tongue the way I wanted to fuck her pussy with my cock, claiming her with desperation as her hands moved to my head and her fingers clenched my hair, pulling tightly enough to pull a mixture of growl and purr from my chest.

The mattress dipped and shuffled as she rose and threw a leg over my lap, straddling me and settling her core directly over my cock. There were too many layers between us. I wanted to feel her heat.

Wrapping an arm around her waist, I lifted her with one arm so I could shove my sweats down my legs as far as I could reach. When she settled again, I could feel the dampness of her slick through the thin material of her pajama shorts.

Little mewling sounds escaped her lips as she began to rock against me, sending sparks of pleasure through every nerve ending in my body.

"More," she moaned against my lips. "I need more."

I was tempted to grab the sides of her shorts and rip the fucking things from her body. But we'd bought them for her, for her comfort. Instead, I tugged at the sides, shoving them over her hips, chuckling against her lips when she practically stood on the bed to help me pull them down her legs.

She lifted first one leg then the other as I pulled them away and tossed them onto the floor.

When she lowered back onto me, I hissed at the contact. She began to rock again, sliding her sex along my shaft, coating it in her slick.

"You're so fucking wet," I growled, cupping her heavy tits in both hands as she continued to use her tongue to explore my mouth.

Lifting slightly, she put her hand between us and wrapped her small hand around my cock, holding it in place for her until the flared head touched her opening.

As she slid down with ease, I clenched my jaw and squeezed my eyes shut at the sensations. I had never felt anything like it. I had never felt as though I would blow my load before I'd had a chance to rut inside of her, before I felt her pussy clenching around my knot.

Not yet. I needed to see her fall apart. I needed to feel her clenching around me before I allowed myself to fall over that edge.

Hands on her hips, I held her in place, fighting my alpha instincts when she whimpered. That fucking sound would send any alpha into a frenzy. And this was my omega. This was my woman.

This was my mate.

Violet

"Please, Mac," I breathed out.

His hands were on my hips, keeping me from moving.

"Not yet, sweetheart."

This wasn't like with Andrei. He wasn't withholding my release. A muscle ticked in his jaw and I wondered if he was trying to hold back for fear of our first time together being too short.

Or, was it as he'd said and he feared he would lose control with me?

I wasn't afraid. There wasn't a single thing about Mac that scared me. Unlike the others, he was a steady, calming force in the house. Almost as quiet as Chase, there was something extra about him, something that told me he would do anything to protect me, no matter the price.

His hands lifted from my hips to smooth along my sides and cup my breasts in his hands. He lowered his head and pressed kisses to each swell before taking one pebbled bud between his lips and sucking hard, nipping it lightly with his teeth.

I hissed in a breath at the sharp pain then moaned when he soothed it with soft sweeps of his tongue.

"Hmm. You're clenching around me. You like that," he said, his voice deep and gravelly, full of lust and need.

Lifting my other breast, he showed it as much attention, using teeth and lips and tongue while pinching and rolling the other between his fingers.

He wasn't dominant like Andrei, didn't try to push me past my threshold, didn't ask for a safe word. But he was definitely demanding when he ordered me to look at him.

"Watch me," he ordered as he sucked my nipple until it was bordering on pain, releasing it with a pop of his lips. "That's my girl," he cooed.

I swore his words alone were strumming my clit even as we stayed still, his cock filling me, his swollen knot pressing against my opening.

It would be so easy to shove myself further, take his knot inside of me, feel him fill me until I was bursting.

But curiosity got the better of me. Each of my alphas were so different in their lovemaking styles. Even with Liam's playful and horndog personality, he'd shouted his confession of love when he'd filled me.

How would Mac sound when he shot heat into my pussy, as he stretched my opening with his knot, when he locked us together?

How would he sound when I wrapped my lips around him and took him into my throat? How would he feel with my tongue teasing his knot?

So many things I wanted to do with this ruggedly beautiful man below me. Yet, my body refused to let me move as he nearly brought me to orgasm simply by showering my breasts with attention.

He wrapped an arm around my waist and urged me back until I was bowing over his forearm. His free hand smoothed between the valley of my breasts, his fingers circled each of my nipples and a growl began to vibrate between us.

"Mac," I breathed.

His hips rolled beneath me, his cock pushing in and out of me in shallow thrusts. *More. I need more.* I needed so much more.

Wrapping his other arm around my waist, he pulled me to his chest and slammed his mouth over mine, his growl vibrating against my tongue and sending shocks of pleasure directly to my core.

He took control, then held me in place as he fucked into me from below, his cock rubbing all the right places.

Whimpering and mewling into his mouth, I shuddered against him as the first ripples of release rolled over me, slick coating his dick and causing a slurping sound as he continued to pump into me.

"Fuck," he growled, his voice deep, his face tense, his jaw clenched.

In one swift move, he rolled us until he was on top, nestled between my thighs.

He shoved my knees toward my chest until his hips were slapping against the backs of my thighs, his balls tickling my virgin ass.

Mac's grip on my legs was so tight I began to wonder if there would be bruises in the morning. As long as he continued what he was doing, he could leave as many bruises as he wanted. Because I was already climbing the hill to another climax.

"Mine," he growled, lowering my legs and urging my feet around his back.

I locked my ankles and reached for him, pulling him to my mouth with my hands on the back of his neck.

"Mine," he growled again, this time against my mouth.

He dipped his head and nuzzled my throat, his tongue darting out and swiping along my pulse point as he tasted me, as he drank in my scent.

"Violet," he panted as he pushed harder until his knot began to stretch me.

"I'm yours," I said, pulling his hips down until his knot pushed past the tight opening of my pussy.

A loud rattling growl was nearly deafening as he dipped his head and a sharp pain shot through my shoulder followed immediately by a dizzying, earth shattering orgasm.

He grunted over and over as he rutted into me, his cock rubbing, his dick bottoming out, pushing me to another, softer orgasm, one that clenched my heart.

As his cock twitched and he filled me with his release, I was instantly filled with a sense of affection so strong my eyes watered. That wasn't from me. That strong emotion, the intense love I felt was coming from Mac, coming through the bond.

He'd marked me. He'd sank his teeth into my shoulder and bonded me to him. He would feel everything I felt, and I would feel everything he felt.

As he pulled his mouth from me and lapped at the tender wound, his attention caused my pussy to clench again as a new rush of lust washed over me.

"It'll be sensitive for a while," he muttered against my shoulder.

And then stiffened.

"Fuck," he grunted. He tried to sit up, but we were locked together until his knot deflated. "Fuck," he said louder.

Seconds later, feet began to thunder through the house as though a herd of elephants was surging through the house.

"Violet!" Andrei called out.

"Uh oh," I said, smiling up at Mac.

But he wasn't smiling. A deep groove was etched between his brows as he refused to meet my gaze.

He'd been afraid to lose control with me. He hadn't been afraid he would hurt me. He wasn't afraid he would scare me.

He'd been afraid he wouldn't be able to hold back from bonding me to him, to his pack.

Well, I had zero regrets. Even as doors began to be thrown open, I felt little threads of anger and fear from the other guys. I could feel my pack through Mac's bond.

Mac's door slammed open and Andrei's large body filled the frame.

"What the fuck did you do?"

CHAPTER 23

ndrei

I HAD BEEN ASLEEP, although lonely without Violet at my side. Then I felt the threads of my pack bond being strummed until I was dragged awake.

Mac. Lust. Fear. Ecstasy. He'd finally given in and taken our omega to bed.

And then I'd felt the first glimmering appearance of something different. Something softer and sweeter and bright.

Shooting from the bed, my feet were running before I was fully aware of what the fuck was going on. Liam and Chase exited their room, the same confusion on their faces. I'd known through the bond she was no longer with them.

I slammed open Violet's door first, calling her name.

But the paint fumes overrode anything else. She wasn't in there.

Which meant there was only one other place she could be.

The door hit the wall when I threw it open and found Mac on top of Violet, her legs locked around his ass, his knot deep inside her core.

Her fingers trailed along his back, but I could feel his fear and regret.

That fucker had marked her. We'd all discussed it and had decided to wait until her heat, waited until she was one hundred percent sure she wanted us as her pack permanently, and he'd sank his teeth into her skin and tied her to himself.

Tied her to us. While he was now her main alpha, her first alpha, all four of us could feel hints of her through the bond.

"What the fuck did you do?" I bellowed, causing Violet to wince.

Mac couldn't turn to look at me, couldn't roll away from our omega. They were locked together until his knot released her.

Violet leaned her head to the side and smiled at me, the look soft and drunk as she blinked a few times.

"Shh," she said, as though I'd merely disturbed them during a nap.

As though she wasn't currently filling the room with pheromones that nearly overrode the anger I felt for Mac and almost sent me charging toward the bed to shove Mac out of the way so I could feel her.

I forced myself to take shallow breaths rather than sucking that sweetness into my lungs in hopes of calming my body.

But it would take a lot more to calm my fucking anger.

Chase pushed past me until he was directly beside the bed. He climbed onto the side and turned Violet's head with a gentle hand on her cheek. His eyes lowered to Mac, but the fucker refused to raise his head.

"Are you okay, Lil' Bit?" Chase asked her.

"Mmm," she purred. Literally fucking purred. And the feeling was like a line straight to my dick. "I'm perfect. Except you're killing my buzz," she said, and pointed a finger directly at me. "I can feel your anger. You don't get to be mad. You've been with me, too."

"You think I'm mad because you slept with one of your alphas?" I said with a humorless laugh.

Her brows drew together a brief second. "Then what…Oh. 'Cause he marked me first?"

She tilted her chin down to try to get a glimpse of where Mac had bitten her. I couldn't see it from here and worried if I got close enough to see I would either start beating on Mac while he was still locked inside of Violet or I would latch onto her free shoulder.

Neither was an option.

One hand reached for Chase. He willingly bent forward and accepted a kiss from her. But when she wrapped her fingers in his hair to deepen it, he pulled away gently, taking her hand and kissing the tips of her fingers.

"You need time with your alpha," he explained when she released a frustrated whine.

"You're my alpha, too."

He leaned forward and pressed a kiss to her forehead and pulled away before she could get her hands on him. "He'll help your mark heal. We'll talk tomorrow."

Leave it to Chase to smooth things over. Or at least explain why we couldn't all climb into bed with her when that was all we wanted to do. The thickness of her perfume was intoxicating and irresistible. And that was exactly what the three of us had to do – resist the temptation to leave our own marks on her body.

I turned on my heel and stomped from the room, ignoring the grin on Liam's face. If it had been up to him, she would have been bonded before we'd left the cabin. I had marked the other three to complete our pack bond. Liam had marked Chase during a heated night of fucking.

And now, we could all feel our omega along that thread, could feel her desire, could feel the heady joy she felt of lying beneath Mac's weight, and the confusion over why we hadn't joined them. Or maybe it was confusion over my anger.

Yeah. We'd discussed waiting. But if I were honest with myself, I was pissed, jealous. I wanted to be the first to mark her. I wanted to be her alpha, her first alpha.

Once I was behind closed door, I shoved my sweats down my legs and flopped naked onto my back. There was only one way to prevent the overwhelming urge to rush back to that room.

Wrapping my fist around my cock, I pulled, picturing the many things I'd yet to try with Violet. I'd pushed her a little our first time together, testing her boundaries, testing her limits, and had yet to find one. I pictured putting her over my knee and slapping her ass pink.

Better. I pictured slapping her tits and watching her pussy grow shiny with her slick. I fantasized about tasting her, teasing her, keeping her release just out of reach before giving her my knot and my permission to come.

Hot spurts hit my stomach as I came hard, clenching my teeth to avoid roaring with the release.

She was ours, now. For better or worse. As I focused on that faint hint of her presence along our bond, I closed my eyes and smiled softly to myself. Now that the anger was fading, I had to admit, I liked feeling her with me. I liked knowing no matter what happened, we would know if she needed us.

And we would know the moment her heat began to creep in and could take care of her the way she deserved.

I had plenty of time to test her limits. I had plenty of time to live out a few fantasies with her, some that involved just the two of us – and maybe a few toys – and some that involved the pack.

Violet

Pulling my arms over my head, I stretched, pointing my toes as the feeling of floating on a cloud swept over me.

Then a twinge of anxiety touched my heart. I wasn't anxious. What the hell…

A light finger touched a tender spot on my shoulder and slick instantly coated the lips of my pussy.

"Are you okay?" Mac's voice was gravelly as though he'd just woke.

"If you keep doing that, we'll both be more than okay."

The bed shook lightly as he chuckled soundlessly.

His finger grazed lightly over it again, pulling a moan from my lips. "You think that's good?"

He rolled to his side and ran a tongue over the twin crescents on my shoulder, sucking it lightly.

Stars exploded as I came instantly. "Holy fuck," I breathed as aftershocks rippled through me.

The bed shook again, his breath warm against my skin as he chuckled. "The guys are all waiting for you to get up."

He threw his legs over the side of the bed and reached for the sweats he'd kicked off when he'd been able to pull from me last night.

The memory was hazy, more like the best kind of dream, but I remembered everything. I remembered the exact moment my life felt as though everything had clicked perfectly into place. The moment my heart felt like it would explode with love.

Then the moment Andrei had crashed through the door. My three other alphas had refused to join us. I wanted more of that feeling. I wanted to be bonded to all four of them. I wanted to feel that thrum of heat and bliss that had pulsed from my shoulder to my heart…and my clit.

As Mac stood to pull up his sweats, I watched the muscles in his ass bunch, watched the muscles in his back tense.

"What?" I asked when he refused to turn to look at me as he found my clothes and handed them to me. "What's wrong?"

"They're pissed."

I felt the anger, but wasn't aware it was aimed at me. "What the hell did I do? I thought being bonded was the end goal. Isn't that part of my job? To be tied to you guys?"

As much as I'd begrudged growing up beta, being an omega was confusing as hell.

"They're not mad at you. And I don't think they're mad as much as they're worried about you. It'll be like this each time any of us mark you."

"Why won't you look at me?" I asked.

He'd just brought me to climax simply by sucking on the mark he'd given me and now he refused to make eye contact.

Mac's head wagged side to side as he lowered to the mattress, his back to me. "I should have asked permission. I told you I was worried about losing control."

"You didn't lose control."

I tugged on my tank top, then lifted my ass to tug on my shorts, then crawled over to where he still sat facing away from me and curled against his back. "Last night was…perfect."

If he could feel me through the bond, why couldn't he feel how happy I was? How…right everything felt now?

Gripping my hands that were wrapped around his neck, he turned his head to kiss the back of one hand then did the same with the other.

"You're not mad?"

"You tell me. Can't you feel me?"

He shook again with that soft chuckle. "I feel those tits I love pressed against my back."

I leaned forward and playfully bit his earlobe.

He squirmed, then turned so he could tug me onto his lap. "I can feel you," he said, looking into my face. He leaned forward and kissed the tip of my nose. "But I still should have waited. I should have asked permission. I should have kept my dick away from you until one of the others marked you."

"Why does that matter? If it's going to happen, if I'll be tied to all four of my alphas, why does it matter who marked me first?"

Rather than answering, he dipped his head to claim a quick kiss. "Take a shower and meet us in the kitchen. Time for breakfast."

I pulled his head toward me for a longer, deeper, licking kiss.

"On second thought, maybe forgo the shower a while longer. I like my scent on you."

Looking up at him through my lashes, I tightened my hold on him. "You could always shower with me then leave your scent on me again."

I squealed as he lunged to his feet and practically sprinted toward the bathroom, never setting me on my feet until it was time to strip to get under the spray. He washed me from head to toe, then lifted me in his arms again, this time settling me over his cock and taking me hard and fast against the wall. But he never knotted me. We needed to join our pack and have breakfast, not spend the next hour locked together.

CHAPTER 24

hase

THE MOMENT we allowed Violet to see the changes we'd made to her nest she'd instantly demanded we all have our first official cuddle in the room.

Andrei had given a few suggestions and let Wilder choose the paint color and the rest of the crap he'd brought. The walls were a creamy color, closer to tan. It was warm and cozy. There were twinkly lights hanging across the ceiling like stars, the curtains looked sheer but would black out the sun completely when our omega needed the dark comfort of her nest.

And there were dozens more pillows and blankets littering the floor and leaning against the walls.

"Can't we just live in here?" she asked, her head using my stomach as a pillow while her feet were propped on Mac's lap.

Mac huffed a laugh as he kneaded and massaged her feet.

A shrill beep sounded from Andrei's pocket. He pulled his phone free and glanced at it, then pushed to his knees, bending over Violet to claim her lips in a quick kiss before leaving the room without saying a word.

"I hate when he does that," she admitted.

"Does what?" I asked, threading my fingers through her silky soft hair.

I was an alpha and even I was ready to take a nap on the cloud of softness below us.

"Sneak around like that. You and I both know it's some kind of news. Why not just tell the room instead of making me ask? I can feel his anxiety right now."

It wouldn't be as strong for her as it was for each of us. He was the alpha of a pack of alphas. But only Mac had bonded her. She would feel a shadow of what we felt through that bond.

"He's probably waiting to say anything until he has something to report," Liam said.

Liam was lined along her left side, his arm draped over her stomach, his chin resting on her shoulder. He looked as relaxed as I felt and I could feel the contentment and love for Violet pouring through our personal bond.

"Or he thinks he's protecting me," she said.

"Need a distraction?" Liam said, humping against her hip without opening his eyes.

"Idiot," Mac muttered.

"What? Can't have our sweet little omega stressed, now, can we? I say…we play spin the bottle. Ohhh. Or truth or dare. I dare you to… give me a blow job."

Being as Liam barely moved, I knew it was nothing more than a ploy to distract her by pretending to think of ways to distract her.

The pack and Violet knew him as a tease, a flirt, a goofball. But my mate, my *first* mate, was loving. He was kind and had a big heart that wanted to make sure those in his life were happy and safe.

Hell, he'd been the first to tell Violet exactly how he felt, even if he'd declared it when he'd blown his load while knotting her.

"Hmm," she hummed as though considering it.

Liam's eyes flew open and his head popped up. "Blow job? I dare you. Double dog dare you."

Her giggle was so girly and like music to my fucking ears. She'd already been such a bright spot in our lives. But since last night, another layer of her had been peeled away. Or maybe she finally felt as though she belonged.

She had a family. And, yeah, it was cool as fuck that she was an omega, but I knew each of us would have wanted her regardless of her designation.

We wanted Violet because she was…Violet. Because she was beautiful and strong and funny.

And had the most amazing tits.

Anger thrummed through the bond a second before Andrei's head peeked around the corner.

"No negative shit in the nest," he declared, jerking his head for us all to follow him.

"Damn. So close," Liam teased, but I could see the tightness around his eyes and feel his worry.

Mac set Violet's feet on the floor, stood, then offered his hand to pull her up. I instantly missed her head on my stomach.

Liam pushed to sitting and put his hand in mine when I offered. I helped hoist him up. He pressed a quick peck to my lips before following Mac and Violet out of the nest.

We'd been lacking in affection between the two of us as we all learned to live with an omega, especially one who was reluctant to let us do our damn jobs of spoiling her.

Somehow, the two of us needed to reconnect while absorbing her into our little family of two. I knew Liam would love to be with the two of us at once, but we needed more than just sex, we needed a full connection.

Once we were all seated around the kitchen table – none of us had any desire to move the couches back since it was the easiest way for us all to be near Violet at once – Andrei lifted his eyes from his phone.

"We've got a suspect," he announced.

Shock rippled through the bond. Then a huge rush of fear when Andrei's eyes settled on Violet.

"He did it again. He killed another omega," she choked out the words.

Andrei nodded once, then scrubbed his hands down his face as though he carried the weight of the world on his broad shoulders.

"Another compound?" Mac asked.

"One of the omegas refused to stay in a safe house any longer. He went off on his own, returned home. He was found early this morning, his pup cut out of him."

All eyes turned to Violet in time to see her face drain of color and her eyes widen. She swayed in her seat a little.

"They...he was pregnant? They took his baby? Why..." She was having difficulty finishing a thought let alone a sentence.

Her hand fluttered to her stomach and she lurched like she was going to throw up.

"Shit," Mac said, lunging to his feet and grabbing the trash can from under a cabinet.

Setting it at her feet, he knelt beside her and rubbed circles on her back as she dry-heaved and gagged. But nothing came up. She hadn't eaten since dinner the night before.

I wanted to comfort her, to drag her onto my lap and wrap my arms around her. I wouldn't admit it – and knew the others wouldn't, either – but this was a good time to have Wilder here, as well. All the alpha pheromones would be more potent with our rising anger and fear for our own omega. Wilder would be a calming source for her.

But that would mean he would have to have her close and there was no way Mac's alpha instincts would allow that after being so newly bonded.

"Why would they do that? I don't understand. They forced us into heat. They dragged...that fucking building. That room. I never saw it, but I heard the guards laughing their asses off about all the things they'd done to the omegas there." She wrapped her arms around her middle. "They made sure we weren't on any form of birth control. They wanted us pregnant. I saw those pregnant omegas..." She blinked a few times. The wheels were turning in her head. "They took the baby," she repeated, lifting her eyes to mine. "But they killed the pregnant omega when you guys came. Is there a way to test for future designation in the womb?"

I looked to Mac first then Andrei. Andrei pulled open his laptop and started rapidly tapping keys. He leaned forward and read for a few minutes, stringing everyone's nerves tighter, then leaned back.

"It looks like they were experimenting on that at some point, but I don't see anything from the government sites saying it's being widely used."

"Could they be killing those who aren't carrying what they consider desired? Could they be killing anyone carrying…I don't know, an omega? Or a beta? Hell, an alpha?" Her eyes darted around the room as though she were deep in thought. "Why kill omegas if they were trying to breed more omegas?" She wasn't asking anyone in the room. She was trying to work what she'd heard through her mind. "None of this makes any fucking sense," she all but screamed, lunging to her feet and shrugging away from Mac when he reached for her.

Her steps were somewhat jerky as she began to pace the kitchen, her eyes holding a faraway look. Was she mentally back at that compound? Was she running everything she'd heard through her head in hopes of making a connection?

When she whirled around to face us, we all waited silently as she looked to Andrei. "You said you had a suspect. Who is it? Was he law enforcement? Do you know his name? How did you find him?" She was firing off the questions so rapidly we had to wait for her to run out of breath for Andrei to answer her.

He held his hand out to her, but she moved to sit back in her chair, leaning against Mac. A flash of jealousy sung through the bonds, but Andrei hid it well.

"His name is Mason Hawke. He's a local real estate mogul and somewhat of a…purist. He believes betas are a waste of resources."

"But he killed omegas. He's hunting us."

"His men killed omegas either while shooting at us, or because they were pregnant with a beta. That's the only connection we've found with the dead pregnant omegas. Only one of the five of you who we got out was pregnant. We're working under the assumption the child is either an omega or an alpha."

Violet told us she hadn't been touched any further than being dragged to the infirmary where she received injections and inspections of her body, as though they were making sure she was fertile.

How much longer would she have had before one of those fuckers would have raped her? How much longer before she would have been forced to carry a pup she hadn't asked for?

And what happened to the omegas who birthed betas? Did they simply take the child then try again, or assume the omega was useless and end both lives?

Every option made me sick to my stomach.

"So, do you know where he is?" she asked, gripping Mac's hand when it rested on her knee. He still knelt beside her, pressing as close as he could without lifting her and setting her on his lap. Or burying himself knot deep in her.

"Several teams infiltrated the three addresses we found attached to him but he wasn't there. They did find records."

"What kind of records?" Liam asked.

"Names, ages, designations of family members, addresses…"

"Of us. Of the omegas he took. They'd chosen us. I hadn't been snatched by chance. They hadn't simply detected my perfume and decided I was a trophy. He had somehow found evidence of me. Of us."

Color had returned to her cheeks and I knew it had everything to do with the rage that was burning through our bond, as strong as if she were bonded directly to me.

Our girl was a fighter. Our sweet, beautiful omega wanted blood.

And I didn't give a fuck what headquarters or our commander said. We would do everything in our power to make sure that Hawke fucker was found. We would put a bullet directly between his eyes so he would never hurt another omega again.

. . .

Violet

For the first time since it had been purchased and delivered, I found myself curled in the comfy egg thing Andrei had chosen for the house. I'd wrapped one of my new blankets around myself and all but fell into it, doing everything I could to avoid taking my bad mood out on everyone in the house.

They were doing everything they could to find Mason Hawke. The whole of ORE was searching for him, following any trail of money he might have been stupid enough to leave, questioning any and every contact he'd had in the last ten years.

I was shocked they were actually leaving the house in rotations, always making sure at least two were in the house with me at all times. Even Wilder had been sent to babysit me when Mac, Andrei, and Chase had had to head out to scope out a possible location of another of Hawke's compounds with several teams from Omega Rescue and Extraction.

Someone had warned of the upcoming raid. There wasn't a single guard left behind, but at least the omegas were still alive and had been taken to various safe houses around the state.

Now, I struggled to ignore the niggling anxiety rolling through the bond with Mac like someone was plucking a guitar string. They were each watching me from the corner of their eye as though they expected me to…what? Cry? Scream? Start throwing stuff?

Honestly, all of the above sounded pretty damn satisfying, but wouldn't solve anything.

Struggling to sit up from the deep cushions of my seat, I looked at each man in turn when they immediately gave me their full attention.

"What if I leave?" I asked.

"What?" Mac nearly bellowed.

"You want to leave?" Chase asked, his sweet face full of sorrow and fear.

"Not like…" I waved my hand in the air. "You said they tracked down the pregnant omega. What if I make a scene of moving out of here, get a place where you guys can keep me under close surveillance, then wait to see if this douche or one of his cronies comes out of hiding to get to me? I won't be in danger because you will all be there."

"You're seriously not offering yourself up as bait. I'm sure you've noticed by now there isn't a chance in hell any of us would–" Liam started to say, but Andrei cut him off.

"We could put cameras around the property. Inside the building. Keep teams hidden and on the ready," Andrei said.

"What?!" Mac and Chase bellowed at the same time.

"You can't seriously be fucking considering this," Mac said, his voice loud and growly.

Andrei held up his hands to silence the protests, but his eyes remained on me. "You realize how big of a risk this is."

"Of course I do. But I trust you guys. I know you won't let anything happen to me. I know you won't let Hawke drag me away. Just wait for him to show up and *BOOM*! Put a bullet through his heart."

"And if it's not him? If he sends a group?" Liam asked, his usual playful manner completely gone as he glared at me.

"Then you pick a few to question and…do whatever you do to those kinds of people. You won't hear a peep from me if they happen to disappear."

I wasn't a violent person. I had never wanted to hurt another person in my life. I had no desire to see anyone in any form of pain. But Mason Hawke? People like him? I hoped every single one of them suffered slow and painful deaths.

Growls rattled around the room as my alphas considered the possibility of putting me directly in the line of fire. It wasn't like I wanted to be that close to Mason Hawke or any of his people ever again. But if I was the key to stopping him, I would gladly set aside my own fear to make it happen.

Mac pushed to his feet and walked toward me. No. He stalked toward me. That was the only appropriate word for the way he moved as his eyes stayed on my face and his body tensed, the muscles I'd finally felt pushing me into the mattress nearly straining against the fabric covering them.

When he was within touching distance, he lowered to his knees in front of me and cupped my face in both hands. "Andrei might be our team lead, but you're my mate. There is no fucking way I will allow you to put yourself out there like a worm on a hook."

While I was fully aware what he was trying to say, a certain word rubbed me the wrong way. "You won't *allow* it? Do I need to remind you how long I've been taking care of myself? How long I protected myself before you big, bad alphas came along. And yes, before you try to throw it in my face, I know I was taken by some sick, twisted fuckers who thought they would use my body for some kind of experiment. But even then, I had fought. They had to sedate me to keep from burying my knee so far in their balls they would choke on them every time they tried to touch me."

Chase huffed a surprised laugh.

Frustration and a sense of terror rang through our bond. Mac lifted a hand and grazed his fingers lightly over the crescents that were healing on my shoulder, sending heat to all the right places and giving me a buzz like I'd just taken shots of liquor one after the other.

Reality slowly trickled in and I glared at my first bonded mate. "Are you seriously using your mark to disarm me?"

I hated to admit it, but it had almost worked. I'd been close to forgetting everything we'd discussed and begging Mac to carry me to his room so he could ravage my mouth and body for a few hours.

"No weaponizing affection or sex," I said, taking his fingers in mine and pulling them away.

"I wasn't…that's not what I was doing," Mac grumbled, a frown creating a deep crease between his brows.

Bull shit, he wasn't. He was trying to distract me from the subject. I wasn't naïve.

It did feel good, though, and I already missed his touch.

"We'll find another way. A safer way," he muttered softly, returning his hands to cup my face so I couldn't turn away from him. "If we can't find another way, then we'll consider your plan."

"You'll *consider* it?"

"Don't turn everything I say into an argument. I can't stand the thought of that mother fucker being within a hundred feet of you, let alone showing up at your door. We have a lot of good soldiers out there looking. Law enforcement from around the state have all received every piece of information we have on him and are on the lookout, as well. We'll find him."

My biggest fear was they would put me first and cause another omega to be taken or killed. I feared it would take too long or Mason Hawke would find a way to drop off the map.

And I wasn't sure I could live with myself if there was another murder simply because my alphas refused to let me do the only thing I could to contribute to Mason Hawke's end.

CHAPTER 25

iolet

IT HAD BEEN two weeks since I'd attempted to talk my guys into letting me try to help track down Mason Hawke. Every time I'd brought it up since that day, I had been shot down and reassured it was simply a matter of time.

They still hadn't found him.

Cramps had started low in my belly a few days ago, heralding the arrival of my heat. It would only be a matter of days before I was in full swing, until I would require my nest and my alphas.

Liam talked me into snuggling with him and Chase in their room for a few hours while Andrei and Mac were out with a few ORE teams. Honestly, I hated when any of them left, but at least I could feel Mac's presence. It was like he was there in my chest, like his heart beat the exact same cadence as mine.

It was comforting to know I would be aware if he was in danger. So why couldn't they trust that Mac would feel if I was in danger?

Why couldn't they simply rely on that same bond and allow me to help in the only way possible?

Each of our rooms had television sets hanging on the wall that weren't much smaller than the one over the fireplace in the family room where the pack tended to congregate at the end of the day. Or when we all felt like being lazy since we were pretty much on house arrest.

Or at least *I* was on house arrest. The four of them had left at intervals, staying gone for hours at a time while all I could do was worry whether they would come back to me in one piece.

"Why do you always pick horror?" Liam whined as I clicked through the selections.

"You gave me the remote. If you wanted to pick the movie, you shouldn't have given me control," I teased as I leaned back against his chest.

He reached over my shoulder and plucked the remote from my hand and flipped up until he landed on new releases, trending, and anything not horror related.

"With the stuff you see on a regular basis, how does fake blood and pretend monsters freak you out?" I asked with a giggle.

Chase leaned into my right side and pretended to whisper in my ear. "I think he uses his fear as an excuse for extra cuddling after."

"Yep. We'll stick with that," Liam said after settling on a series about a girl who went back in time by touching some kind of magical rock.

It started off a little slowly, but then everything was rolling at an exciting pace. This was definitely some kind of romance.

"Awww. Is my big, flirty alpha into chick flicks?"

His arms snaked around my waist and he nuzzled his cheek against my temple. "Why, yes I am. Especially when they include sex scenes."

"Has anyone ever told you you're a bit of a slut?"

Liam's arms shifted enough so he could dig his fingers into my sides. "Take it back."

"Never," I squealed as he continued tickling me.

"I think he prefers nympho," Chase said with a chuckle as he watched me struggle to get away from Liam's torture.

"Oh, you both think you're funny."

When his hand snapped out to dig at Chase's ribs, Chase was able to move in time. I, on the other hand, could not squirm away.

Or maybe I didn't want to. I loved to play with Liam. I loved to play with all my guys, but Andrei and Mac were usually on the more serious side. The only time I saw the playful side of either of them was when we were alone behind closed doors and had finally come down from the high of good sex.

By the time I'd moved halfway across the bed, Liam was practically lying on top of me, his fingers still jabbing at my ribs.

"We're going to miss the whole show," I said with a giggle, doing my best to pry his fingers loose.

"I can put on a live show for you. Give you the highlights." He finally stopped with his fingers and lowered his lips to mine, just a sweet, soft caress of his mouth against mine.

The kiss might have been chaste but it heated my blood nonetheless.

Of all four of my alphas, Liam had been the only one to declare his feelings for me, and that had only been the one time, the first time he'd knotted me. He'd shouted it as he'd shot his release deep inside of me, then collapsed into an emotional ball of love beside me, holding me close and running his fingers along any part of my body he could reach for well over an hour.

But that had been it. He hadn't said it again. And none of the others had uttered the words.

I hadn't said it back to Liam, either. It wasn't because I didn't feel it. It was because I was scared. Not that I had a clue why I would be scared. I knew these men. These alphas were mine as much as I was theirs. I had claimed them back at the cabin. They had told me I belonged in their lives.

Yet Mac was the only alpha who'd left his mark on me, the only one who'd bonded me to him.

Maybe they were as scared as I was.

Although Liam lifted off me, I'd still felt his boner pressed against my stomach. I hated to see such a glorious thing go to waste, but Chase had made a plea for some down time, some snuggle time, just the three of us hanging out with no interruptions.

But...couldn't our down time also include a threesome with two of my favorite people on the planet?

I'd had so many fantasies involving these two since that first night I'd awakened to them making love. And then, Liam had joined Chase and I when we'd finally had some time alone. But my back had been to them. And...I hadn't been able to enjoy them at the same time.

Problem was if either of them knotted me, that would be the end of sexy time until that knot began to deflate enough to pull from me.

One of the few things about my first heat with my pack that I was actually looking forward to was alpha biology. Since the heat was a way of reproducing, the alphas' bodies would react accordingly. They would still lock inside of me, but would be able to pull free faster than when we were simply enjoying each other's bodies. Meaning, we could go over and over without having to wait upwards of an hour before I could take another of my alphas.

Were they my alphas? Technically, only Mac had marked me. I was only bonded to him. Did that make the other three simply my guys and Mac my alpha?

"I have a question."

Liam and Chase raised their brows at me, twin looks of confusion on their gorgeous faces.

"If Mac is the only one who's marked me, does that make him my only alpha? And...if you guys ever get around to it, does that make him top dog or are you all equal?"

Liam's brows shot up as though I'd challenged him. Chase smiled softly.

"We are all your alphas. You're pack, Violet. And no, Mac won't be top dog *when* we all mark you. But you'll probably feel him stronger than the rest of us," Chase answered.

"*If?*" Liam said, a growl rattling from his chest.

I was still at the foot of the bed where I'd squirmed when he was tickling me. He leaned forward until he was on his hands and knees and began to crawl toward me.

Scooting back, I gasped when my hands hit air and I started to teeter over the side.

But hands on my ankles pulled me back until I was positioned directly beneath Liam. "*If?*" he growled again. "I know my sweet omega isn't having doubts."

"No. I..." My mouth was suddenly dry as his heavy cock pressed against my stomach and slick dampened my panties. "I don't have doubts. I just…you said you…but then you didn't say it again. And no one else has…but Mac…"

"Cat got your tongue, little omega?" Liam said, a purr rattling his chest, the vibrations doing all kinds of delicious things to my sensitive and hardened nipples.

Andrei was dominant and demanding. Chase was sweet. Mac was wild. Liam…was unpredictable. I never knew what side of him I was going to get on different days. A few times, he'd simply sat beside us and watched as Chase and I had made love, using his own hand for release. Other times, he had tossed me over his shoulder like a caveman and carried me to the bedroom, demanding he taste my slick covered pussy.

Tonight…I had apparently pushed some button and was now seeing a rougher side of him. And a thrill went through my body at what he might have in mind for my punishment for daring to entertain a single doubt about my new pack.

Liam

Even after the time we'd spent with her, with everything we'd done to try to show her how important she was in our life, Violet still harbored doubts. Or maybe they were fears.

Fear of rejection? Fear we might change our minds?

How the fuck could she not see the clear and obvious affection in Chase's eyes every time he so much as looked in her direction? Or the way Mac could barely stay more than a few feet from her. Or the way Andrei constantly found ways to leave his scent on her, to touch her, to give her everything she could possibly want while we were all locked up in this house.

Well, we weren't locked up. Just her. And it was temporary. The second the threat was eradicated, we would take turns taking her on real dates, courting her the way we should have if we'd met her like a regular pack meeting their omega.

Andrei had been livid when Mac had marked her. But the lack of the remaining three of us was setting her on edge. So…fuck Andrei. He could be pissed all he wanted. Because by the end of the night, I was going to have her begging for my knot and my teeth. I would wait until she couldn't take anymore, until I'd milked her body of her very last orgasm for the night, then Chase and I would mark her together, locking down our bonds with her.

Her perfume floated around me until I could taste her arousal on my tongue. Her chest heaved with deep breaths, pushing those big tits every single one of us were obsessed with against my chest. Her thighs had parted when I'd dragged her under me as though her body had a mind of its own.

No. It was her omega recognizing the need for her alpha.

Rolling my hips, I smiled when her tongue darted out to wet her bottom lip the same time her thighs opened wider.

Chase moved into my periphery, his hands smoothing over her hair.

"You're ours, Violet. For better or worse, you're our omega. You're the only one we want. The only one we've ever wanted."

The fucker dipped down and took her mouth in a long, wet kiss as I continued to rock my hips against her.

Lifting my weight up and holding myself on my hands, I watched the two loves of my life tasting each other, watched as Violet's nipples pebbled until I could practically see their full outline through the thin material of her tank top.

Fuck. I wanted to be inside of her, but I wanted to taste her. I wanted to taste all of her.

I wanted the three of us to share something she wouldn't share with the others. I wanted tonight to be a moment we would cherish, a moment she would dream about. A moment that would reassure her once and for all she was one hundred percent a part of this pack.

Pushing back onto my haunches, a sense of warmth spread through me as her arms wrapped around Chase's shoulders and tugged him closer.

Too many clothes. We were all wearing far too many clothes. Especially Violet. I could forgo my own release. I had found holding out and feeling the lust through our bonds was kind of a kink for me. But...I wasn't sure I could withhold for very long tonight, not with my omega's sweetness coating my tongue, seeping into my every pore.

Chase maneuvered himself until he was practically draped across her torso, his hands running over her hair, her face, before brushing down her throat to cup one of her heavy tits. He tweaked and rolled a pebbled nipple between his fingers, drawing a gasp from Violet's lips.

As Chase lavished attention to her top half, I hooked my fingers into the sides of her shorts and panties and dragged them over her legs. For a moment, all I could do was smile at the way her cunt glistened with slick. A soft whimper escaped her lips when I slowly dragged only a fingertip through her folds, then tested her opening. She needed to be wet and ready for what I had in mind for her tonight. For what I had in mind for the three of us tonight.

Sure, I looked forward to having her on my tongue, to having her wet heat wrapped tightly around my cock, to feeling my knot filling her until we both lost our minds.

But it was more than that. This, tonight, was for us. For Chase, Violet, and I to share a true bond. And I couldn't find a single fuck to give when I thought about how pissed Andrei would be when he felt our connection grow through the bond.

As I brushed my tongue over her clit, the urge to turn my head and latch onto her thigh was strong. But I would wait. I had to wait. I wanted Chase and I to share that moment together. I wanted us to choose where we would leave our mark and clamp down on her together so that we could take the time to soothe the bites, to help the wounds heal under our care.

Glancing up, I smiled against Violet's slick covered lips as Chase raised her tank above her tits, exposing them to the room and to his mouth. He lapped and sucked each nipple into his mouth while using his hand to massage the free one.

Violet was whimpering in earnest now, her hips rocking against my face as though trying to fuck my tongue. I was more than happy to give her what she needed.

Hooking my arms under her thighs, I held her in place and ate her as though she was my last meal, lapping at the slick as she shuddered and cried out, her sweetness covering my tongue and sliding down my throat.

Not done yet. I wanted to hear her cry out again before either of us gave her our cocks.

Sucking at her clit, a purr rattled from my chest as she squirmed, one hand landing on my head as though to push me away from her sensitive sex.

That lasted all of a few seconds before she melted back into the mattress and began riding my face again, rocking her hips against my tongue.

"I need to feel her," Chase said, his voice deep and husky with need.

"Not yet," I muttered before diving back in.

Her cotton candy and lollipop taste was always stronger when she came and I planned to lap at her until I was on a sugar high.

"Fuck. Liam," Chase muttered.

Rolling my eyes up, my heart stuttered when I found his eyes on me, on my mouth on our omega's slick soaked pussy.

With a growl, I pushed away and made room for my mate to settle between her thighs.

Taking his length in my fist, I stroked it slowly, then guided him to

Violet's opening, watching closely as he slid into her, his throbbing, purple knot rutting up against her until she began to stretch. From this angle, it looked as though her pussy was trying to draw him in, trying to suck his knot deep inside of her.

As an alpha, I wasn't built for a knot. That had never stopped the wish for my mate's inside of me, of feeling every inch of him, of loving on him and bringing him as much pleasure as possible.

Chase was on his haunches, his hands massaging Violet's thighs as he took her in long, slow thrusts. Crawling around, I wrapped my arms around his chest and pulled him against me, running my lips and tongue along his neck.

Had this been any other day, I might have taken my mate from behind while he made love to our omega. But not tonight. Tonight was all about tying Violet to us in the most profound and permanent way possible. I wanted her lying in a puddle of our release and her slick before we bit her.

Her dark hair fanned out around her as her head lolled side to side, her mouth open, the most beautiful sounds escaping her mouth as Chase finished what I had started.

"I need..." Chase said, his body tight under my hold as he tried to hold back.

"Knot our omega, mate. Give her what you both need."

Chase's thrusts became hard, faster, more desperate. Reaching down, I dragged my fingernails over his knot, teasing him until he thrust forward hard, seating the swollen base of his cock fully inside of Violet.

He fell forward, falling from my arms, and rutted inside of her as they both cried out as the release washed over them in wave after wave.

My eyes dipped to where slick and cum seeped between them to pool on the mattress. I couldn't fucking help myself.

Coating my finger, I slipped it into Chase's puckered ass and milked him of another release. His orgasm tore another from Violet as his knot pulsed inside of her, rubbing along her inner walls and touching all the places our omega needed stroked.

"Fuck," Chase groaned out as I pulled my finger from him and smiled at the two people I loved most in the world.

He held his weight from Violet on his forearms and his ass was practically presented to me from his position, but I resisted. Took damned near every ounce of control, but I managed to resist the temptation.

CHAPTER 26

iolet

Liam didn't give me much time to catch my breath or for the aftershocks of my last release to subside before he took the place Chase abandoned the moment his knot deflated.

"Liam," I breathed out as he flipped me onto my stomach, pulled my hips until my ass was in the air, then positioned the velvety head of his cock against my opening.

"Do you want me to stop?" he asked, but there was a playful tone to his voice.

He knew damn well I didn't want him to stop. Even without my heat in full force, I couldn't seem to get enough of my alphas.

Bite or not, Liam and Chase were right – they were my alphas. I might only carry the bond from Mac, but I could feel every one of them inside my heart, though Mac's connection was far stronger.

I wanted that with all of them. I wanted to feel that thread to their emotions. I wanted to feel their love, their affection, even their fears if it meant I could help ease them.

"Hell no," I answered.

Liam chuckled softly, then pushed into me slowly. There was no reason to take his time. Chase had stretched me with his knot and I was coated and wet with both of our release. There was no resistance as Liam slid into me with ease, moaning softly when he was bedded as far as his knot would allow.

Opening my mouth, I was ready to beg for it, beg him to lock us together, beg for the ultimate release. But he was pumping into me already, a faster and harder pace than Chase had set.

His hands were on my hips. Chase stretched alongside me, one hand fondling a breast while the other thread through my hair.

"You're so beautiful," he cooed.

I smiled at him, at the sweetness on his face and in his tone. I loved this man. I loved this man so much it scared me. I loved all of them, really. Each of them were so different yet so similar and had each won a place in my heart that no other could ever fill. They had filled a place in my heart that I hadn't been aware was empty until their presence, until they'd rescued me from that compound.

They'd rescued more than my physical body that day. They had given me something I had craved and longed for my entire life – a family. A family who loved me with everything they had.

"Do you know how good you're making your alpha feel?" Chase asked.

Had Andrei said it, it would have come out as dirty, kinky even. But with Chase, he reveled in the way I made love to his mate, in the way we connected.

"I wanted to mark you tonight," Chase said, a finger lightly grazing down my cheek as Liam continued to thrust into me.

"Yes. Please. Mark me. Bite me," I begged, unable to stop the words from falling from my lips.

"Not yet." Liam chuckled from behind. "I want to make sure you're unable to walk on your own before we tie you to us."

A shudder worked through me at his words. I knew exactly what he meant. They planned on taking turns knotting me until they'd milked the last orgasm from my body, until I was too exhausted to take anymore.

And I didn't have a problem with that.

I didn't know when Mac and Andrei would return from whatever mission or hunt they were on. And part of me wished they were here with us. But that time would come. They had given me a beautiful nest where we would spend days and nights together as I begged and whimpered for their knots until the fever broke and my mind was no longer fogged with lust.

Liam hadn't exaggerated. Chase and Liam knotted me over and over until my legs shook and I was unsure whether my body could take any more. I would definitely be sore in the morning.

"Bite," I nearly screamed as Chase shoved his knot inside of me, his shaft pulsing as he filled me with jet after jet of his hot cum.

"I love you," Chase muttered as he lowered his mouth to my right breast.

Liam lowered his mouth to my left. Their teeth sank into my flesh nearly in unison, dragging out the ripples of release and causing the walls of my pussy to clench tighter around Chase.

He growled as he stayed latched onto me, shooting more release into me.

As our bodies began to come down from the endorphin high, they each took turns lapping and kissing the tender bites that were so close to my nipples.

They'd chosen a place they knew would already be sensitive. *Damn sadists*, I thought to myself with a silent huff of laughter.

Even without hands or lips on me, every time my shirt or bra shifted along the bites, I would end up horny. They knew exactly what they were doing.

"I love you, too," I whispered, raising both hands to thread my fingers through the hair of the alphas who sung through the bond we now shared.

I felt the moment of surprise then the warm tendrils of affection they felt from my words.

I didn't say either of their names. I didn't need to. They could feel me in the bond. They could feel that when I said the words, I was answering both declarations – Liam's from weeks ago, and Chase's from tonight.

Chase

A *bleeting* sound made its way into my dreams and dragged me awake. That was the alarm from the perimeter censors.

"Shit," I muttered, pushing up and shaking Liam hard. "Get up. Incoming."

Liam was on the move before his eyes were fully open. He was dressed and arming himself as I struggled to wake the exhausted omega who now belonged to me. There was no turning back. She could no longer wonder if we would change our mind and see her as nothing more than a damsel we'd saved from slavery.

"I need you to get up, omega," I said, putting the urgency in my voice.

Her lashes fluttered, then her eyes shot wide open when the sound made it to her brain.

"Oh no," she cried out, crawling to the end of the bed and running for her room.

"What are you doing?" I asked, chasing after her.

I rounded the corner in time to see her shoving her legs in sweats. "I'm not about to fight naked."

"You won't be fighting."

Another alarm went off. Without checking the system, I didn't know which directions the enemy was coming but that was a different section of the property. They were trying to circle us, to flank us, to cut off any chance to flee with Violet.

"Well, I'm not hiding under the bed in hopes they won't find me, either. I'm not going down without taking one of them with me."

A mixture of pride and fear clenched my heart. Pride because my new mate was more than ready to go toe to toe with any enemy to protect herself. Fear because the last thing I wanted was those fuckers anywhere near her.

"They always check under the bed first," Liam said as he passed her bedroom door and double checked the alarms for the windows and doors.

The alarms would do nothing to keep anyone out, but it would give us a heads up if they were able to enter the house from any point.

"Gun?" she asked.

We had all agreed she should be trained to fire a gun. And none of us had taken the time to teach her. While there wasn't much to it more than point and squeeze the trigger, the recoil alone could cause her to miss her target.

It was better that she was armed, though. We would keep her as isolated from any intruders and guard her the best we could, but she still needed a way to protect herself in case we fell.

While I knew the anxiety would have already alerted Mac and Andrei to approaching danger, I jogged back to the bedroom and snatched my phone from the nightstand. It began to ring before I had a chance to pull up the phone icon.

"What's going on?" Mac barked over the phone.

"Incoming. From at least two directions –" *Bleet. Bleet.* "Make that three directions. We're officially under attack."

"Fuck!" Mac bellowed. "Get to the house," he said over the line, his voice a little muffled as though he'd pulled it away from his mouth. "We're on our way. I'll put in a call to headquarters to send any and all available teams. Keep Violet as far from those mother fuckers as possible."

"That's the plan," I said before ending the call.

I needed to focus on who was approaching from three sides of the house. For them to have tripped the sensors, we still had a few minutes before they attempted to enter the house. The woods surrounding the property was too dense with trees and foliage to get anything more than a dirt bike through without crashing.

Liam was piling weapons on the kitchen table, checking magazines and pulling on holsters to hold several weapons at once. We might not have time to retrieve others, might not have time to reload.

"Take her downstairs," Liam said.

The basement wasn't much. We had never bothered doing anything with it as it was primarily used for storage. There was a small home gym, but even that was rudimentary at best; the walls concrete as were the floors, and nothing more than a weight bench with a barbell and a few free weights lined up.

But the windows to the basement were too small for a grown man to wedge through. For the moment, it was the safest option.

Once my omega was dressed, I grabbed her wrist and began dragging her from the room, down the hall, and toward the steps leading to the basement.

Stopping only for a few moments, I grabbed two handguns and two magazines, and prayed she wouldn't have to use them. But she was right – she deserved the chance to defend herself. If Liam and I fell, it might buy her some time until Mac and Andrei – or any other local teams – arrived.

I waited until we were downstairs and I had her tucked into a corner as far from the door as possible before pushing her to her knees and setting the guns by her side. Moving quickly, I dragged the weight bench and some boxes around her, hoping to camouflage her while giving her enough line of sight should the enemy make it down to where she hid.

My heart clenched at that thought for so many reasons. I would plant my ass right in front of that door. The only way for one of Hawke's men to get to her was if one or both of us fell. I could lose Liam. He could lose me. She could lose us both.

I had never met an omega who'd lost one of their alphas. I wasn't sure what would happen to the bond if either Liam or I died after barely just bonding her to us. What kind of pain she might experience if our mark was never properly tended to and the thread was cut.

Taking her face in my hands, I pressed my lips to hers in a hard, lingering kiss. When I pulled back, fear caused her bottom lip to quiver as her eyes glistened with unshed tears.

"I swear to you I won't let them touch you." Kissing her once more, tears burned the backs of my own eyes as I found her so easily in our bond. "I love you, Violet."

"I love you," she whispered against my lips.

Her fingers were clenched around my wrists as though she didn't want to let me go. When the fourth alarm sounded through the house, it was time to go. It was time to protect our omega.

It was time to protect the woman I loved more than my own life.

"Do not move from this spot," I ordered. Pushing to my feet, I leveled a look at her and poured every ounce of alpha into my bark. "Do not move from this spot until someone you recognize comes for you. If someone makes their way down here, you aim and pull that fucking trigger. Don't think, just shoot."

"What if I shoot one of you?"

"You'll feel us. And if it's another team, they'll identify themselves. Do not hesitate," I barked.

Backing away, I tried to drink in her face, hoping it wouldn't be the last I looked upon it, before turning and rushing up the stairs, pulling it shut behind me.

There was no lock on the door from either inside or out. After tonight, that would be rectified.

Actually, after tonight, I would be the first to suggest we find a new house, one that was paid for with cash and not so easy to find. I wanted our omega safe. I wanted our pack safe.

I wanted us whole, and that wouldn't happen if the enemy was always able to track our location.

"Andrei said he's sending in other teams," I told Liam as he paced from one window to the next, trying to see into the dark night, trying to track any movement from the encroachers.

Liam nodded, but didn't speak. Anxiety, fear, and rage burned through the bonds and I was having a hard time tracing the thread to which of the pack those emotions were coming from. Could be all five of us.

Personally, I had no plans to hold anyone to question. I would execute every single cock sucker who'd trespassed onto our property to steal our omega.

Had Hawke ordered her execution? Or were they here to drag her to another compound in hopes of forcing another heat cycle and breeding her?

It didn't matter. Their plans didn't fucking matter. They wouldn't get near her. Grabbing one of the long-range rifles from the table, I found a spot near the back of the house and lowered to the floor of the dark kitchen. All lights were off, hiding our location while hopefully allowing us to see theirs.

Normally, we would each be wearing comms in our ears, would be able to dictate to each other whether there was a target rounding the house. Neither Liam nor I had bothered to put them in our ears before going into full battle mode.

As carefully and quietly as I could, I disarmed the alarm to this window and pushed it open silently, propping the muzzle on the ledge and peering through the sight. Since so many of our ops tended to be at night, I was able to see the forest in shades of green and saw the slightest of movements nearly twenty yards out.

Tapping the floor, I waited for a tap back from Liam. I warned him that I had at least one coming in my direction. Moments later, Liam tapped the ground three times. He'd spotted three on his side.

The two of us couldn't watch over the entire property alone. Even if we were to pull up the surveillance cameras on our phone, we couldn't cover every side of the house.

Where the fuck was the backup Andrei was supposed to send?

I had to remind myself it had only been minutes since I'd hung up, though it felt like hours since I'd done my best to hide Violet in the basement.

For a brief moment, I wondered if this was how they'd felt at the Alamo. That moment passed when several more bodies passed through the woods, their green forms slightly streaking as they jogged.

Nope. I wasn't going to wait until they were close enough to open fire or make their way through any of the windows.

Inhaling deeply, I blew the air out slowly and aimed at the first of my targets. And fired.

CHAPTER 27

ac

I HAD FELT the moment Violet's arousal spiked. I had felt the moment love bloomed like a fucking bouquet in her chest.

And I had felt the moment Chase and Liam had bitten her and bonded her. I had no idea how much stronger our connection could be once the entire pack was tied to her. Well, not the entire pack. Andrei was stubbornly holding back.

I had also noted the moment Andrei felt that clicking into place by the way his jaw had tightened and his hands gripped the steering wheel until his knuckles grew white.

So many things were on my tongue, insults, jabs. It was his own fucking fault. There was literally nothing standing in his way to tying Violet to him, of completing our pack bond.

A rush of panic flared in my chest and clouded my vision for a split second. And it wasn't coming from one source. Liam, Chase, and Violet all felt the same sense of panic, the same fear, and there was a touch of anger.

"Fuck," I growled out the same time Andrei hit Chase's number and filled the car with ringing coming from the speakers.

"What's going on?" I asked the moment Chase connected the call.

"Incoming. From at least two directions…make that three directions. We're officially under attack." Several beeps sounded over the line, meaning the perimeter had been breached.

"Fuck!" I bellowed, raising my fist to punch the dash then thinking better of possibly breaking my hand when we were rushing into possible battle. "Get to the house," I barked at Andrei as though he hadn't already shoved his foot against the gas pedal as far as the floorboard would allow. "We're on our way. I'll put in a call to headquarters to send any and all available teams. Keep Violet as far from those mother fuckers as possible."

"That's the plan." And then Chase ended the call.

"How far out are we?" Andrei asked, his eyes frozen on the dark street ahead of us.

"At least ten minutes."

A growl filled the cab of the SUV as the spicy scent of black pepper overrode Andrei's warm leather in his rage and fear.

That same emotion pulsed through our bond like someone was plucking at a bass string. It was uncomfortable. Fuck, it was downright painful.

Mostly because I needed to be with my omega. I needed to be there to shield her, to protect her, to end this fucking threat now.

I didn't wait for Andrei to put in the call to headquarters, just scrolled through his contacts until I found the number and waited for someone to answer.

After running down the situation, I insisted as many teams as possible be sent to our pack house. "And tell them to shoot to kill."

"We need answers, Mac. Unless Hawke is there—"

"I don't give a fuck. They're on our property to steal our omega. Kill on sight."

There was a heavy sigh over the line, then, "Copy."

The line went dead.

No timeline was given as to when backup would arrive for Liam and Chase. As far as I knew, we might make it to the house before any others. Which normally wouldn't be a problem, but we had no idea how many assailants were flanking the house. It could be four against a dozen as far as we knew.

But it would be four pissed off alphas defending their bonded omega. The fuckers now trespassing on our property were dead men walking.

I reached into the backseat and grabbed a few weapons when the SUV's headlights bounced over the mouth of the long driveway. I nearly pushed the door open and took off at a sprint. But the car would be faster, especially with how recklessly Andrei was driving, yanking the wheel to steer around vehicles that cut across the wide, paved way to our house, to our pack. To our omega.

Pops sounded from ahead, gunshots echoing through the dark night. Our home was far enough from any others that the police wouldn't be notified by concerned residents. This was not one of those times I was thankful for our isolation. But at least headquarters had been alerted. Not only would teams from ORE arrive, but hopefully the local law enforcement would be rushing this way, as well.

More vehicles crossed over the driveway, causing a damn roadblock.

Fuck it.

Lunging from the passenger seat, my feet hit the ground and I ran as fast as my legs would carry me before Andrei had a chance to put the SUV in park. I heard his feet hitting the pavement half a second later as he raced after me.

Our guns were raised, our eyes scanning the area around us for threats as we charged forward to join our packmates in defending our omega.

The succession of gunfire increased and decreased and seemed to come from so many directions. Too many directions. Our home had been surrounded by the enemy for no other reason than the beautiful woman inside.

Fuck. Had they been able to put her somewhere safe? There was no way there weren't bullets passing through windows and walls. It would be far too easy for Violet to get hit by a stray bullet.

Or maybe that was the plan. To eliminate one of the last witnesses to Hawke's crimes.

Hell no. No one was getting near my omega. No one was getting near my mate.

She was mine. She was ours.

The moment a person came into view, I lifted my rifle and pulled the trigger, not taking even a second to aim. The man whipped around as a bullet ripped through his shoulder, surprise widening his eyes.

Got you, fucker.

Popping off another round, I took him out before he could rebound and open fire on me or Andrei.

Feet thundered behind us. Whipping around, rifle raised, I yanked my finger from the trigger when I noted the patch on the tactical vest of an ORE team member racing to catch up with us. Only six men appeared behind us, but it was better than only the two of us fighting those outside.

As rifles and pistols fired round after round, my ears began to ring; the only sound I could make out was blood rushing through my ears.

Fear sent bile into my throat at the sight of the front door hanging wide open, at the windows lining the front of the sprawling ranch shattered, leaving plenty of access to those who'd attacked.

Without saying a word, I rushed in, rifle raised. There were sounds of a scuffle in the kitchen near the rear of the house. Several dead bodies littered our living room. Our makeshift nest of couches was covered in blood and glass.

No way would I allow my omega to stay here after this. We would move the entire pack, find a more populated area in hopes of keeping her safe from another sneak attack.

The entire property had been wired with alarms and cameras, yet that hadn't stopped our home from being infiltrated by the enemy.

Why the fuck had I left? Why the fuck had I allowed headquarters to send me on another mission when our own omega was at risk?

We should have been here. Andrei and I should have been with our packmates to protect Violet.

Liam and Chase were fighting off five men, their weapons laying on the floor as Liam was restrained by two men while another pummeled him. Blood coated one side of his face and he looked as though he was struggling to stay on his feet.

Chase wasn't faring much better, but at least he was only fighting two men, swinging wildly then lunging forward to tackle one of the men to the ground.

Instead of taking the time to assess the situation, I rushed forward and used the butt of my gun to incapacitate the man beating the piss out of Liam. That left the two holding him.

Fuck a fair fight.

Letting the rifle drop to hang from its strap, I pulled my pistol from the back of my pants and put a bullet into each of the enemy's heads before turning and doing the same to the men attacking Chase.

"Where the fuck is Violet?" Andrei asked, his voice loud. His ears were either ringing as loudly as my own or he was fighting the same panic that rose in my own chest when I didn't scent her sticky sweet smell on the air.

Violet

The guns Chase had left sat on the floor near my knees. Lifting a little, I tried to peek through the cracks of the stuff Chase had surrounded me with as he'd tried to hide me in case anyone made it downstairs.

Reaching down, I wrapped my fingers around the hilt and held it with shaky hands, keeping the muzzle pointed toward the only way someone could approach.

The first pop overhead made me jump with a squeak.

Shit. Shit shit shit. There had been a glimmer of hope the backup Chase mentioned would arrive before any action started. Instead, two parts of my soul were upstairs alone with an unknown number of attackers.

And they were risking their lives for me.

I would have rather left and tried to stay hidden as I had for years before Hawke and his asshole buddies found me. Then my pack would be safe.

This was the downside of allowing someone into your heart, the downside of allowing your soul to claim its mate. If one of them fell, a part of me would die with them.

More pops. Louder. More rapid. Smashing glass. The tinkling sounded overhead as it rained down onto the hardwood floor.

Where were Mac and Andrei? Searching the bond, I felt them, felt their fear and determination. They were rushing to us, rushing to protect the pack. To protect me.

There had to be more I could do than cower in this damn basement. I felt like a coward, but we had never gotten around to actually training with any of their various firearms. I might end up being more of a liability or distraction.

Cramps squeezed in my torso and I gasped in a breath, doing my best to ignore them. My skin felt as though I'd been placed under a heat lamp. This was not the best time to be experiencing the symptoms of my heat cycle. I needed to stay focused, and couldn't do that if my hormones took over and flopped from sending pain radiating through my body to causing slick to dampen the sweats I'd hastily donned.

More glass shattered overhead. Then feet thundered across the floor. Too many to belong to the only two people who should be inside the house.

Shouts. More gunfire. Heavy thuds.

New pain rocked through me and it had nothing to do with my heat. I could feel Liam and Chase, could feel the injuries they were incurring as they battled the men who'd made it inside.

Trembles shook my entire body until I wondered whether I would actually be able to hit anything if I ended up having to use the gun clenched in my hands. Chase had left me two pistols and two magazines along with those inside the semi-automatic handguns. I could assume there were enough bullets if anyone made it down here.

I hadn't even bothered to learn what the hell kind of guns I was holding. As far as I knew, they all served the same purpose – to end a threat to my life. I just hoped it wasn't like in the movies where I had to line up the target with the sight at the end of the gun purposely or miss my assailant completely.

No. Those thoughts had to stay away. And I was half-tempted to see if I could block the bond with my mates. Their pain was distracting me and causing a new sense of panic to bubble up and stir bile in my stomach.

It was so freaking dark down here, not even moonlight making it through the small windows up high on the concrete walls. All I could do was stare into the darkness and wait for a familiar voice to tell me whether we were all safe.

If we were all safe. What would I do if I lost one of my alphas? What would happen to me? I couldn't imagine the severing of that thread would leave me feeling whole. It would feel like someone had reached into my body and ripped away a part of my soul.

The door at the top of the stairs squeaked as though someone had opened it. Pushing up onto my knees, I peered through the gap of boxes and watched for…anything.

A light flipped on over the stairs, casting a shadow of an imposing figure descending slowly.

"Omeeega," a man said. Not any man. I knew that voice. I still heard it in my nightmares.

Oh god. If he had gotten past Chase and Liam, did that mean they were…

I searched the bonds and found them. They were hurt, but they were still alive. Yet Mason Hawke had gotten not only into our home but past my alphas and was now searching for me.

Part of me hoped he was simply going room to room. But with my heat so close, I knew I was practically leaving bread crumbs with my perfume. All he would have to do was follow the smell and he would find me cowering behind the boxes and weight bench and whatever else Chase had piled up.

Was there enough between us to buy me time?

Don't hesitate. Shoot, Chase had said.

But I couldn't see Mason, only his shadow. It would do no good to start firing blindly. I could run out of ammo that way.

No. I would bide my time. Wait until I could fully see his body outlined by the overhead light. Then I would do as my alpha had barked. I would follow his instructions then wait for them to find me. I would keep my eyes away from the body I would leave dead on the concrete floor until my alphas came for me.

"Mmmm. Someone is hurting," Mason purred. The fucker actually purred as though he were simply an alpha enjoying the perfume of his omega.

But I wasn't his. I never would be. I would rather put the gun to my own head and pull the trigger than be dragged to another compound. I would rather die here and now than lose my alphas, than lose my soul mates.

Someone is hurting. He knew I was nearing my heat. He knew my mind would turn to mush in a matter of hours or days.

I hated that. I hated that I couldn't hide something so personal, so intimate from someone like Hawke.

He didn't move closer, his shadow merely staying near the stairwell. Did he know I was armed? Was that why he wasn't moving closer?

"I can help you," he cooed, his voice full of faux sweetness. He wasn't sweet. He wasn't kind. I'd seen what this man was capable of, had felt his fingers digging into my biceps until he'd left bruises when I'd fought against his hold.

"Omega," he barked, and my body jolted.

No. No no no. He wasn't my alpha.

"I know you hear me. I can smell your sweetness. Come out now," he barked the last words, and my traitorous body stood before I could stop it.

Shit. I had to fight. I had to fight my own fucking biology.

The shadow head turned as though he'd spotted me. If he could see me, that should have meant I could take aim at him, right?

Or had my perfume simply grown stronger as I came out of hiding?

"Closer, omega," he barked, his voice no longer holding even a hint of sweetness. His bark was as strong and demanding as Andrei's, and I shook as I tried to fight my body's reaction.

"No," I snarled, squeezing my eyes shut and reaching for my pack.

They had to have felt the moment Mason had found me. They had to know I was now in the predator's sights.

"Now, omega."

A whine worked up my throat as my feet began to shuffle forward, the gun still clenched in both my shaking hands.

If I moved away from my little hiding spot, I would be leaving my backup gun and ammunition. And I would be at the mercy of one of the most sadistic alphas on the planet. Hell, he was probably one of the most sadistic people in history after the atrocities he'd committed and would continue to commit if he wasn't stopped.

He had to be stopped. Tonight. But my body and mind refused to cooperate.

It was hard to climb through the boxes, to push them out of the way. But I made it through before planting my feet in place.

"Closer," he barked.

This time, he moved out of the shadows and I could see his face clearly.

Raising my arms, I pointed the gun directly at the center of his chest. I didn't trust my ability to actually hit him if I aimed for his head.

"Put the gun down, omega. Put it on the floor."

That fucking bark felt like someone had taken control of my body. My muscles screamed and strained as my arms lowered as though someone was dragging them down. But I didn't release my grip, didn't drop the gun.

I had at least a tiny amount of control over my body and I

wouldn't relinquish that control without a fight, even if I was beginning to feel as though I was being manhandled by a grizzly bear.

In slow steps, Mason walked closer, his moves like a predator stalking its prey.

"We're going to leave," he said.

This wasn't bark but a statement.

"Fuck you," I snarled.

"Oh, you will. A lot. Once we get situated again, I'll be the only one allowed to touch you. I'm going to make sure you stay in heat as long as possible. I'll record you begging for my cock so I can play it for you later. Then, once you get pregnant, I'll pass you on to my guards. Until after the pup is born. Give me an omega or alpha, and you get to live–"

"To continue as your sex toy," I growled, the sound nowhere close to the one I'd heard come from my alphas.

He chuckled softly and nodded. "Exactly. I'll breed you over and over until your body gives out. Had you behaved and stayed in your room or returned to me, I might have allowed you to leave after a few times. Now?" He shrugged as though we were discussing the weather. "I'm going to wreck you, wear your body out until you're no good to anyone."

Rage rippled through me. And it wasn't solely coming from me. I felt my pack burning through my veins. I knew they couldn't hear the words coming from Mason, but they must have picked up on my own anger and fear.

"But first, we need to make sure your alphas are out of the way. Can't have those fuckers tracking us down again."

Those words broke whatever spell Mason Hawke's bark had put on my body. Raising the gun, I snarled as my finger twitched on the trigger.

"Put it down, omega," Mason barked.

But it had no affect on me. He wanted to kill my pack. He wanted to kill my alphas.

A snarl rippled from my mouth as my vision attained a red tint. No one would touch my alphas.

Finger on the trigger, I squeezed. Then squeezed again and again, watching as Mason danced backward in a macabre display, blood blooming on his shirt.

My ears rang. Gunpowder and the coppery smell of blood tickled my nose. But all I could do was continue to snarl at the man dying on the floor, at the asshole who'd dared to threaten my pack.

CHAPTER 28

ndrei

THE TEAMS WERE CLEARING the outside as I checked over Liam. "Where the fuck is Violet?"

No more did the question fall from my tongue before a series of gunshots echoed from the basement.

No. God no.

The four of us nearly tripped over each other to get to the basement door. "I left her down there," Chase said, his voice garbled with a swollen and split lip but obvious dread and fear in his words.

My feet nearly slid down the stairs as I sprinted down, not caring it I tumbled head over heels onto the concrete floor. As long as I got to my omega's side.

The basement was dark, the only light coming from the single bulb hanging over the stairwell.

Cotton candy. Sticky lollipop. Acrid, burning rubber of an alpha. Coppery blood. And gunpowder.

My eyes could barely make out the shape of a body on the floor before the basement was flooded with light as someone flipped on the fluorescents that hung from the rafters.

Violet stood twenty feet away, her hands raised, a gun pointed at the man on the floor as her lips parted on gasping breaths. She was visibly trembling, her eyes glued to Mason Hawke dead on the floor.

Our omega had done what the whole of Omega Rescue and Extraction had failed to do – she'd killed him. She'd eliminated the threat to omegas in the area.

"Violet," I said softly.

"Lil' Bit?" Chase said, stepping closer.

Her arms jerked up and the muzzle was suddenly pointed in our direction. Our sweet omega was in shock. After everything she'd survived, her mind had splintered the moment she'd taken the life of another. It was yet something else we would help her heal from.

Stepping ahead of Chase and Liam, who were injured, I raised my hands, palms out.

"Violet," I barked. "Look at me."

Her eyes jerked to my face, but her gun didn't lower.

"I need you to lower the gun. Your alpha needs you to put the gun on the floor."

"My alpha," she whispered barely above a breath.

"That's right, sweetheart. Your alphas are here. You're safe. Set the gun on the floor."

Her arms shook a few heartbeats then finally began to lower until the gun barely hung from one hand. I feared it would drop to the ground and accidentally fire a round.

Lunging forward, I took the gun from her limp fingers, flipped on the safety, and shoved it into the back of my pants.

With both hands, I cupped her face in my hands. "Look at me, omega," I barked. Her pupils were blown. Her perfume was heady. Not only was Violet in shock, her heat was charging forward, muddying her thoughts further.

"We need to get her out of here," Mac said, pushing forward.

She stiffened, her eyes darting to his face. But just as quickly, she relaxed, then lunged for Mac, throwing her arms around his neck as sobs shook her body.

Mac hugged her tightly to his chest before lifting her and cradling her as closely as he could.

I moved to stand at Mac's back so she had to look at me. "Omega," I barked. She opened her eyes to look me in the face. "Mac is going to carry you upstairs and out of the house. I want you to close your eyes and keep them closed. Can you do that for your alpha?"

Her head nodded in jerky movements.

"That's my good girl," I cooed, pressing a kiss to her forehead.

I was overwhelmed with so many emotions and was having a hard time weeding through them, having a hard time deciphering my own from my pack's. Her presence was so much stronger since Liam and Chase had claimed her. Her body still lacked my own mark. That would be rectified the moment everything was calm and we helped her through the trauma and her quickly rising heat cycle.

Her lids lowered and she buried her face in the crook of Mac's neck, her breath coming in long pulls as though she was grounding herself with her alpha's scent. Or perhaps her omega was reacting to her alpha's pheromones.

There were splatters and pools of blood everywhere. Furniture had been destroyed by bullets, by bodies crashing upon them, or stained with crimson.

Nothing in the main area would be salvaged. I didn't care whether we could get the stains out with a professional company. I never wanted my omega near this shit again.

I wanted my omega out of this house. We could sign it over to ORE as a safe house and buy something new for Violet. Build her one from scratch with a nest designed specifically for her.

Mac's hold on our omega was nearly crushing, but she didn't protest. In fact, her arms around his neck made me wonder if she wasn't cutting off his air supply. He didn't offer a protest, either.

Liam and Chase followed us up the stairs, Liam with a heavy limp. The two would need medical attention as soon as possible. They would need to be checked for broken bones and possible concussions.

Violet didn't appear to have any wounds, but I wanted her checked over, as well. As soon as we were far enough away from the house that she couldn't see the absolute destruction or the bodies we and the other teams had left littering the yard and inside the house.

Blue and red lights lit up the night, flashing on trees, vehicles, and faces.

Several ambulances waited at the very end of the driveway, either unable or unwilling to move any closer when there could still be a possibility of more gunfire.

Raising my hand, I waved one of the local police forward and filled him in on who was in the basement, then barked at one of the EMTs to attend to my pack.

When a woman touched Violet's back, she tensed and whined, pushing herself further against Mac's neck and tightening her hold until he grunted.

Well, shit. I couldn't have Mac passing out because our omega strangled him.

"Omega," I barked. She stiffened and opened her eyes, focusing on me. "You're safe now. I need you to let Mac set you down. I need these people to look you over."

"I'm not hurt," she said, her voice small.

Even as she spoke, the female paramedic shone a flashlight in her eyes. "She doesn't appear to have a concussion or anything. I don't see any blood."

"Did he touch you? Did you hit your head?" I asked her.

Violet shook her head.

"Can you stand?" I asked, lowering my head to be face to face with her.

Her head nodded, the same jerky movement as she had in the basement.

Mac growled softly as he set her on her feet and stepped away enough for the paramedic to check her over.

"She's fine. She's in shock and going into heat. Take her to her nest–"

"We can't," Chase said, his voice a constant growl.

The woman looked over our heads toward the house that would be shielded by trees. With a nod, she turned back to me. "Find somewhere safe for her. She'll be ready to deal with...all that in a few days."

After her heat. She would have to suffer mentally and emotionally all over again once her hormones were no longer in control of her body.

And we would be there. I had every intention of asking for at least a month off. We all deserved it at this point. Liam and Chase would need at least that long to heal from the beating they'd taken.

As much as I would have loved to pretend they wouldn't participate during our omega's heat, I knew better. They would want to be in the room with her, to ease her pain, to knot her so she could rest. They would be right there with me and Mac, making sure she ate and drank water and bathed.

Right now, though, all I wanted to do was find somewhere to take my beautiful girl so I could smother her in my scent. I wanted to line my body along hers, to rub my face against her cheek, to hold her as long as she could handle.

Mac

I STARED through the windshield of the SUV from the backseat, Violet cradled in my lap, Chase gripping her shins like he was afraid she would disappear it he wasn't touching her.

Liam was in shotgun, Andrei behind the wheel.

It had taken hours at the hospital before Chase and Liam were given their walking papers. Andrei and I had wanted to take Violet somewhere, but she'd refused to leave the other two.

Now, we were parked outside of a house that was just short of a mansion.

"You sure this is safe?" I asked.

"It was my great grandparents'. It's in my parents' name. They're dead. No one lives here. At least not full time," Chase answered as he reluctantly pushed through his door.

We all followed and waited as Chase punched in a code and pushed the door open, waiting for the rest of us to step inside.

"What the fuck, Chase?" Liam said. "We could have used this place as a vacation home." He was doing his best to keep his tone light, trying to be his usual, playful self, but I could see the tightness in his expression as pain caused every step to send ripples through our bonds. Both he and Chase were hurting.

I was tempted to tell them to shut down the bonds so our omega didn't have to feel it, but knew it would be damned impossible with their energy so fucking low.

"Kitchen is through there," Chase said, turning on lights as he moved through the house. "Family room."

Violet craned her neck to look into the room as we passed. Her breath caught at the sight. The family room was more like a grand room from those historical movies she liked to binge. The ceilings were no less than eighteen feet high. A large fireplace was on the far wall, the exposed brick all the way up. A tv that made ours look like a child's was on another wall, a deep wrap around couch facing it.

"The nest is up here," Chase said, peeling my attention from the room that could have easily engulfed half of our pack house.

My omega perked up at that. Of course she did. Her skin was hot, the warmth flowing through my shirt as her perfume tickled my senses and made my dick hard.

Who was I kidding? I'd walked around with a chubby since the day we'd brought her to the cabin, no matter how hard I'd fought against it.

Chase led the way to a room on the second floor, opening the last door in the hallway and flipping on more lights. It was a bedroom. And by the lack of smell, it hadn't been used in years.

"She won't want to be in a used nest while she's in heat," Liam grumbled through swollen lips.

"It's never been used. My dad had it installed in case one of my sisters perfumed. Didn't happen so it's sat empty all these years."

A soft whining worked from Violet the closer we got to the space at the far end of the room.

The nest was far nicer than what we'd had at the pack house. The floor was one big pillow, as though the builders had made sure the room was a wall-to-wall bed. Pillows and blankets were piled up against the walls, some folded and ready to be used. This room lacked any smell short of the faint hint of cleaning products.

I was almost rendered drunk when sweetness filled the room the second I carried Violet through the door. Her hands pawed at me, her face nuzzling against my neck as though she was trying to climb into my skin.

"Almost ready, sweetheart," I said, holding her tighter against my chest as she tried to pull my shirt over my head.

Any minute she would be lost to her biology. Liam and Chase had seen better days, but they would do what they could to help her. But the bulk of it would fall on Andrei and me. It was time to help our omega through her first heat with her pack.

We would worry about the emotional and mental healing after.

"Lie her down," Andrei said, shaking out blankets and spreading them around, grabbing pillows from the sides of the room in case she needed them.

If this had been a normal situation, we would have had time to court her. We could have showered her with gifts, with pretty things, soft things. I'd bought her that sweater that was designed to capture our scents, but it was back at the pack house. And as far as I was concerned, everything there was tainted and needed to be destroyed.

We hadn't been the ones to equip this room to her needs. We hadn't been able to do as we had the first time and let her pick out exactly what she wanted for this space, for her bedroom, for her nest.

But it would do for now. It was comfortable and clean and provided plenty of room for the four of us to help our omega through her heat. We would do anything and everything she asked as long as it brought her comfort.

A keening whine preceded a whimper as I set her on the heavily padded floor. Her fingers tangled in my shirt as she tried to tug me down on top of her.

Her skin was hot, feverish. She had barely escaped going into full-blown heat during that fucking attack. Would Mason Hawke have been able to manipulate her in her weakest moment? Or would she have had enough forethought to fight against an alpha's demands?

"Please," she begged, the whimper nearly taking my legs out from under me.

Omegas were susceptible to their hormones during this time. But alphas were no better when their omega was in need.

"Tell me, sweetheart. Tell me what you need," I said, following her down and lining my body along hers, pressing her into the padding while holding the bulk of my weight on my elbows.

"Touch me. Someone, please touch me. It hurts."

I was yanked away by my collar and then three sets of hands frantically started removing her clothing. She was bare and spread before us like a sacrifice within seconds as alpha pheromones nearly crowded out her sweetness and dragged a growl from my chest.

Mine.

Fuck. No. *Ours.* She was ours. Violet was our omega. I had to share her, no matter how badly I wanted to be the only one to knot her, no matter how badly I wanted her covered in my scent.

My fingers shook as I grabbed the collar of my shirt and yanked it over my head, then fumbled with the button and zipper of my jeans.

Liam dove face first into her tits, sucking one of her nipples between his lips and plucking the other between his finger and thumb.

"More," she begged.

Her skin was hypersensitive. It didn't matter where we touched her – she would still feel pleasure. But the only thing that would help ease the cramping and fever that rolled in waves for the next few days was orgasms. More specifically, being knotted by her alphas.

CHAPTER 29

iolet

FINGERS WERE ON ME. Mouths. My alphas were touching me, but it wasn't enough. Pain swelled low and my body felt as though I was boiling alive.

"Please," I begged the room. I didn't care who fucked me, as long as someone slid into me now.

"Hold on, omega," Andrei said.

A whine, high pitched and long, escaped my lips before I could stop it.

Andrei tensed and leaned over me, his face a breath away. "You're going to be knotted, my sweet little omega. We're going to make sure you get everything you need. I want you to tell me exactly what you want. Can you do that for me?"

My body shuddered at the demanding and hungry look in his eyes.

"Kiss me," I breathed out.

He bent and took my lips in a bruising kiss, his tongue diving into my mouth, tasting, warring with my own.

That fucking whine continued. I needed more than lips on mine. Pulling away for a brief second, I said, "Someone please touch me. Lick me."

"Where, little omega? Where do you want a tongue?"

"My pussy. Please. Eat my pussy?" I begged, unable to ignore my alpha's instructions.

Andrei returned to fucking my mouth with his tongue the same time a slow, long swipe worked through my folds. I hummed and moaned into Andrei's mouth as one of my alpha's began to flick their tongue against my clit, sucking it between their lips.

Hands were on my breasts. Lips wrapped around one nipple, sucking hard enough to pull a gasp from my chest.

Fingers entered my sex, pumping at a slow, lazy rhythm.

No. I didn't need slow. I didn't need gentle. I needed the pain to go away and I needed the fever to fade.

Shoving at Andrei's chest, I reached between my thighs and gripped Mac's head, rocking my hips against him and fucking myself on his mouth.

"Mmm. My sweet omega needs to come," Andrei purred as he rested onto one elbow and watched as I rubbed myself on Mac's mouth.

Liam was currently helping himself to my breasts, plucking them between his fingers, rolling them, sucking them between his lips and laving them with his tongue.

So much. Not enough.

More.

Fire blossomed, tingles built, then ripples of pleasure exploded from me as slick left me and rolled down to the crack of my ass.

Any other day, that might have embarrassed me. But when Mac sat up, his face shimmering with my relief, his tongue lapping at his lips and his fingers as though he couldn't get enough of my taste, I found myself needing more.

Before the aftershocks stopped rippling through me, I was tugging at Mac, trying to drag him up my body. "More. Please. More."

A growl and purr mixed in his chest as he spread my thighs wider and settled himself between them, gripping his shaft and positioning it against my opening. His teeth gritted as he tried to push in slowly.

"No," I cried out.

Mac froze, the head of his cock barely penetrating my pussy.

"Harder," I begged.

A heavy rattling sound filled the room as Andrei dove back at my mouth the same time Mac slammed his dick into me, his knot pushing to the point of stretching me without entering.

More. I needed more.

Andrei pulled away and stared down into my face. "So beautiful," he said, his fingers caressing my lips. "Such a beautiful mouth."

He shifted until his cock bobbed over my face and I hungrily took it between my lips, one hand reaching up to run my fingers over his swollen, throbbing knot.

He grunted, wrapped his fingers in my hair, and began to pump his hips, fucking my face as the sounds of Mac's thighs slapping against mine filled the air.

I didn't know where Liam and Chase were. No one was touching my breasts. No one was fondling me. All I felt was Mac. All I tasted was the peppery warmth of Andrei's cock on my tongue.

"Fuck," Mac grunted after a few minutes.

"Give our omega your knot," Andrei ordered.

Mac leaned over me, stretching my thighs further, and pushed hard. The moment his knot stretched and filled me, I cried out around Andrei's shaft as my body seized with pleasure. Mac rutted inside of me, his release hot as his dick twitched over and over.

When he pulled free, our mixed cum slid from me, soaking the padding below me.

Andrei was looking into my eyes as he fucked my mouth.

"Do you want another knot, little omega?"

I wasn't sure what it was, but when Andrei got all demanding like that, I would have given him nearly anything he asked for. Or maybe it was the lust haze of my heat sending me into a spiral.

I'd just had two orgasms, yet I still needed more.

Trying to speak, I gagged around Andrei's dick. How the hell was I supposed to answer with him nearly touching the back of my throat?

"I'll take that as a yes." Andrei chuckled, reaching down to play with my breasts. "I still plan to take these tits before the week's over. I can't wait to see how pretty you look covered in my cum."

"Fuck, Andrei," Liam said. But it wasn't a protest. It sounded more like he was as turned on by the idea as Andrei was. And as turned on as *I* was.

Fingers slid through my folds, coating my already soaked cunt with my slick. Then the blunt head of a cock pressed against my opening and pushed home without preamble.

Yes. That was what I wanted. That was what I needed. We could do slow and easy later. For now, I needed relief. I needed this pain to stop. And the only time I wasn't fighting the urge to cry was when someone was touching me, when someone was fucking me, when the orgasm was stronger than any cramping.

"Be careful," Chase warned. "You'll tear your stitches."

Liam. Liam was now fucking me.

Andrei pulled from my mouth with a pop of my lips, then helped me to a halfway sitting position so I could watch Liam entering me.

"Look how well you take your alpha, little omega." He shifted until he was sitting behind me, his length pressing against my back. "You take him so well. Do you know that? You're taking your alpha's dick like a good girl."

A whimper escaped my lips at his praise. I wasn't sure whether I would have reacted the same way had anyone else said those words to me. But when Andrei praised me, it felt like I could take on the world.

Or at least four dicks.

"Tell him what you want, Violet," he whispered in my ear, then nuzzled that sensitive spot below it.

Of my four alphas, Andrei had yet to mark me. He had yet to bond us. And I would demand he bite me before the week was up, even if I had to tie him down and force him. I would use every tool in my omega bag to convince him.

His hands massaged my breasts, plucking and rolling my nipples. My eyes rolled closed until he pinched to the point of pain. "Nope. Keep those pretty eyes open. I want you to watch your alpha knot you."

Liam smiled a second before shoving hard into me, his knot almost painful. His hips jerked as his dick twitched inside of me. Ripples worked through me, clenching my cunt around Liam's dick until he barked out with another release.

I WOKE TO PAIN. Doubling over, I squinted in the dim light of the nest and tried to get my bearings. I'd been nearly drunk when we'd arrived in this place. I hadn't had much time to get a look around as need had taken hold.

My heat was doing its best to drag me down again. But after the past few hours, I knew I didn't need to ask for anything, even if Andrei enjoyed hearing me beg. It was as though my alphas knew what I needed when I needed it. Andrei enjoyed prolonging it, enjoyed hearing me beg for release.

But my other three were more than happy to feel me clenching around their knots as I fell apart.

We were asleep in a puppy pile, Chase spooned behind Liam, Andrei still at my back, Mac draped over my legs.

Just the sight of my pack naked, their bodies there for the taking made my pussy wet and my mouth dry.

But who to ride first?

Even in their sleep, their cocks were in various stages of hardness, even if their knots weren't swollen. I could still get off with a hard fuck.

I supposed it wasn't a matter of who, but how. Chase was sweet and gentle, even when I begged him for hard and rough. Mac liked to touch and suck on my bonding mark as he took me.

But Andrei.

Carefully pulling my legs from under Mac, I rolled until I was stretched on top of Andrei. His arms immediately wrapped around me and rolled me under him.

"Did you think you were going to take control, little omega?" he whispered as he opened his eyes and stared down into my face.

I couldn't speak. I could barely breathe. Especially not when his hands trailed down my body, his fingers found my folds, then dipped inside. "Mm. Does my omega need me?"

"Please?" I begged.

His fingers began to thrust into me, slowly at first, spreading as though preparing me. I was stretched plenty from my alphas' knots.

But when another finger joined…then another.

Pushing back onto his haunches, he reached forward and gently wrapped his hand around my throat. "Do you remember your word?"

I swallowed hard. "Clover," I squeaked out as he slid another finger with the first three.

My alphas were long and thick. Their knots stretched me more. But what Andrei was doing to my body now was beyond anything I had experienced.

"You say the word and I stop," he said.

The stretch burned a little at first, like the first time I'd taken one of their knots. There was a slight ache, and then Andrei pushed his entire hand inside of me.

"Do you know what I'm doing?" he asked, his voice deep and growly and demanding.

I shook my head.

"Words. I want you to answer me," he barked while keeping his voice low.

With another hard swallow, I said, "No, alpha."

No, sir, had been on the tip of my tongue, but he had never set any ground rules as to what he wanted to be called when we played like this.

Oh, but this was beyond play. He was sending so many sensations through my body I almost forgot that my skin was on fire.

"I'm fucking you with my fist. It'll be like having a knot filling you to the brim."

And then he started a hard, brutal rhythm, my body rocking against the cushioned floor of the nest.

My mouth opened, but I couldn't make a sound, simply thrashed my head side to side as he kept his gentle grip on my throat, barely restraining me while reminding me he was in control.

"Holy fuck," Mac muttered from somewhere behind Andrei.

He moved until I could see his face, his eyes focused on what Andrei was doing to my slicked cunt.

"Take her mouth," Andrei ordered.

"Fuck you. You're not my alpha," Mac said, but crawled forward until he was beside my face.

And take my mouth he did. He fucked my mouth hard and fast, his knot bumping my chin and nose with each thrust. He gripped the hair at the crown of my head and grunted, hot jets shooting to the back of my throat.

I swallowed every drop, savoring the warmth of it, comparing Mac's whiskey warmth to Andrei's peppery spice.

"Fuuuck," Mac groaned out, finally pulling from my mouth and sitting back.

He bent and pressed his lips to mine, kissing me deeply, no doubt tasting himself on my tongue.

That mixed with Andrei's fist driving into me sent me over the edge. I cried out, my body convulsing and twitching until I collapsed back onto the floor, feeling boneless.

Andrei slowly pulled his fist from me, licking and lapping his fingers, cleaning himself of my release.

"You realize that just makes me want more," I said as I watched him.

"It's the hormones," Chase said.

"It's you guys. I swear I've been horny for weeks."

Liam chuckled. "Why the hell do you think I'm always fucking you or fucking him," he said with a jerk of his head toward Chase, "begging for a blowjob, or jerking off in the shower? You do the same thing to us."

"Mmm," I purred.

I saw the moment Liam's dick twitched at the sound. I had only slept for a few hours since the last time we'd collapsed into a slick and cum soaked pile, yet my body was revved and ready for more.

They could blame it on my heat, but I don't think there would ever come a day when I didn't crave these men.

CHAPTER 30

hase

By the third day of Violet's heat, we had almost begun to fight over who would fuck her next. Liam had played with her ass, but we hadn't gotten her ready to take one of us there yet. That was something that would have to be remedied soon. There were four of us and only one of her.

For the moment, Mac fucked her pussy, Andrei slid between her tits as he'd promised, and I was lying on my back while Liam blew me. I wanted to shoot down his throat, but my alpha needed to knot my omega. Our primal instincts were as strong as hers. It was that need to breed, regardless of whether our omega was on birth control or not.

"You watching Liam suck off Chase?" Andrei asked as he held Violet's heavy tits closed around his dick.

"I like watching them," she said, not an ounce of embarrassment or shame on her pretty face.

The first night she'd woken to Liam and I making love, I'd noted the hesitation in her voice and the pink hue to her cheeks. But then... she'd fallen into place with us as though she was born to be our mate.

Fuck. She was born for all four of us. No matter what each of us asked of her, she didn't bat an eye. And vice versa. Even when she'd asked Liam to eat her pussy when it was coated with the release of the entire pack, he hadn't hesitated to suck her clit between his lips. Because it brought our omega pleasure.

"Knot," she suddenly blurted out. "Please, Mac. I need your knot."

He gripped her thighs and shoved forward hard, stretching her and filling her. I couldn't see as much as I wanted from this angle, but it was enough for me to have to pull Liam off my dick before I finished on his tongue.

"Hey. I was enjoying myself," Liam whined.

I only held out a few more minutes. I waited just long enough for Mac's knot to begin to deflate. Then, like a fucking caveman, I nearly plowed through both Liam and Mac, shoving Mac out of the way, and taking my place between her legs. I didn't have time to fuck her. I simply gripped her hips and pulled her toward me as I thrust in.

She cried out, her fingers clenching the blankets strewn around her.

"Fuck yes," Andrei ground out. I craned my neck in time to see him cover her chest and throat with his release.

He was right – she did look pretty all shimmery with his cum.

"Shit," I said as my knot instantly swelled and I began to rut inside of her. It would normally take time for our knots to relax enough to pull from her. But the need to breed made it possible to go again and again.

But normally, it wasn't seconds after getting off. The most I could do was cover her body with mine and pump my hips forward, shoving my knot deeper and deeper until another wave washed over me, filling my omega's cunt with release.

The wet sound that filled the room when I pulled from her was by far the best sound I had ever heard in my life. It was the sound of the pack inside our omega. It was the sound of a well-pleased omega.

Pushing back, I grimaced at the soft pop of our bodies separating, my chest now covered with Andrei's cum, too.

Oh well. This wasn't the first time or last time I would be covered in my pack's cum. Although it was normally Liam's.

Violet's eyes fluttered shut and her body went slack. Moments later, her breathing came slow and steady. She'd fallen back to sleep.

Liam chuckled as he pushed to his feet and sauntered across the nest, his dick bobbing with each step. "Where's the bathroom? We need to get her cleaned up. She's going to end up stuck to the damn floor."

With my own chuckle, I joined him, showing him the door beside the nest that opened onto a bathroom perfect for an omega.

After I'd presented as an alpha, my parents had truly believed my sisters would be alpha or omega. Nope. Both betas. But at least they'd been prepared. And, unlike Violet's family, hadn't batted an eye that they hadn't perfumed.

We both piled wash cloths and towels on the counter, wetting a few with hot water, while keeping the others dry.

Andrei stroked his fingers through her hair, nothing short of affection in his eyes. He still hadn't marked her. We'd been locked in this nest for days with her and he'd yet to sink his teeth into any part of her body.

Mac was situating blankets and pillows around her body, making her more comfortable. Only after Liam and I fully cleaned her did Mac drag a soft blanket over her body all the way to her chin.

He laid down along her side, draping an arm over her waist and closing his eyes.

He was exhausted. We all were. Liam and I had received a hell of a beating, Liam receiving stitches in the hospital. But there wasn't a thing Violet could ask for that we wouldn't give her.

Sure, we would hurt later. We might have even done more damage to our injuries. But it was more than worth it.

. . .

Violet

I hummed at the sensation of fingers gently threading through my hair. Peeling my lids open, I smiled sleepily at Andrei.

"Hi," I said, my voice scratchy from four days of screaming with my orgasms. Or maybe it had been four days of begging mixed with the screaming.

"How do you feel?" he asked.

"Less…needy," I said.

His fingers stilled, then lowered until they settled on my shoulder near where Mac had left his mark.

We laid there staring into each other's eyes in silence while the rest of the pack slumbered around us.

When Andrei sat up, I instinctually rolled onto my back. But he didn't force my knees apart, didn't bark any orders for me to touch him or myself. Simply lowered his head and pressed a gentle kiss to my lips.

"I want to mark you," he said against my mouth.

Elation and excitement skittered through me.

"Finally," I said.

His lips stretched into a smile, still pressed against mine. "Do you want me inside you when I bond you?"

"Yes. Please," I said, only this time, it wasn't the needy beg of the heat, but rather the need to feel as much of a connection to my alpha as possible.

He shifted until his body covered mine, lining us chest to toes … well, sort of. Mine only touched his shins because of our height difference. He urged my knees apart with his own, his cock instantly rubbing through my folds.

"How are you already so wet for me?" he whispered as though he didn't want to share me in this moment.

"I'm always wet for my alphas," I admitted.

Andrei's eyes stayed on mine as he slowly slid into me. In the times we'd been together, Andrei had never taken his time to make love to me. He took from me, demanded I come, teased me.

But this time, he seemed content to take all the time he wanted, rotating his hips until his cock was rubbing all the right places while his knot pressed against my opening.

"I don't want you to come yet," he said when my breathing became quicker. There was my dominant alpha. "I'm going to shove my knot into that tight little cunt of yours, then sink my teeth into your shoulder. When you feel my dick twitch inside, that's when I want to feel that pussy clenching around me. Can you do that for me?"

All I could do was nod as I struggled to keep from coming. He reached between us and toyed with my clit, stroking it, pinching it.

"Tease," I whispered as pressure began to build.

How the hell was I supposed to hold off when he was doing everything he could to shove me over the cliff?

His smile was equal parts sweet and deviant. He pulled his fingers away, winked, put the hand covered in my slick over my mouth, then slammed his knot into me. My scream was only barely muffled behind his hand.

Lowering his head, he sucked on my shoulder, then latched on hard and tight, marking me the same way he fucked me.

His hand stayed over my mouth as I bucked and cried out. I couldn't hold back. As I came, my inner walls clamping around his dick, he grunted and began to rut hard against me before finally relaxing, his weight heavy on top of me.

His tongue gently lapped at the seeping wound, soothing the ache, but also sending new tingles of pleasure all the way to my toes.

Nope. No way would I ever get tired of my alphas.

Andrei's hand slowly pulled from my mouth as he kissed and lapped at his mark, sending zips and zaps of tingles through my body.

When he pushed up to look into my face, he made sure I was looking directly into his eyes.

"I could have lost you," he whispered, his face pained.

"I could have lost you."

Wrapping my arms and legs around him, I secured him in place against me. Not that he could have pulled free yet. My heat was finally subsiding and we were locked together for a bit.

One of his hands smoothed over my hair as his gaze bounced between my eyes. "I should have told you before. I should have told you weeks ago. I love you, Violet. I love you so much. If I had lost you–"

I lifted and silenced him with a deep, but soft kiss. Dropping my head back against the padding, I smiled up at him. "I love you, too."

His smile was slow and tentative, then stretched into a grin. "What the hell did I do to deserve you?"

"Well," I said, pretending to be in deep thought. Snapping my fingers, I pointed at him. "There was that time you saved my life. And then brought me home. And gave me a family."

"It's too much!" I giggled as Mac lifted me from the ground and plopped me on my bed so I had to watch as deliverymen piled into my room carrying bags and boxes.

Chase had talked to his siblings and gotten the go ahead for us to move into the massive family house. His sisters said they'd already thought about putting it up for sale since no one had used it in years.

According to Chase, this was the only house fitting for his omega.

Me? I was still having issues with getting lost when I roamed the halls.

I'd seen larger houses in the past, but had never actually been inside them. I felt like one of those women from the historical romance shows and movies I'd always been obsessed with. Except there were no exposed concrete walls or torches and candles to light our way.

"Why didn't we just bring my stuff from the other pack house?" I argued when my guys would traipse through with bags.

"Nope. Tainted," Andrei said as his only answer.

That had been his argument since the decision had been made to abandon our old home and move into here. I would have been just as happy finding another house similar. I really didn't need the opulence nor the excessive amount of clothing, blankets, and pillows they were currently piling into the bedroom and nest.

We'd been perfectly comfortable through my heat. Yet they thought I needed more. They'd also ordered nearly every scent of body wash and bubble bath, including scent blocking for when I left the house. Not that any of them would let me leave without an escort.

Wilder stepped through my door, and I widened my eyes, hoping the beta would be on my side. He shrugged up his shoulders. "You really think anything I say will help?"

My alphas had grown more comfortable with Wilder visiting since it was obvious there was no sexual attraction between us. It wasn't like Wilder was a bad looking guy. He just didn't tug at my heart – or other parts of my body – the way my alphas did.

"You don't think it's too much?"

He set a bag of what looked like new sheets beside the bed. When he turned to lower onto the mattress, he was warned with a growl from Mac as he passed.

Holding his hands up, Wilder stopped mid-sit and turned to face me. "It's normal. It's in their blood. Get used to it." His expression turned serious for a moment. "That – they could have lost you, Violet. Let them spoil you."

They could have lost me. And I could have lost them. Yet I wasn't able to run around buying them pretty things and spoiling them like the kings they were.

I huffed and crossed my arms over my chest like a petulant child. "Fine. But can you at least help me reign them in a little? They're talking about building another wing onto the house."

His brows drew together as a huff of laughter escaped him. "For what?"

My cheeks grew hot. "Because we're thinking about..."

"Are you pregnant?" he asked as a grin stretched across his face.

"Not yet. But you better believe we're going to do our best to knock her up as soon as possible," Liam said as he passed.

My four alphas stopped outside the nest, their eyes roaming over the excessive number of bags littering my room.

There was plenty of space in this bedroom. Hell, my old duplex could fit inside this one room alone. But since we'd left everything we all owned in the pack house that, according to the only person who would tell me the truth about that night – Wilder – had been littered with bullet holes or spattered with blood, it made sense to get all new stuff.

The guys refused to entertain getting anything cleaned and instead wanted a fresh start as a fully bonded pack.

"Yep. Time for me to go," Wilder said the same time my alphas' pheromones filled the room, heating my body from head to toe.

It never took more than a touch from any of my alphas to make my body burn or my blood boil. But when they all four looked at me as though all they wanted to do was strip me naked and replay the events of my heat...

"Are they gone yet?" I asked, jerking my head toward the front of the house, indicating the deliverymen.

Liam held up a hand, five fingers out, and began folding them down as he counted aloud.

When he hit one, the front door closed and the alarm beeped as it reset.

"One," he said, then dove at me.

I squealed as he pinned me to the bed and dug his fingers into my ribs. "Say you love it," he playfully demanded.

Chase jumped to the foot of the bed and began tugging my pants down my legs.

"Say you love every single thing we bought," Liam demanded as I giggled and tried to squirm away.

"That's not how you bark at your omega," Andrei said as he and Mac climbed onto either side of me.

Oh, they didn't have to bark. They didn't have to make any demands. These alphas had me. They had me body, heart, and soul.

* * *

IF YOU LOVED Violet's story of discovering here inner strength, finding her pack, and building a family, I would love if you could take the time to leave a review on your favorite site. And don't worry, more stories of love, laughter, and knots to come soon!

You can contact Raelynn Rose at authorraelynnrose@yahoo.com

Printed in Poland
by Amazon Fulfillment
Poland Sp. z o.o., Wrocław